W9-DJK-943

ACKNOWLEDGEMENTS

First of all, I'd like to thank Allah for allowing me to complete this project. To my beautiful family, thanks for being patient with me while my mind was concentrating on getting this novel done.

To my people running the book business in the streets, Omar Traore "Rubbish" from 125th Street, Tony Brown, Balde, Ishmael Sangnan, Massamba Amar Jamaica (Queens), Mustapha, Konate Moriba "le Gouru", Yigo Aboubacar, Abdou Boussou, Abo Ndiaye, 23th Street, 6Ave, Cheikhona Ba, 44th Street, Lex. And a special thanks to the two beautiful models, Sidibe Ibrahime "Papito" and Maimouna Ouedraogo "Mai La Princesse".

Special thanks to: J P Morgan Chase Bank-Harlem, Branch 61, Sean Burrows, Sarah, Jacinth Fairweather, Sharyn Peterson, Sharon Font, Sonya Merriel and Bonita Veal.

To my brother-in-law, Fadiga Aboubacar, Sidibe Hadja, Amy, Sidibe Zenab, and Aicha(Ohio) thank for support and believing in me.

Special thank to my friend, Hubert Daleba Gnolou. I know you been always there for me.

To my best friend, Meite Ibrahim Jean. Thank you for holding me down.

To my friends James W. Martin Jr. aka Jalike Ashanti Heru Herukhati, and Norma van Demark aka Ewunike Adesimbo.

Thanks to A & B and Culture Plus for their support and for believing in me.

Thanks to all of the readers who sampled the manuscript and gave me their feedback. There are too many of you to name individually, but you all know who you are, and I'm extremely grateful.

To my special friends from Sweden, Jaqueline Carleson, Lisa Erickson, and Haddy.

To one of my dearest brothers & friend, Sidibe Siaka, his wife, and two sons. I can't thank you enough for what you have done for me.

To my big brother, Ousmane Fofana "Restaurant bon appetit". Thank you for believing in me.

To my friend Marlon. L. 162+Jamaica do your thing.

To my friend from Burundi, Aimable Rulinda.

To Christine Jordan "28 Precinct Harlem". Thank you for keeping our community safe.

To my brother, Inza Sangare "Brikiki", and Kashan Robinson, best-selling author, of Veil of Friendship. Thank you so much for your support.

To my friends in Germany. Thank you so much for your support.

To my brother-in-law, Graig, and his beautiful wife, Corinne. Thank you for encouraging me.

To my man from Paris, Aaron Barrer, "le Congolais blanc". Grand merci.

To my best friend, Ahmed Kaba "Bajo" le prince charmant de New York". Keep doing your thing.

To my friend & partner, Raphael aka Pepe, Trazar Variety Book Store, 40 Hoyt Street, Brooklyn, NY. Thank you for your support.

And a special thanks to Kevin E. Young. If it weren't for you the project would not have been completed.

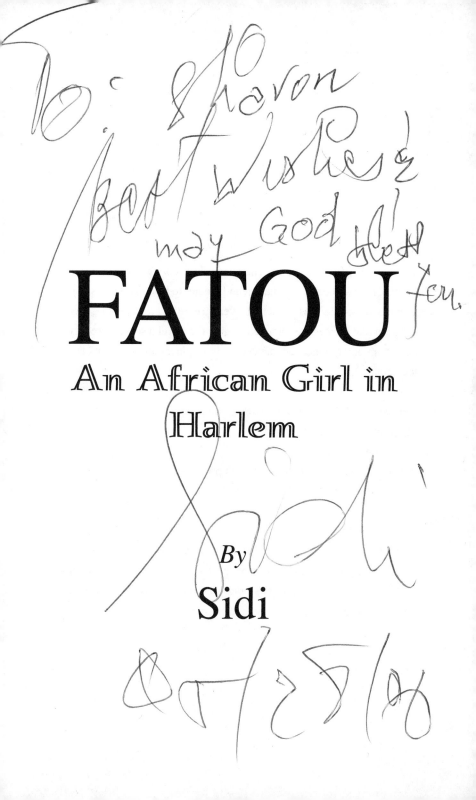

To: Sharon
best wishes &
may God bless
you.

FATOU

An African Girl in Harlem

By

Sidi

Published by

Harlem Book Center, Inc.
106 West 137th Street, Suite 5D
New York, NY 10030
Tel: +1/646-739-6429

Warning!
This is work of fiction. All the characters, incidents and dialogues are the products of the author's imagination and are not to be construed as real. Any references or similarities to actual events, entities, real people, living or dead, or to real locales are intended to give the novel a sense of reality. Any similarity in other names, characters, entities, places and incidents is purely coincidental.

Cover Design/Graphics: www.mariondesigns.com
Photography: Alexei Production
Editor: Barbara Colasuonno
Models: Maimouna Ouedraogo "Mai la princesse" and
          Sidibe Ibrahime «Papito»

© Copyright 2005
ISBN 0-9763939-0-5

DEDICATION

I dedicate this book to

Sidibe Arravian. E.Wilson "Missy"

Sidibe Mabana Hallary

Sidibe Mamadi, and Keita Maimouna

PROLOGUE

The blazing hot sun of West Africa's Ivory Coast beats down on twelve-year-old Fatou La Princesse as she navigates the path to her village. She hopes her mother is busy and too preoccupied to notice her walking alone. "There is safety in numbers," her mother always tells her. But today, Fatou has left the other children behind her in her haste to find out what surprise awaits her. Her curiosity has gotten the better of her, and she's excitedly rushing to discover what her father meant when he told her, "Today your life will change forever."

Fatou is a very beautiful girl. She has long, finely textured hair that touches the small of her back. Her eyes are a mesmerizing shade of gray, and her face is flawless, like a supermodel's. It's as difficult to believe that she is only twelve years old as it is to believe that her family is dirt poor. She possesses the grace, charm and poise of royalty.

As she hurries along the path, she wonders if her father was made an elder tribesman, securing for her family a home in the developed portion of her village—a place that isn't all mud-hardened fixtures and tents, a place of amenities and lots more privacy. *What else could father mean when he says my life will change forever?* she asks herself. *He has to be becoming an elder. He has to be improving our lot in the world.*

Fatou stops dead in her tracks. A snake has cornered a field rat not far ahead of her. It's a bad omen to witness such things, and she wonders why today of all days her positive thoughts are interrupted by such negative images. *This cannot be a bad omen,* she thinks. *My life is about to change forever. I am about to experience things that I never dreamed of.*

Not far away, Lama Contravene, a forty-five-year-old West African immigrant to America, nervously scans the cabin of United Airlines Flight 666 from West Africa to New York City's John F. Kennedy Airport. He pats his suit jacket to confirm that his digital camera is still in the inside pocket. Now reassured, Lama fidgets in his seat, anxious to go to the lavatory. With each passing minute, beads of sweat gather in his gray, slightly balding hair and trickle down his huge, malformed forehead. When the captain finally turns off the seat belt sign, Lama rises nervously from his coach seat and uneasily creeps down the aisle, nearly knocking over an elderly woman also heading toward the rest room.

His heart is racing a thousand miles a second as he locks the rest room door. Although he is anxious to get back to Harlem, all he now wants is to remember is how to operate his new toy so he can return to his homeland via the mpegs he'd videotaped.

Just four days ago, he'd learned about his father's death. He'd convinced his friends, Binta and Alpha, to wait for him to arrive before before burying his father. He wanted to be there.

Three days in West Africa reminded Lama that his homeland was all he remembered it to be. The unaccomodating tents and rocky terrain did nothing to comfort his aging back. Same with the manmade axes he used for chopping the wood he gathered for his father's funeral ceremony bonfire. And the wrestling of wild antelope for food was the definitive reminder of why he now despised West Africa.

In the cramped rest room, Lama pulled down his pants and leaned against the wall, trying to get comfortable. But now, instead of being on a plane back to Harlem, the only place he wanted to be was inside the digital camera that housed the images of Fatou.

Fatou's thighs were lusciously plump and supported a backside that looked like two cassava melons resting side by side. Before seeing Fatou again, cassava melons were Lama's favorite source of nectar. But now, he longed for the juices from Fatou's melons.

He was amazed at how Fatou's melons, both her breasts and her backside, jiggled as she danced at the ceremony. When she leaned back on his digital camera's screen, he imagined he was behind her, rubbing his aging manhood against her luscious bottom. He closed his eyes with Fatou's image securely affixed to his memory and took himself back to her tent in West Africa. He began to massage his groin.

He thought about how tempting she was when he peeked through the hole in her tent and watched as she bent over and rubbed oil on her naked body. The memory caused his whole body to shake as he aimed his eruption at the screen on his digital camera. When he finally opened his eyes, his semen was running down Fatou's belly.

He suddenly became aware again of his surroundings. Banging on and fumbling at the door made him realize that he'd better clean his body and camera in a hurry. *These wretched Americans,* he thought. *They don't know anything about our culture and definitely wouldn't understand this.*

As he wiped the sperm off his fantasy girl, he addressed the people outside the lavatory door and let them know he'd be just a few seconds more. Then he wondered what Fatou was doing back in Africa.

Twelve-year-old Fatou La Princesse was navigating the path to her village, clinging to an innocence that Lama Contravene wanted lost. After he placed the digital camera back in his pocket, he emerged from the lavatory and tried to put a distinguished look on his face. The waiting passengers scowled at him, wondering how he could be so selfish and unconcerned about other their needs. They didn't know how right they were.

CHAPTER ONE

La Dotte

Binta and Alpha Kone lay on their backs staring at the top of their tent. Fatou hadn't returned from school, so they had the privacy they needed to resume the only conversation they'd had since Lama Contravene had left the village. As she laid her head on Alpha's chest, tears flooded Binta's eyes as she lightly stroked his arms.

Alpha had a king-like stature, broad shoulders, a massive chest and a six-pack abdomen. Binta's long hair was twisted into her customary two braids. Her modest robe revealed thunderous thighs and a hint of ample backside. Her breasts were plump and tender, and her face was as lovely as it had been when she was a teenager, graced with gray eyes that would stop any man in his tracks. There was no doubt that Binta and Alpha were Fatou's parents. They were the most handsome family in their small West African village.

Alpha wiped the tears off Binta's face and softly protested. "Why do you act as you are? This was your idea. We've already sent Lama letters telling him we'd follow through with our promise to his father."

Lama's father, Daleba Contravene, and Alpha had been companions for years prior to Daleba's death. They were so close that they promised each other that whoever had a daughter would give her up to the other's son so that their families would be united forever. They were both so fond of their promise that they each tried to birth a daughter despite the fact that they were years past child rearing. In the end, Binta had become pregnant with Fatou, and the child's fate was cinched the moment she was brought into the world. Yet Binta began to question the fate they'd determined for their only daughter.

"I know this was my idea," she said. "But shouldn't I be allowed to be wrong? Lama is almost as old as we are, and Fatou is just a baby. And Lama doesn't care. Shouldn't that mean something to us? Knowing that Fatou will be his one day, shouldn't Lama want to wait? Why is he in so much of a hurry to take away our baby's innocence?"

"He's already given La Dotte," Alpha replied. "And we've told him that she's his wife till death, just as the traditions instruct us to do. Besides, Fatou may be a baby in age, but her makeup is that of a woman. We can't blame Lama or any man for that matter for being smitten with her. What are we to do? We've already used some of La Dotte."

Binta thought about La Dotte, the dowry, that Lama had given them for their daughter's hand. They'd already eaten four of the ten coconuts and one of the five antelopes. The robes she and Alpha were wearing were among the twelve pieces of clothing they'd received from Lama, and Fatou was headed to school in a pair of the ten pairs of shoes. In total, Lama had given them about $5,000 worth of goods to secure their daughter's hand in marriage.

"We've sold our daughter to the devil," Binta screamed. "We've given her away for scraps! I know things have been hard, but she's our child. Our stomachs will be full for a spell, but they will know hunger again. We will be draped in a fine wardrobe, but soon it will wither away to rags. And in the end, Fatou will never be the same. Our little girl will never be the same."

"May I remind you again," Alpha rebutted, "that this was your idea..."

"Yes," Binta said, interrupting. "It was my idea. But at some point before my idea became a reality, one of us should have spoken up for our baby. You should have shaken me like a tree branch and asked me what was wrong with me. We could have done something."

"Yes, we could have," Alpha said calmly. "But we didn't. Now it is written and only Allah can protect Fatou. We've already summoned him through the juju we've sent to Lama in our letters. The juju will protect them from all danger and bring them much happiness. Now we must prepare Fatou for her wedding. We must let her know that she is to go to the Americas to meet her groom."

"I can't bear the pain," Binta pleaded. "Can't we tell her that she is to continue her studies in America? I won't be able to look into her eyes knowing I've done this to her. I'll never be able to look into her eyes again."

Fatou is told of her impending trip as soon as she arrives home from school. She is excited about going but disappointed that she'll miss the wedding ceremony she'd heard the other little girls whispering about.

"Well, we'll just make sure that you're a part of a ceremony before you leave," Binta says, smiling. Her words put a smile on Fatou's face as well.

Yet, little does Fatou know that the ceremony she is excited to be in is all for her. Little does she know that in less than a week, her twelve-year-old innocence will be lost to a man old enough to be her father, her own father. And there is nothing that Fatou can do about it.

"What am I to do in America without you, Mama?" Fatou asks.

"Allah will protect you, my dear," Binta says, crying. "Allah will have to protect your little heart and keep you strong." Binta repeats her words to herself in her thoughts and prays that Allah be with her little girl in the big cities of America. Then before rushing out of the tent in anguish, she prays that Lama will be patient. She knows that once she loses her little girl, she'll never get her back.

The ceremony is amazing. Fatou is wrapped in white cloth and she dances and dances until her young bones get tired. She grows weary of waiting for the bride and begs to be excused. *I guess I'll have to learn of the bride in my parents' letters*, she thinks.

The ceremony had turned into a send-off party for her. Everyone hugged and kissed her with tears in their eyes. The attention felt good, but she adored hugging new brides. *Such is life,* she thought as she unwrapped the white dress and prepared herself for bed.

Binta remained talking with the other women of the village as Alpha prepared to give his daughter her final lesson in womanhood. He peeked through the same hole Lama had peeked through days earlier and watched his little girl's womanly features emerge from the white cloth.

"Allah forgive me," he said. "Fatou is too much for any man to resist."

While staring at his daughter, Alpha was taken back twenty years to the days when Binta's body was so young and so tender. *Yes, Binta is impeccable right now,* he thought, *but her body doesn't have the ripeness it once had. Fatou's tight skin is amazing considering how plump her breasts are. Look at her thighs and backside. Where did all of that glory come from in such a young girl?*

"Allah forgive me," he said. "Please forgive me."

When Alpha entered the tent, Fatou shyly turned away, oil still fresh on her hands, and said, "Daddy, I'm naked."

"I know, sweetness," Alpha replied. "But believe me; this is for your own good. No matter what, you have to remember that this is for your own good."

Fatou looked at Alpha curiously as he approached her and told her to rub the remaining oil on his chest. She obliged, trying to cover up her nakedness as best as she could. Then she watched as Alpha took her hands and rubbed the last fragments of oil on his own before softly placing her hands at her side.

After surveying his daughter and reveling in her beauty, Alpha took his hands and started massaging her breasts. As he lowered his head to nurse on her nipples, he whispered again, "This is for the best, sweetness. After the wedding ceremony, this is always for the best."

Fatou stood in shock as her father's hands caressed her breasts, her backside and her thighs before fumbling with her womanhood. He licked his fingers, then brought them down to her inner thighs before sticking them inside of her. Fatou shuddered and didn't understand what she was feeling. She hated what her father was doing but couldn't argue with him. It was against tradition to disrespect any man, especially not your father.

Fatou also hated the signals that her body was giving her. She was

9

hypersensitive and didn't understand why she was yearning to discover these new feelings. *Besides,* she thought, *Daddy must really love me to be trying so hard to make me feel good.*

She looks at his closed eyes and serious face and how he seemed to be utterly enjoying himself. She gasped as he continued to nurse her breasts and play inside her womanhood with his fingers. She wondered what he was going to do next when he grabbed her backside firmly and lifted her up before placing her down on the cloths that made up her bedding. Then he did it.

In an instant, all of the tingling she'd felt became pain as he placed himself inside her.

"Daddy, no," she moaned. "It hurts. It really hurts."

" No matter what happens," he replied, "remember that this is for the best. Your father always knows what's best."

Fatou cringed as the pain continued unbearably. Occasionally, she shrieked when she thought that something might feel good. But she couldn't concentrate on deriving pleasure. Her young body was in too much pain.

Before long, her dad took himself out of her, and she felt a warm liquid on her belly. When she wiped herself off, the cloth showed what appeared to be a clear gooey substance mixed with specks of blood. Because she hurt so badly, she knew the blood had to be hers.

"Remember, this is for the best," her father said one last time as he gathered himself and left the tent.

Fatou remained inside, alone except for her tears. She wasn't exactly sure what had just taken place, but she hated it.

"Why would Papa hurt me?" she whimpered. She finally cried herself to sleep.

Outside of the tent, Alpha told Binta, "She's a woman now."

And oh what a woman she is, he thought as he remembered how good his young daughter had felt to him.

The next morning Fatou rose early and packed all of her belongings before heading to the foot of the village to meet Kouadio, the only person in town with a car. She couldn't bear to look into her father's eyes after what had just happened the night before. She also felt guilty about her mother, thinking that she'd stolen something that was meant only for her.

Fatou quietly escaped the village without a goodbye to her parents. There were no tears or endless embraces. All that Fatou had was guilt, pain and a hunger to succeed in America.

I can't believe that Father hurt me so, she thought. *I'm going to America now and Lama will protect me. Allah, please allow Lama to be my new father and guide me in the right directions. Please allow me to prosper in my schooling and to make the most out of the chance that Lama is giving me. Father, I am so disappointed in you, but Lama, I love you so for choosing to be there for me. I just hope that I can make you proud. And I hope that one day I can make it up to you.*

As Kouadio guided his car toward the airport, Fatou was not aware of how soon that day would arrive. She soon would be making things up to Lama. He had paid $5,000 to guarantee that she make it up to him in any way he saw fit. And as her father promised in his letter to Lama, Fatou was Lama's until death.

CHAPTER TWO

Fatou Goes to Harlem

Lama Contravene strolled into Sister Fifi's Hair Braiding Salon on 125th St. and told her he wanted his hair washed and his scalp greased. Then he winked at Fifi and nodded his head in the direction of a hair stylist named Patra who was originally from Africa but had entered the US illegally several years back. Fifi grabbed Patra's hand and walked with her to the back to have a few words with her.

As Patra walked away, Lama marveled at how her backside swished perfectly inside of her sweat pants. Lama chuckled to himself, remembering how Jell-O shook in the television commercials. He thought that he should start calling Patra the Jell-O Girl.

Fifi emerged from the back and asked Lama, "How much?"

He looked surprised and let her know as much when he replied.

"I'm about to give you an amazing hair braider straight from the motherland. This should be on the house."

"And will be, my brother. Relax," she replied. "But for what you really want, you can't expect to pay nothing. Be reasonable."

Lama smiled and pulled forty dollars out of his pocket. "Should I give this to you or her?"

"Wait," Fifi replied before taking the forty dollars from his hand and handing him back eight dollars. "Give this to her. It is enough."

Lama walked to the back of the salon and smiled widely at Patra. "Let's get this over with," Patra said nonchalantly as she opened her robe, revealing her nakedness underneath.

When Lama approached, her she backed up and held out her hand. He gave her the eight dollars then rushed at her aggressively, palming her breasts and backside as if he'd never felt a woman before. Patra leaned back in the tall chair, and Lama entered her roughly. He moved his face toward Patra's as if he wanted to kiss her but she pulled her face away. Not even three minutes into their sexual adventure, Lama started to shudder and released his fluids inside of her. Then he stood up proudly as if he'd just won a gold medal and strutted toward the door. "Hurry up, girl," he said. "I have to get my hair washed and oiled before I start my shift in the cab. And I can't be late tonight. I have to be at JFK early tomorrow to pick up Fatou La Princesse."

Patra shook her head, acknowledging Lama, and grabbed two cloths. She wet one, and when Lama didn't take the other from her, she threw it down. Lama didn't wash himself afterwards, or at least he hadn't the countless times he'd been with her.

After Patra finished with his hair, Lama felt handsome despite his balding gray-black hair. He believed that Fatou would covet him the moment she saw him.

"Don't I get a tip?" Patra asked as he approached the door.

He shot her an angry look. "I keep you in business, girl. Isn't that enough?"

Then he sashayed out the door looking as proud as a peacock.

Lama's night was uneventful until he saw a white hooker while he was dropping off a fare in Harlem. He barely remembered to ask for the money.

He made a quick u-turn. He didn't want anyone else to pick her up. He reveled in the fact that for twenty dollars he could make a white woman do anything he wanted her to do. Things like that never happened in his homeland.

She approached his taxi and asked what he wanted. He gazed down between her legs, pleased that he had the chance to pick up the white hooker.

"Money first," she said matter-of-factly, then reached in her pocket to grab a condom.

"What's that for?" Lama protested. "I love the way it feels when two bodies are together. I don't want anything hindering that."

A small argument ensued, but she relented. As she removed her pants and sat on top of him, he noticed the first streaks of daylight as the sun rose.

I don't have much time, he thought as he pulled the hooker's hair, bringing her face to his. He kissed her passionately before coming inside of her. Then he let her out of his cab and headed toward the base. He wanted to check in before going to get Fatou.

On the plane, Fatou is sleeping deeply, dreaming. Suddenly, she starts moving her head back and forth, and before long, she is shaking in her seat. She shouts, "No, Daddy, no!" and jumps up in her chair. Her eyes fly wide open, and she begins to be aware of her surroundings.

"You must have really gotten that tail licked good, young lady," says the passenger in the seat beside her.

Fatou smiles, acknowledging the older West African gentleman, but she doesn't comment. She tries to relax for the remaining forty minutes of the flight.

As the captain informs everyone that they are starting their descent, Fatou wonders what made her father turn on her as he did. She'd done everything her parents asked of her, so she couldn't imagine why he was so upset. And she was certain that her father enjoyed being with her mother, since they often put her out of the tent to have privacy.

Regardless, what he had done to her was the most cruel and unusual punishment she'd ever received. She is unsure if she will ever be able to forgive him.

That's OK, she thinks. *I have a very long time to make up my mind about Papa. Lama will be filling his shoes now.*

Fatou thinks about Lama giving her piggyback rides up and down the streets of New York City, then buying her American hot dogs. She can't wait for him to introduce her as his little girl from the village as he takes her to quaint little eating spots and lets her sample some of the best cuisine that America has to offer.

"Yes, Papa Lama," she says softly to herself. "We're going to have so much fun!"

As the flight attendants prepared the plane for deboarding, Fatou could barely contain herself. She skipped along the walkway, following the passengers who'd had better seats, wishing that they'd hurry.

When she saw Lama, she dropped her two bags and ran to him. She leaped into his arms and wrapped her legs behind his back. Oblivious to his palms on her backside, she became teary eyed thinking about how he would be her protector.

"Oh, Lama," she swooned, "thank you so much for bringing me here. Thank you so much for saving me."

Lama had expected Fatou to be reluctant to be his young bride, so he was glad that Fatou was much happier than he'd imagined she would be. Suddenly, he wasn't so tired.

"I must hurry and get you home," Lama exclaimed. All thoughts of his obligations to finishing his replacement's shift drifting from his mind.

After placing Fatou's bags in the trunk, he told her to sit up front. And in her African dialect said, "Excuse me for one moment, Fatou."

Lama called the base of the Gypsy Cab Company and pleaded his case in a heated debate. He closed the passenger door and argued with the dispatcher so that Fatou couldn't hear him but since she didn't speak English, it didn't much matter.

"I have just brought my mate here from West Africa," Lama said. "How can you allow your brother to back out on me at the last moment? What am I supposed to do with her?"

"Drop her off, then return to accepting fares," the dispatcher said.

"That will take too long! By the time I drop her off and get her settled, I will only have about forty minutes left to drive. Then I will have to drive another twenty minutes back to my home. That is all too much!" Lama argued.

"Shall I play the violin for you?"

"You are an asshole!" Lama shouted.

"It doesn't matter what you say I am. You don't have anyone to take your shift, so you'll have to finish it."

"Well then, Fatou La Princesse will sit up front with me for my last two hours of collecting fares."

"You know that we don't allow such things."

"It is my cab. I paid for it."

"But you work for my company."

"Don't remind me," Lama shouted, slamming shut his phone. He tried to compose himself for a few minutes before joining Fatou inside the cab. He sat quietly for a moment, took a deep breath, then struck up a conversation.

"So how is everyone in the motherland?" he asked. "And how was your flight?"

"Everyone in the motherland is OK," Fatou replied. "But I'd rather talk about America! The metal bird was awesome and shook something horrible. It made my ears feel funny and my stomach turn. I even vomited. But the most surprising thing of all is that white people served me. On the little television we have in the village, I saw only blacks serving whites. So to see it the other way around was really odd!"

"Slow down, Fatou," Lama said jollily. "You have the rest of your life to tell me of your adventures. Now I want to show you around New York City."

CHAPTER THREE

Til Death

Fatou's heart raced as they walked up to the house in Harlem. Compared to the tents she was used to back home, it was a miracle .

Lama's house, a two-bedroom brownstone, had running water in both bathrooms, and a kitchen with a stove. *Gosh, we won't have to collect wood to start fires*, Fatou thought.

Lama told her that he had other African immigrants staying with him (they were actually Jamaican). But the brownstone was roomy and had more amenities than Fatou was accustomed to.

This will do just fine, Fatou said to herself and smiled.

Lama called out to the others.

As planned, music familiar to Fatou began to play. A group of ten African women dressed in traditional garb started to come down the stairs. One held the source of the music, a palm-sized cassette player.

Fatou looked around the large room she was in, the living room, and saw that it was decorated similarly to her village when ceremonies were held.

When the women approached her, they began to sing the wedding song. And in horror, Fatou suddenly understood. She looked at Lama, who was smiling from ear to ear, and backed away.

Fatou was panicked. The women came at her from all sides, grabbing her and pulling at her. They finally dragged her into a bathroom but Fatou was unaware. She had fainted.

Her unconsciousness didn't faze the women. They dutifully stripped her of her clothes, bathed her, oiled her skin, and sprayed perfume on her before wrapping her in white cloths.

When Fatou regained consciousness, she screamed, but no one heard her, not even her mother in West Africa.

After emerging from the bathroom, the women escorted Fatou to Lama's bedroom. They told her to relax until her husband joined her at midnight, then they closed and locked the door.

She screamed repeatedly and thought about how her parents had betrayed her. Then she wondered if she would be allowed to complete her studies.

"Oh, my God!" she hollered. "The ceremony, the new clothes, Papa touching me—my family has sold me into slavery! I am nothing to them but a meal and a piece of cloth!"

Fatou wailed uncontrollably until one of the strange women came into the room.

"Sweetheart, I am Mati," she said. "Do not trouble yourself so. We have all been where you are, and it is just a part of life. But you are in America now in much more than a dirt or cloth hut. You have a lot to be thankful for. You have made it out of poverty."

Fatou glared at her. She could not respond. She knew what was going to happen to her. More pain. From Lama this time, not her father.

Not far from Sister Fifi's, Lama sat in his cab with Patra.

"Hurry, child," he said while unbuckling his belt.

After pulling down his pants, Patra protested. "Lama, you haven't washed! I cannot do anything with you like this."

"Why do you fuss, you little whore?" Lama replied angrily. "You defile tradition by speaking to me as such. Let's just get this over with so I can go to meet my wife."

"Relax," Patra replied more calmly. "I will only be a second. I must go retrieve something from the house."

Patra exited the cab before Lama could stop her and went inside Sister Fifi's. She emerged with two hand towels, one wet and one dry. She returned to the cab and sat next to Lama.

"You must really be more careful, Lama," she pleaded while washing his groin. "You don't know what can happen to people, and you have too much trust when it comes to things like this. You know of the epidemic in our homeland."

Lama didn't comment as Patra cleaned and dried him. She then flipped a condom she was hiding in her hand onto her tongue and held it in her mouth. Lama started to protest, so she softly placed her hand on his mouth before lowering her head to his groin. After placing the condom on Lama, she briefly moved her mouth up and down his manhood before raising herself up on top of him.

Lama climaxed, and Patra rubbed his head as she removed herself from him. Then she wiped him off again with the wet towel and dried him with the other.

"Lama, you should never contaminate one woman with another woman's spirit. You must always wash yourself in between so that everyone remains happy and prosperous."

"I like to feel all of you, Patra," he said. "You must know this by now."

Patra sized Lama up with her eyes before saying, "I thought I knew you. But you go out of your way to bring someone from the motherland here when I thought you loved me! And now you lay with me before rushing home to your bride, knowing full well that your bride should be me."

"Am I to marry a whore?" Lama asked sarcastically.

"A whore?" Patra shouted angrily. "Is that what you think of me? You think I'm a whore?"

"Well, what should I call it when I pay for it all the time? When have you just given yourself to me?"

Patra glanced at Lama in amazement. "Lama, I love you. I've loved you for a long time. But a woman doesn't just give herself to a man. We are no longer in the motherland. You cannot just come into a tent and take a woman freely. You must show her that you care."

"Show her that you care," Lama said, laughing.

"Quiet!" Patra snapped back, cutting him off. "You came into Sister Fifi's demanding to have me. You never once asked me if I liked flowers or walks through a garden. You didn't try to romance me. You just offered Sister Fifi money to defile me, knowing that I would get fired if I didn't agree. And with her contempt, she might have called the authorities and have me sent back to Kingston. Now you stare at me with that foolish look! No, Lama. You never did a thing to show me you cared. Still, the only reason I allowed you to do what you have done all this time is I thought one day you'd realize that I was made for you. I thought one day you would make me your bride. But today another has become your bride, and you've proven to me that you never really cared about me. For that, I despise you."

Patra rushed out of the cab angrily, and Lama followed her into Sister Fifi's. "So, why do you lay with me now if you despise me?" he asked.

"I despise you, but I still love you. Now go take your citizenship and give it to another woman while I still worry about being here illegally. Show her around your home while I lay on Sister Fifi's floor wondering when some maniac will come in the middle of the night and hurt me. I've given you all that I have, and all that you have, you've chosen to give to another. Be gone, Lama. Just return when your loins crave me. That is all you value me for anyway."

Lama stared at Patra in amazement. He'd always fancied Patra but never imagined she had feelings for him as well. At that moment, he felt contempt for Fatou.

I could have kept my $5,000, he thought.

His eyes pored over Patra, and he noticed that her breasts were just as marvelous as Fatou's. *They are actually bigger,* he thought. Lama walked slowly around Patra, almost as if he were in a daze, studying her closely for the first time, and caressed her thighs. He marveled at their firmness and recalled some of the females who ran on Jamaica's track team. He palmed her backside and was amazed at its plumpness.

At that moment, Patra's womanly features were suddenly too much for Lama, so he backed away from her and fumbled for the door.

He drove home, thinking of his predicament. Before today, he had never noticed how beautiful Patra was.

What have I done? he thought.

He parked his car in front of his house and banged his head on the steering wheel, feeling contempt for Fatou. *I slave and slave like a dog to bring you here and you cry!* he said to himself. *You have no fucking appreciation!* It didn't matter to him that Fatou was crying out of joy.

Lama angrily pulled himself out of the cab and violently slammed the door. He stomped inside the house and ran up the stairs, not acknowledging the women who happily greeted him from the living room.

He went into his room, and Fatou stirred in bed. She stared at him and didn't say anything. As Lama approached her, she timidly backed away into the bedpost, tears in her eyes. The sight of her wet cheeks made him even angrier. He snatched off his belt.

"I work and sweat and beg to bring you here to give you a better life, and how do you repay me? With foolish tears!" He lashed her with his belt. "I hate you. I fucking hate you!"

Fatou's cried even harder, not understanding his anger. "I'm sorry, Papa Lama. I'm so very sorry."

"I am not your fucking papa!" he hollered, lashing her again with his belt. "I am your husband, and you will love me!"

"OK," Fatou pleaded. "Let me love you. Come and let me love you."

She grabbed his hand and brought him to her. He eagerly approached her, wildly pulling away the white cloth. He licked his lips at the sight of her young perky breasts bouncing about. As he pulled away the cloth from her loins, he moved closer as if inspecting her.

Her young vagina was very smooth and had only a tiny stubble of pubic hair.

"This is what I've always wanted," he said as he took her into his mouth.

Fatou summoned everything she had inside to act like she was enjoying herself. *I do not wish to be beaten anymore,* she thought as Lama lapped away at her with his tongue.

Eventually, Lama pulled himself up on top of her and kissed her with glistening wet lips. His spit disgusted her, but she wanted no more trouble. He put himself inside of her. She cringed from the pain but didn't cry out.

Fatou was relieved that Lama didn't hurt her as much as her father did. She didn't know any better, but Lama wasn't as well endowed as her father.

Her thoughts actually went back to her father and how he had caressed her. Lama seemed to be a man with a purpose, hastily satisfying his own pleasure, oblivious to hers.

Why did you do this to me, Papa? she thought. *And, Mama, why did you let him?*

Lama released his fluids inside of her and flopped onto the bed. Within a minute, he was fast asleep, his snores filling the silence in the house.

Fatou laid there and wondered what else was in store for her.

Without stirring Lama from his sleep, she quietly inched her naked body out of bed and knelt on the floor. She stared at Lama briefly before bowing her head to pray.

"Allah. Please watch over me as I sit alone in this large forest, defeated and scared. Please mend Papa and Mama's hearts and remove the contempt they must have for me to leave me in this predicament. Yet do not punish them. Forgive them for their misgivings. Also, forgive Papa Lama, for he knows not his indiscretions. He cannot know how much he's hurt me thus far by taking away my hope. America is no longer a dream to me. It is a harsh and painful reality. Allah, please bring back the dream. Please bring me hope for a better tomorrow. Because today... today..."

Fatou started to sob uncontrollably. She was very afraid of waking Lama, but she couldn't help herself. Luckily, he didn't stir. His snoring only became louder.

Fatou pulled herself together and went to clean herself. She soaked for hours in a hot tub.

CHAPTER FOUR

Prisoner of Love

"She hasn't been here a day and she prances around like she owns everything. She pays no rent but makes us wait for hours as she soaks like a high priestess," Nefara protested to her mother, Mati.

"Well, I'll do something about that," Lama replied. Then he turned to Mati. "She seems to be fond of you, so be sure that she is bathed and fed. I will buy two round tubs so that she won't be required to go into the rest room until she has learned her lesson. You can fill one with water for her baths, and the other she can use to relieve herself. It is settled."

Lama started to walk away, but Nefara stopped him with her words. "But what if she defies us? What if she runs away?"

"I will call a locksmith," he said. "Have him place bars on the bedroom window. Mati will keep one key, and I will have the other. Fatou is to be locked in the room at all times. Now, I must go to work."

Lama hurried out the door, and Nefara wielded a vicious smile.

"Why do you hate her so?" Mati asked.

"She thinks she is so special," Nefara replied with contempt. "Lama won the lottery and can have any of us, but he chooses to bring her here. But is she thankful? No. She prances about as if someone should feel sorry for her."

"But she is just a baby," Mati said, defending Fatou. "She has yet to have her cycle. What does everyone expect from her?"

"I just want her to stay out of my way," Nefara said harshly as she shut off her bath water. "Today I will soak for hours as if I am a queen. Fatou can just wait in her plastic tub."

For two months, Mati brought food, water and companionship into Fatou's room. Twice a day she bathed Fatou and secretly taught her English. "Do not tell anyone I am helping you to speak American," she said. "Always speak to people in our native tongue so I won't be found out. Everyone wants to keep you ignorant."

"Why does everyone hate me so?" Fatou asked.

"Nonsense," Mati replied. "No one hates you. They are merely jealous, that's all."

"But why?" Fatou asked innocently. "What makes them jealous of me?"

"You don't understand," said Mati calmly. "Lama was a nobody until he was chosen in the lottery. Then every woman he ever batted his eyes at thought they had a chance to be his bride and to become legal naturalized citizens of the US. But when you came, their chances of getting a green card went away. So it is not you that they hate you. They hate their own circumstances."

"So why does Lama hate me?"

"Lama is just full of a big head. He's coveted you for a long time, and now that he has you, he is showing you his backside just as any man will do. That is just the way of men. Child, you have a lot to learn."

With that, Mati left Fatou locked in the room with her thoughts of West Africa. "This place is nothing like home," she whispered to herself. "Everyone is at each other's throats. This is not such a nice place."

Four months later Nefara met her cousin, Patra, at Sister Fifi's. They embraced, and Patra asked about Fatou.

"Oh, she is locked in her room like an animal," Nefara said, laughing. "She has to have food and drink brought to her by Mati. Mati even has to wash her."

"Nefara, you are wrong," Patra said harshly. "You have not been in America so long that you are disrespecting you own mother. How do you call her Mati and not Mama or Mother? Anyway, I see nothing funny. You and I slave twelve hours a day or more for a rental fee and mere scraps while Fatou has the world given to her on a platter. Some days you and I cannot eat, we are so busy, me here and you at your salon. On those days, Fatou's belly still is full. It seems as if she has the last laugh."

Patra's words sunk in as Nefara sat quietly for the rest of her visit. Then she went home, storming through the door.

"Good. I caught you before I left. Today is the day for your rental fee," Lama said cheerily.

With disgust Nefara reached into her purse and grabbed forty dollars. She screamed, "Fatou has the world on her shoulders, enjoying your master bedroom while the rest of us slave to share the smaller one. It may as well be a closet."

"Now, what has you upset today, Nefara?" Lama asked. "Fatou has been staying out of your way. I can't understand why you are so agitated."

"Everyone brings money into this house but her!" Patra replied angrily. "And Mati can no longer work as much, since she cares for Fatou all day. So who has to cover her share? Me, that's who."

"Well, this was supposed to be a surprise, but I see no reason for holding it back any further," he said. "Fatou reached womanhood over three months ago when blood stained our sheets for the first time. A month later, it happened again. But it hasn't happened for almost two months now. So Fatou cannot work. She is with my child."

"Well, if she stays for free," Nefara shouted angrily as she snatched her forty dollars out of Lama's hand, "I stay for free."

Lama watched her backside switch up the stairs and called for Mati. "Mati, it is time," he said. "Prepare Fatou to start at Sister Fifi's. She will begin next week. And have Nefara give you my rental fee before I return. She is very abrasive and needs to remember how to respect a man as she did in the motherland. I will not tolerate her nonsense any longer."

The next day Lama took Fatou to Sister Fifi's to get her hair braided. After explaining to Patra how he wanted it, he went to converse with Fifi.

"Fifi, she already knows how to braid," he said. "You will just need to make her familiar with the styles they want here. And I will need to know what her wage will be."

"Well, all the other girls make $150 a week," she said. "But they are not ignorant like Fatou."

"What do you mean, ignorant?" he asked. "Fatou is very intelligent. She just needs to learn a little English."

"No, she doesn't," Fifi replied sneakily in English, thinking that Fatou wouldn't understand her. "We only need to teach her words that have something to do with braiding hair. And we will show her how to take the buses and subways between your home and here. I will give her fifty dollars and keep the rest."

"No. That is too much," Lama replied. "You keep forty dollars for her rental fee and let me worry about the rest of it as I have been. I will get fifty, and Fatou will get sixty."

Fifi smiled.

"So it is settled," Lama said as he sat at Patra's station and leaned back to take a nap.

Patra started to interrogate Fatou while Lama snored in. "So…are you really pregnant?" she asked.

"I hope not," Fatou replied fearfully. "I am certainly not ready for childbirth. What gives you the idea that I am pregnant?"

"Lama told me of course," Patra said, looking at Fatou strangely.

"He talks to you?" Fatou asked. "He rarely says two words to me. He just jumps on me and does his business. I cannot believe that Lama talks to you."

"Foolish child," Patra said, laughing at her before calling out to another worker. "Can you wash and dry her hair? It is already too flaky to be braided. I have some quick business to tend to."

Patra tapped Lama on his leg until he stirred. "Why have you awakened me, woman?" Lama asked irritably.

"And why do you raise your voice?" she asked, but didn't wait for a response. "Don't you want to go in the back?"

Lama relaxed and got up from his chair smiling broadly.

"Go on back," she continued. "I will be there in a second."

Fatou watched Lama walk away, amazed at the control Patra seemed to have over him.

"You are here because he can control you," Patra said. "But Lama is truly mine."

"Really? But we have had the ceremony," Fatou replied, not knowing what else to say.

"The ceremony!" Patra repeated, laughing. "Listen closely and I will let you hear a ceremony."

Patra nodded her head at the sink closest to the door Lama disappeared into, then went in, careful not to close it all the way. She grabbed the money from Lama, and when he looked at her oddly, she said, "Do not tell Fifi. Today will be special for you, since I get to keep all of it."

Patra caressed Lama's groin with her hand and straddled him once he became erect. Then she bounced on him like a wild woman.

Lama was very pleased that Patra had not forced him to wear a condom. He could not believe how good she felt.

Fatou heard Lama and Patra frolicking inside the back room and didn't understand. Tradition said that Lama could have many wives, but she was sure she would have been a part of the ceremony had he wed Patra. Fatou didn't understand her own jealousy but felt it none-the-less.

When Lama came inside of Patra, she smiled to herself and wiped herself off. Lama looked at her as if he was waiting for her to wipe him as well.

"No. Take my scent home to your wife and sleep with her," she said wickedly. "And be sure to make her take you in her mouth."

She smiled as she walked out of the room. Lama was gathering himself together while Patra approached Fatou and whispered in her ear. "You see," she said. "Lama has always been mine. You are only here to do what I won't do."

Fatou's eyes started watering. "But I cannot have his child if he is yours."

"No problem," Patra replied. "When you come to work on Monday, we will deal with that situation, and you will no longer have to worry. Just stick with me, and I will make sure of it. Now hurry and get back under the hair dryer so I can show you how to braid once your hair dries. I do not harbor any ill feelings against you. I just want what's best for you."

And more than that, I want what's best for me, Patra thought to herself. *And I will have what's best for me.*

CHAPTER FIVE

Thanks For My Child

On Monday, Fatou arrived at Sister Fifi's and asked Patra about her pregnancy. Patra told her that they should wait until Fifi left for lunch before talking further.

As soon as Fifi was gone, Patra summoned Fatou into the back room. "I have a way out for you," she told Fatou, "but it won't be easy. You will feel lots of pain."

"I don't care," Fatou replied. "How can I have his baby when he sleeps with you, a woman who is not even his bride? I have no other choice."

Patra told Fatou that she should take off her clothes and put on a robe. Then she leaned her back in a chair and placed a blindfold on her.

"You won't allow me to finish if you are able to see," Patra said before taking a needle filled with anesthesia that her doctor friend had given her out of her bag.

Finally, Patra retrieved a wire hanger from off the coat rack and twisted it until she was satisfied with its shape.

After grabbing all of her materials, Patra lurked over Fatou with an evil grin on her face. Then she jabbed the needle into Fatou three times, once below her belly button and once on each inner thigh, just as the doctor had instructed her to do. Fatou shrieked, and Patra smiled, knowing she stuck Fatou harder than was necessary.

Patra watched the seconds tick by on her watch. She wanted to be certain that Fatou felt very little pain after she gave her the type of abortion that had been outlawed for many years. Patra pinched Fatou after a few minutes to make sure that it was OK to proceed.

Satisfied, Patra took the hanger and shoved it inside Fatou's young vagina, twisting it around several times. When Patra saw Fatou's blood, she got excited and started twisting the hanger even more.

Patra was surprised when she heard a key being inserted into the back room door. She turned to look and saw Fifi.

"Girl, why you gon' lock the door back here with all those customers up front?" Fifi asked before she noticed Fatou bleeding. "Girl, what the blood clot are you doing? You gon' mess around and kill that child."

"No," Patra said innocently. "I was just trying to help. Fatou is pregnant and doesn't want to be. No, she cannot be. She is merely thirteen years old. I am trying to save all of us."

Fifi slapped Patra and told her to get her doctor friend to come there instantly. "Move it girl! Now!" she screamed.

Patra's doctor friend stopped Fatou's bleeding but told her she would be in intense pain once the anesthesia wore off. Then she pulled Fifi aside and whispered her opinion about Fatou's health.

"I don't think she'll ever be able to have children now," she said. "Her insides appear to be damaged yet we won't know for sure unless she is cared for in a hospital."

"But what will we tell them?" Fifi asked, whispering. "She's a baby who has just had an abortion."

"That's it," the doctor said. "We can drop her off at the Emergency Room. I will help her sneak out of the hospital later when she's better. I can't think of any other way without someone getting into lots of trouble."

"Alright," Fifi said agreeably. "That is what we will do." She turned to Patra and said, "Watch the shop, girl. Do you think you can do that without screwing things up?"

Patra shook her head yes and watched Fifi leave the shop with her doctor friend. When they were no longer visible, she called Nefara at her salon.

"Nefara's Hair Care," Nefara said, answering the phone.

"It's me," Patra said matter-of-factly. "The little bitch is no longer pregnant. And she almost died," Patra added, laughing.

"And the world would have been a much better place," Nefara responded. "Well, it is very busy for a Monday. I will call you later. But thank you so much for the good news."

"It was my pleasure," Patra said smugly. "Next time I'll try to do a better job."

Patra hung up the phone and pranced around the shop like she'd just won a million bucks.

Several hours later, Lama entered Sister Fifi's looking for Fatou.

"You are to meet Fifi at the hospital," Patra said before Lama had the chance to open his mouth. She pushed him toward the door. "Just go," she said. "It is imperative that you don't waste any time. Fifi will explain everything to you once you get there."

Patra paused before continuing. "Oh. I will expect to see you back here at your regular time. If you enjoyed yourself Friday, I guarantee that things will be even better when you return tonight."

At the hospital Lama learned that Fatou had lost their child. Yet Fifi couldn't bear to tell him about Patra giving her the abortion.

"Are they saying that she will never have children?" Lama asked, highly disappointed.

"Yes. That is what the doctor says," Fifi replied. "But we can't see her. I'm waiting around until the doctor helps sneak her out. You should leave. If the authorities come, and I get caught, at least I can say that she works for me. What will be your excuse?"

"You are right," Lama said, standing up wearily. After dragging himself out the door, he sat in his cab for a few minutes, then drove around town. After a while, he parked his car in front of Sister Fifi's salon and went in.

"How is Fatou?" Patra asked, feigning concern.

"She is still at the hospital," he answered. "But it is horrible. She has lost the baby." He paused briefly. "I'm sorry I didn't tell you, but Fatou was carrying my child. Now I may never have a chance to father a child."

Lama lowered his head and started to weep silently. Patra grabbed his arm and guided him to a chair in the back room. She smiled at him and said, "I guess only I can make you feel better."

Lama surveyed Patra guiltily before reaching into his pocket. Patra didn't give him a chance to pull out any money.

Look, Lama," she said. "I don't feel right about taking your money. In fact, I don't want your money anymore. Whenever you want me, you can have me. We just have to be careful that Fifi doesn't find out. You know that she would want her cut."

Lama smiled widely as Patra continued. "That's not all. If you want, I will give you a child. No more condoms. But you must promise me two things."

"Anything," Lama said hoarsely.

"You must never again sleep with hookers," she said. "And you must promise to buy me things from time to time."

"Of course," Lama said, smiling.

"You know that I've always loved you," Patra said reassuringly. "It is time that I start acting like I love you."

Lama grabbed Patra and hugged her tightly. "I want to tell you something," he said. "The only reason you and I haven't had the ceremony is that I promised my father on his deathbed that I would marry Fatou. We both knew that she was too young to marry. I swear that is the only reason I made you wait."

Patra kissed Lama on the mouth, then told him, "We are in America now. We no longer have to follow every tradition. You and I will have a marriage without rings. And I will satisfy you more than you could ever imagine. Have a seat. I'll start now."

Patra unbuttoned Lama's pants and took his manhood into her mouth. She worked feverishly, pleasing him orally, until he came. Then she swallowed his fluids.

"Look at me, Lama," she said. "I have given you a Lewinsky. Only my husband can ever have that. Do you understand?"

"Yes, I understand, my bride," he said, grabbing her again and holding her tightly. "I most certainly understand."

A year to the day later, Lama and Patra walked hand in hand into Sister Fifi's. "We have the greatest news," Lama said.

"Patra is carrying my child."

All the workers in the shop cheered three times, "Hip, hip, hooray," all except for Fatou. She lowered her head and held back her tears, She knew it was very unlikely that she would ever have a child.

CHAPTER SIX

Sweet Sixteen

Three years later, Fatou scowled at Lama when he visited Sister Fifi's to drop off money for Patra to buy diapers. The diapers were for their third child.

"Why do you tolerate such a mockery?" asked Natali, a student who was in the US on an education visa. Natali was from Paris and was born of mixed blood, an African mother and a french father.

She tossed her red brown hair from her eyes and waited for Fatou to respond.

Natali was very pretty and everyone adored hearing her natural French accent when she was tried to speak in English. Yet they didn't get a chance to hear it much because she and Fatou customarily spoke to each other in French.

"Patra bears his children because I am unable," Fatou said, defending Patra. "Besides, I do not want to have children yet."

"I agree with your choice to not have children, but don't forget that she is the one who has damaged your reproductive organs," Natali hissed. "Now she flaunts her bastard children in your face. You are often forced to watch them for hours at a time. I do not understand

39

why you stay. Your customer base is such that you can work anywhere in Harlem. Yet, you choose to remain here, getting taken advantage of. If anyone should be gone, you should be gone. It's despicable the way you are treated here."

"Haven't you forgotten that Lama has threatened me repeatedly?" Fatou reminded Natali. "He says that he will kill me if I ever try to leave him. La Dotte has guaranteed that I am his until the death."

"Fatou, you are in America now," Natali cut in. "There are rules. Women have equal rights. Besides, you are still a minor. Lama could be arrested for statutory rape."

"Then what would I do?" Fatou asked. "I am an illegal alien whose parents have sold for scraps. If I get sent back, where would I go? I cannot call the police. I doubt that they would help me. They'd only start the proceedings to have me deported."

"So just leave him!" Natali scolded Fatou. "With your looks, any number of men would kill him if they believed you would be theirs."

"Am I to arrange a murder now?" Fatou asked, laughing.

"Why not?" Natali replied. "These people around here have abused you. You can't tell me that this one over here didn't try to kill you. But you defend her! You should open your eyes to see that she is not your friend. I am the only friend you have here."

Natali and Fatou cut their conversation short as Lama approached. He kissed Fatou on the cheek.

"And how is my beautiful bride this afternoon?" he asked.

"You do not know?" Fatou replied sarcastically. "You have been in here speaking with Patra for the last half hour without acknowledging me. You tell me how your bride is doing."

Natali laughed and said in French, "All I've ever wanted is for you to get a backbone." Fatou joined her in laughter.

"Do not mock me in French!" Lama said angrily. "Have you forgotten that I am your husband? Never forget all that I have done for you!"

Fatou noticed Patra staring at them, so she winked her eye at Natali before pulling Lama closer to her and kissing him passionately.

"I am sorry, my love," she said. "You know that you are everything to me."

Patra stomped out the front door and slammed it. Fatou gave Natali a quick smile while hugging Lama.

"I wonder what has gotten her panties in such a bunch!" Fatou asked inquisitively.

"Never you mind," Lama replied. "Just continue braiding hair. I will speak to you later."

As he walked away, Natali whispered, "That's right, man. Run after your bitch."

Natali and Fatou laughed softly.

Moments later Nefara entered the salon and asked for Fifi, who had left to run an errand.

"I am here to collect your rental fee, Fatou" she said.

Fatou ignored her, so she repeated herself.

"Hello! Are you deaf? I am here for your rental fee."

Fatou cut her eyes at her and said, "My husband is just outside those doors, and Fifi will shortly return. I will handle my affairs with one of them as I always do."

"No," Nefara said curtly. "You will give me your rental fee now or I will take it from you."

In French, Natali said to Fatou, "I know you are not about to accept this foolishness from her. You need to whip her little ass.

"Do not be mad at me that you are half of a woman," Nefara said snidely. "Just give me the rental fee so that I can be on my way. I am sorry that you do not have any children to kick at my shins in your honor. We both know that you are not woman enough for that."

Fatou wielded her razor blade at Nefara and whispered in English so that no one else in the shop could hear, "I am woman enough to cut your bitch ass if you don't leave me the hell alone."

Nefara backed toward the door, screaming in astonishment. "She threatened me!"

Fatou and Natali laughed heartily until they saw Lama. Immediately, they both put stern expressions on their faces.

"Nefara, Fatou threatened you? You are being ridiculous," Lama said. "Fatou barely knows any English at all. And she certainly wouldn't have threatened you. She is worse than the cowardly lion from Oz. I think that you are working yourself too hard in your shop."

"No!" Nefara cried. "The little bitch cursed me. And she threatened me. How are we going to handle this, Lama?"

"What do you want me to do?" Lama asked Nefara.

"Let them fight," Patra answered. "You cannot protect her every time she antagonizes Nefara." Patra looked at Fatou and said in African, "Nefara wants to fight you. You must apologize. I do not want to see you get hurt."

When Fatou didn't respond, Patra sat back in Fifi's chair.

"Well, move the chairs out of the way," Patra said. "If Fatou chooses to be stubborn, let Nefara kick her little ass."

Natali whispered to Fatou, "How can someone be so blatantly two-faced? I told you that she is not your friend. But I do agree with her.

You should fight Nefara. You have the opportunity to mop up this shop with her ass. You can take out all of your frustrations on Nefara right here, right now. Repay her for all the wrong that has happened to you since you got here."

Natali stopped talking when she saw Nefara taking off her earrings, got up, grabbed her purse and from it, pulled a jar of Vaseline.

"I haven't been in the US long, but I have learned a few tricks," she said in French as she smeared Vaseline on Fatou's face.

Then she whispered to Fatou to be careful. "Ugly bitches like that will try to scratch you to take away your beauty."

"Relax," Fatou said. "She will never touch me."

Fatou charged at Nefara, totally catching her off guard. She wrestled Nefara to the ground as if she were an antelope, then brought her fists down into her face as if she were West African wood to be chopped. She beat Nefara unmercifully as everyone looked on, totally astonished.

It took Natali to pull Fatou off Nefara. "Stop it, child, before you kill her." Then she gave her a high five. "That's right, girl. I knew you had it in you. That's how you beat someone's ass, especially someone who's had it coming for as long as she has."

Fatou was happy to find that Mati wasn't upset with her when she returned to the brownstone later that evening.

"I am proud to see that you have finally stood up for yourself," Mati said. "Nefara can be a bit much to take at times. Do not think that I will no longer befriend you because of it. I only wish that I had chastised her more in her early years. She wouldn't be so spoiled now."

"I didn't want any trouble," Fatou replied. "But it seemed as if Nefara had a vendetta against me when she entered the shop, just as she has had since the first day I got here."

"Never you mind such things," Mati said. "We need to discuss your sweet sixteen party. Do you want it to be at Sister Fifi's or here?"

"It doesn't matter that much," Fatou replied. "If I really had a choice, I would chose neither. Both places have caused me much hardship and many sleepless nights."

Mati looked at Fatou caringly and said, "Well, we will see," before turning to head to her room.

Mati arranged Fatou's party to be at an African restaurant in Manhattan. She felt it was a shame that Fatou has seen nothing of New York City but Harlem.

Fatou's party was a smashing success. Her customers turned out to celebrate with her, many of them leaving work early or not going to work at all that day. Fatou was well liked by her customers and was surprised to be inundated with gifts. She received a Fendi purse, a pair of Prada shoes, and a Movado watch, as well as many other pieces of clothing and jewelry. To say that both Patra and Nefara were jealous was an understatement. Fifi looked on, wondering how to get her hands on some of Fatou's fabulous gifts.

Later that night Lama asked Fatou what small gift she wanted to receive from her husband. Her reply was that she only wanted honesty. Lama didn't understand what she meant, so Fatou tried to explain herself.

"Lama, why did you bring me here as a baby when you obviously loved Patra?" she asked. "You have taken so many risks."

Lama didn't respond, so Fatou continued.

"Do you think that it is normal to fancy a twelve-year-old when you are well beyond forty?"

Lama still had no response.

"Did you expect me to fall head over heels in love with you the moment I came here?"

Lama's expression was stone faced, and his mouth was shut.

"Don't you think that I would have loved you blindly had you been more patient with me? But you were already fucking Patra."

"You are wrong, child," Lama finally replied.

"Do not lie. Have you forgotten that I needed treatment shortly after I got here? If you weren't laying with Patra, I'm certain you would have been with someone else. But I'm sure you love her."

"Enough, child," he said. "Why are you so concerned with her?"

"Because my entire life was uprooted to fulfill what may have been just your perverted fantasy, and you barely care for me. You are too busy acting as if Patra is your wife and I am your slut."

Lama smacked her. "Fatou, just tell me what you want for your birthday."

"I wish for you to let me leave. You can marry Patra. She is already of legal age..."

Lama cut her off. "You will never leave me. You are mine until death."

"Is this what you are worried about?" Fatou asked, pointing down to her vagina. "I promise that if you let me leave, you can have it any time you want it. I would never lie to you. I do not like how I've been treated, but I must admit that you've opened my life up to many more opportunities. I have to repay you for that. But you know that you only want me for my body. You want Patra for everything else. Why not stop the charade?"

"Look, Fatou," Lama said seriously. "You are the most beautiful woman this world has ever seen and…"

Fatou cut him off. "I used to think that. But Patra is also beautiful. Her face is as pretty as mine. Her hair is just as long. Her breasts are far more immaculate than mine even before she gave you your first child. And I hear the African Americans speaking about her bottom. They say that it is a *padonk a donk*. I don't know what that means, but I do

know that it is more ample than mine. Patra beats me in every category, hands down. So again, why not just be with her? You could never do worse."

"Fatou, look," Lama began angrily. "You will always be mine. When you seriously consider your birthday gift, let me know." Lama turned to leave.

Fatou grabbed his legs, and he dragged her while he walked away.

She repeated several times, "Let me be your bitch on the side, Lama. For my birthday, let me be your bitch on the side."

He ignored her and pushed her off him, continuing to walk away. As he opened the door, he paused and looked back at her.

Fatou looked him in the eyes as if she was about to cry.

"Wait," she said. "Let me show you the difference."

Lama looked at her curiously.

Fatou started to undress. Lama closed the door. Fatou called out to him, "Come to your wife". Then she said in plain English, "I will fuck you like a whore so you will see how it will be if you let me leave. But only if you let me leave."

Fatou remembered all the times that she had peeked in on other girls at Sister Fifi's when they had men in the back room.

She thought about the things that they did, most of which she thought were disgusting. But today she didn't care. She figured that she was fucking for her freedom. *If wild sex is what he wants*, she thought, *that is what I will give him. As long as I get my freedom.*

Fatou stroked Lama with her hands and stared him in his eyes. While keeping eye contact, she put his manhood in her mouth and emulated what she had seen Patra do to him on countless occasions. Next she pushed him to the floor and straddled him as Patra did in the back room. She was on top of him, leaning all the way down with her breasts in his face.

After a while, she leaned back and gyrated her hips and thighs, causing Lama to moan loudly. "Oh, you like that," she said, before gyrating even harder on top of him. He could barely stand it.

She turned around and leaned over so that he could see her backside. Then she braced herself with her hands and started grinding her backside into him, wishing it was as big as Patra's.

Finally, she turned back around, leaned her breasts into his face again and beckoned for him to suck them. Lama didn't know what had gotten into her, but he loved it.

After a short time, he climaxed, but Fatou remained on top of Lama, making sure that he stayed inside of her. Tears trickled from her eyes as they kissed passionately.

Fatou eased her lips away from Lama and started to trace his face with her hands. Her tears dripped onto his chest. Softly, she spoke to him.

"Lama, I can no longer lie to you. This is why tonight I have been so truthful. I love you, my husband. I really, really love you. But you hurt me with your disrespect. And you hurt me because you love Patra more than me. I feel ashamed. Yet I doubt that I would if you'd just let me leave, then summoned for me in the midnight hours as you obviously do now with her. I did not ask to love you. You summoned me from my village. And now that you have me, you hide me away like a rabid dog, as if you never wanted me at all. We spend no time together outside of our bed. You do not take me to dinner or the movies as you do Patra, and you have yet to take me on a tour of New York. I've been here for almost four years and know nothing of the great museums everyone speaks about. And I have never once stepped inside a classroom. My loins have yearned to have you like I had you tonight, but you have only cold fucked me for five minutes at a time. Never once have you taken your time with me. No that is a lie. In the beginning, you may have taken your time once or twice. But I was a baby then. I couldn't enjoy it. Now as I approach womanhood and can enjoy it, you give it to Patra.

"Lama, I love you but you break my heart. Please just let me leave. It kills me to know that you are only halfway here. So today I feel like a gambler. I want to bet double or nothing. I want to risk all or nothing. Let me be your whore. Let me be your love slave. Let me be your floor mat. But let it all be official. I can be all of that and then some. If you allow me to leave, maybe I can reclaim a hint of my dignity."

"And by the way, you will never have to pay me. As the Americans say, you can fuck me for free. Just please let me go. If I stay here, I will die of a broken heart.

"Tradition says that I am your wife. My heart says that I love you. Whether it is for your wife or for the woman who loves you—give the gift of life to me for my birthday. Please allow me to hold my head up high, something I have not been able to do since I came to America. Please allow me proud to once again.

"For that, I will give you anything. For that, I will give you everything. But what else can I give? I have already told you that you have my love."

Fatou finally pulled Lama from inside of her and slumped off of him onto the floor. She stared up at the ceiling with fresh tears flowing from her eyes.

Lama said, "You have said a mouthful."

He steadied himself, thinking that this was the first time Fatou had ever proclaimed her love for him. It was what he had always wished for. But now, after hearing it, he wondered why he didn't feel any differently.

Knowing that Fatou actually loved him didn't make his life any easier. Truly, it made things worse.

After sitting quietly for what seemed an eternity, Lama finally spoke.

"I most certainly do love you too, Fatou. Yet I cannot hide the fact that I also love Patra. I loved her when you were just a fantasy. I loved her when I thought she hated me."

"So why did you send for me, ruining my life, if you knew that your heart was with another?" Fatou asked.

"Please let me finish," Lama said.

"I didn't know for a long time that Patra loved me. I thought that what we had was just an arrangement. Truly, I was very fond of her, but I fought those feelings, since I didn't think I could ever have her.

"I knew that I could possess you due to La Dotte, but I never thought I'd possess your heart. And not being able to ever possess your heart made me so very angry.

"Now I do possess your heart, but I am still angry."

"But why?" Fatou asked.

"Because I wonder if it is too little, too late. My life and circumstances now are so different than they once were.

"I gave you everything and you hated me. Now I give you nothing, and you love me. You are such a foolish girl."

"No. I am not foolish," Fatou said. "I am merely powerless."

"Patra never had any more power than you, but she always demanded respect. You have been a coward. I love you dearly, but I could never be with a coward. You are my little concubine. Patra is the light of my life. That arrangement is perfect for me. So that is how things must stay.

"One more thing. Never fight with your sister again. I must go now. I have to tell you, though, that you were incredible tonight. Still, never think that you can talk to me like that again. Speak only when I ask you to speak. And never expect to get what Patra gets. I made a dreadful mistake giving your parents La Dotte. So I will make that up to Patra for the rest of my life. And you will make it up to her as well. She deserves that. She deserves that because she is so beautiful. You could never be the woman she is, so stop trying. Just be happy with your life as it is. This discussion is over."

Lama got up, pulled his pants up and left. Fatou remained on the floor, alone with her foolish heart, her foolish love, and her foolish tears. Lama was going to Patra. And Fatou's life appeared to be even too foolish for her to bear.

CHAPTER SEVEN

Second Chances

Mati was hysterical as she paced the Emergency Room floor at the Harlem Hospital. Fatou had swallowed a large number of sleeping pills and technicians were pumping her stomach.

She went to the phone booth and called Lama for the umpteenth time. "There is an emergency!" she screamed into the phone. "Your wife is in the hospital, hanging between life and death. Why aren't you here?"

"Fatou is merely seeking attention," Lama said. "I am on Patra's time. You must understand, Mati. I cannot steal away this close to daylight. Our last few moments together are cherished by Patra and me before we each start our work day. You cannot ask me to take that away. You are not being reasonable."

"So you are saying that if Fatou dies, then so be it?" Mati asked. "Are you so insensitive to her that you don't care if she lives or dies?"

"Look, I have given her everything. But what does she do? She attacks my child. Now she is trying to take from Patra and me our most precious moments. She is out of line. She is way out of line."

"Well, I will not help sneak her out of here if she does survive,"

Mati proclaimed. "And they will send her away. You will lose your whipping post. I only hope that when she goes, she will meet another and fall in love."

"Bite your tongue," Lama snapped back. "She will be fine until I come for her. Then I will make sure that she is not sent away."

Lama hung up the phone and caressed Patra. She was enjoying her last few minutes of sleep before the alarm clock summoned her to start her day.

Lama dozed, joining Patra in sleep. He hugged her tightly and snored as if he hadn't a care in the world.

When Fatou woke up, she was pleased to see Mati sitting at her side. She felt lightheaded.

"I had a horrible dream," Fatou said. "I dreamed that Lama told me Nefara is born to you and him. This was after I allowed Patra to maim me."

"Well, it is true, my child," Mati admitted. "Lama did father Nefara many moons ago when he used to say he loved for me. But I am too close in age to Lama. I learned that he fancies women whose bodies are much tighter and whose minds are far less developed.

"Now what is this about Patra maiming you?"

"I thought you knew," Fatou said.

"I know nothing," Mati replied "You must tell me."

"Patra told me how much Lama loved her when I was pregnant years ago. I couldn't allow myself to have his child knowing that he loved her. So I allowed Patra to abort our child. She did it right in the back of Fifi's."

"Child, why have you not spoken up sooner?" Mati asked.

"I felt so ashamed," Fatou confessed. "Taking my child's life was so against Allah's way. That is why he has punished me and has not allowed my body to bear any more children."

"You are wrong," Mati said. "You are foolish. Patra has deceived you. She has done what the younger people call played you."

"What do you mean she has played me?" Fatou asked.

"Patra knew that Lama wanted a child to reclaim his youth," Mati said. "She figured that if you had his child before she did, he would love you more. I guess she purposely ruined your reproductive organs so that you could never bear him children. She knows the effect you have on him."

"So are you saying that my life and well-being were all just a game to Patra?" Fatou asked. "Don't you know that I could have died that day? I lost a good deal of blood."

"Your death would have been merely a bonus for Patra," Mati said matter-of-factly. "Patra is like the serpent, very devious. She does whatever she must to get what she wants. She doesn't care about who gets hurt in the process."

Fatou thought about the things Natali had said to her and wondered if it was possible that Patra deliberately misled her, as Natali and Mati believed.

"What you say of Patra is not the way of the communes," Fatou asserted firmly.

"You are correct," Mati said. "But Patra doesn't care about communal unity. Patra cares about Patra."

"Such is a sad way to be," Fatou said despondently.

"Well, that is the way of the Americas," Mati said. "This is a society where people get ahead by standing on the backs of others. It is hard to trust here. But it is very easy for your heart to get broken. The only way you can make it is to think of yourself."

Fatou thought about everything that she had endured in Harlem, and Natali's words made sense. Mati's insight became invaluable. Fatou wondered if she could only think of herself. She suspected she could never be so selfish.

I have to do something, she thought. *I cannot allow my foolishness to get me killed in this place. For better or for worse, I must make a change.*

CHAPTER EIGHT

Back In the Saddle

Fatou's customers were happy that she had returned to Fifi's. Patra remained unmoved. She felt as if she had already won Lama's heart.

Natali arrived and told Fatou that she was sorry she had missed her party. She was in the middle of studying for her finals. She asked Fatou how her health was and chastised her for what she had almost done to herself.

"Do you think that Lama would have done the same for you?" Natali asked.

Fatou didn't respond.

"Of course he wouldn't," Natali said, answering for her friend. "You persist on being an angel in the belly of the devil. I must teach you what the saying 'when in Rome' means."

Natali cut short her chastisement and started taking things out of a huge bag she had brought with her.

"All of this is for you," she said.

Natali pulled out a mini DVD player with some mini DVD movies and CDs.

"These two movies are *What's Love Got To Do With It* and *The*

Burning Bed. You need to watch them both. Then you need to listen to these Mary J Blige and Aretha Franklin CDs that I compiled from internet downloads. If anyone can tell you about being mistreated by a man, it is Mary J and Aretha.

"You have to grow up, Fatou. You can no longer be defined by a man. You can no longer be obedient to your parents. Yes, you can still love them. But you must understand that you are here fighting for your life. You have to create a brand new rule book. Do not continue to allow yourself to be a victim," Natali said as she handed Fatou a poem by Dylan Thomas. "Read this."

"*'Do not go gently into that good night. Rage against the dying of the light.'* What does it mean?" Fatou asked after she finished reading.

"It means you have to learn to fight back," Natali said firmly. "Now come with me so I can show you my new car."

Natali walked Fatou outside to a bright red 500 series BMW.

"My gosh!" Fatou exclaimed. "How can a college student afford such an expensive car?"

"As the old-timers say," Natali said, laughing, "You have to use what you've got to get what you want."

Fatou looked at Natali oddly.

Natali said, "I have to break everything down for you into their simplest forms! But to elaborate, you must come to my home." Natali looked as if she just had a brilliant idea.

"Fatou," she said, "I will no longer be your enabler at this salon. This will be my last time at Fifi's."

"But what do you mean?" Fatou asked. "You are my dearest friend."

"I want you to come to my house from now on to braid my hair," Natali answered. "Then you can keep all of the fee. It makes me sick to give Fifi anything considering what she's allowed to have happen to you."

"But I am working twelve hours a day as it is," Fatou said. "And I must also include travel time. I do not see how we could pull that one off."

"Relax," Natali said. "I can drive you so you won't be late. And even you will admit that Lama won't miss you most days. It will be an opportunity for you to make some extra money. I will even invite other students to come to my house to have their hair braided. You will be able to save some of your money. As it stands now, you can barely afford to make it back and forth to work."

"Let me think about it," Fatou replied.

"There is nothing to think about," Natali said sternly. "I will be at your house early in the morning to drive you. You mustn't be late, because I really need my hair done."

The next day Natali was waiting in her car when Fatou left the house. They greeted each other and drove off.

Natali's house was not far from where Fatou lived, but it was in much better shape than Lama's. The architecture of the facade was incredible. It was adorned with several large windows.

Inside, Fatou was amazed at the silk drapery that covered the windows. It matched the silk throw pillows on the three piece leather sofa. And she loved the fireplace but couldn't understand why it was not to be lit in summer.

Frustrated with trying to explain, Natali beckoned Fatou to follow her to her spare room. There she showed Fatou her climate-controlled

Jacuzzi and queen-sized canopy bed covered in satiny sheets.

In the corner sat a Sony Trinitron 52" big-screen television connected to a thousand-dollar surround sound system as well as Natali's
Compaq desktop computer with a Pentium 4 CPU, a Voodoo graph-
ics card, a microphone set-up, and a high-resolution camera for
streaming video.

There was also a full-sized pool table and an exercise bicycle.

Finally, scattered throughout the room, were many odd-shaped
lights. Natali explained that they were used by professional photog-
raphers to light indoor environments, controlling glare and hot spots.

Fatou looked around the room again before bombarding Natali
with many questions. "Is this how you amuse yourself—playing with
a table and multi-colored balls? Do you sit here and ride on a bicycle
that does not go anywhere? And how can you do your studies while
watching movies?"

"Relax," Natali said. "You are confused."

"All that I'm confused about is how you can afford such things,"
Fatou said while pushing the balls on the pool table at each other,
thinking that making the balls collide was the object of the game.

Natali grabbed a pool stick and used it to pound the cue ball into
the nine ball, sinking it into the side pocket. This excited Fatou and
she clapped her hands together.

"This game is called pool," Natali said. "And the object is to sink
all of the balls by hitting them with the white ball that is called the
cue. Yet you must save the eight ball for last, or you will do what is
called scratching and your opponent will win the game."

"It sounds very complicated," Fatou said.

"It's actually rather simplistic," Natali replied. "And it's very entertaining. But to answer your question about the money, I run my own business right here. It's very lucrative."

"What type of business can you run from inside of here?" Fatou asked. "I see no animals being raised or large amounts of food being prepared."

"You are correct," Natali said. "But those types of things are for labor-intensive businesses. I get paid for providing a service. Like you do. You braid someone's hair and you get paid. Well, at least that is how it is supposed to be."

"But what type of service do you provide?" Fatou asked.

"I am what they call an entertainer," Natali replied. "But I also manage lots of other entertainers."

Fatou leaned against the pool table and folded her arms.

"Well, you have my attention," she said. "Entertain me. Will you be singing or dancing or both?"

"That is not how I entertain people, silly!" Natali said, laughing. "I record myself and others doing our daily activities and people pay to watch via the internet. They pay me very well to watch, I may add. Sometimes people pay to meet some of the girls I manage in person. But I never allow anyone to meet me."

"And people pay you money for this?" Fatou asked.

"Very much so," Natali said. "That is how I maintain such an extravagant lifestyle."

"I want you to show me," Fatou demanded assertively.

"Well, I can't log on right now," Natali said. "Everything runs on a schedule. I have a couple more hours before I am to greet my admirers online. That's why I want you to do my hair first. I must look my best."

Fatou and Natali talked while Fatou braided her friend's hair. She learned that the fewer clothes Natali wore while streaming video across the internet, the more money she made.

Fatou thought it was odd to make money for showing off your body. She also wondered if it was ethical. Natali told her that she was merely old-fashioned and would never be rich with such an attitude.

When Fatou finished braiding, Natali handed her $150.

"What is all of this money for?" Fatou asked.

"I told you that you are a foolish child," Natali said. "Each week when you braid my hair, Fifi receives this same amount of money. When you braid anyone's hair, Fifi receives this amount of money. Yet she only gives you pennies. She is very greedy, and you are being taken advantage of. But what is even worse is that she sends women to the back room to pleasure men and still keeps most of the money. On a normal week, Fifi makes close to three thousand dollars off her workers, but only gives them a couple hundred. Some of them don't even get that. It is just so very sad that she takes advantage as she does."

Fatou thought about her situation and how she braided about ten to twenty heads per week. "But what would be a fair split since I am utilizing Fifi's place for my customers?" Fatou asked.

"Normally there is no split," Natalie replied. "At most places you pay the salon owner rent. Rent above $300 a week is unheard of. And even in places where the salon owners receive rent and a portion of the proceeds, their take doesn't exceed 25 percent. In any case, you should easily be making a thousand dollars a week. Yet you don't. That is what Fifi makes off of you! She plays you for a fool since you are an illegal alien."

"What you speak of is true," Fatou said. "But if I complain, Fifi will call the authorities and cause trouble for me."

"And risk losing out on all the money you bring in?" Natali asked. "I doubt it. She will act as if that's what she wants to do, but she doesn't want to bring any trouble into her salon."

"So you will speak up for me?" Fatou asked. "You will act as if you are my agent."

"In this country you have to fight your own battles, sweetie," Natali said. "But you can always braid hair here. If you remain at Fifi's, it's up to you to change your circumstances by confronting her."

"And that is what I will do," Fatou said bravely. "That is what I most certainly will do."

CHAPTER NINE

Double Lives

Upon arriving late to the shop, Fatou asked Fifi to speak privately. They walked into the back room.

Fatou told Fifi that she had heard it was not customary for hair stylists to be paid a weekly wage. "They are to keep the money they make and pay the owner a weekly rental fee," Fatou said.

"Where do you get such nonsense?" Fifi asked.

"It is not important how I know," Fatou said. "But I know. Now you must make amends."

"What do you mean 'make amends'?" Fifi asked.

"I am speaking of all of the money you have withheld from me for over four years," Fatou said. "We must find a way for you to make things right with me."

"Child, you have lost your mind!" Fifi said. "Everyone in my shop knows the arrangement before they even start. No one can act as if they didn't know what they were to be paid."

"You cannot pretend that this arrangement has been fair," Fatou said sternly. "And you most certainly cannot expect things to remain as they are. I will not work for pennies while you exploit me."

"And what do you expect?" Fifi asked curiously.

"I want more," Fatou replied. "Rather, I deserve more. I am a woman who needs things—things I cannot get making just barely enough money to travel back and forth to and from here every day."

"So you are merely wishing to renegotiate your contract," Fifi said.

"What is this renegotiate?" Fatou asked.

"That means that you want to change the terms of your employment," Fifi replied.

"Certainly," Fatou said. "I need to change my employment terms. I need to be compensated more fairly."

"OK," Fifi said. "I will give you two hundred dollars per week."

"You still do not understand," Fatou said excitedly. "That is just a pittance of what I'm entitled to. You must do much better than that."

"You do not understand how things work," Fifi said. "I must pay a mortgage and taxes, electricity. You only want to see what you want to see. But I must ensure that the salon remains operable."

"But there are six girls upstairs. Surely what they give up must pay for electricity and other things. It seems as if you are just making excuses."

"I do not know why I am even negotiating with you?" Fifi asked. "I will pay you three hundred dollars a week and not a penny more. I will also let Lama know that you are becoming a royal pain in the ass. Now there are things to do besides wasting time chatting as we are. Take the flyers and go down to the subway entrance. You have no customers for a couple hours, so you can help bring more people into the salon. You must earn this additional money you are requesting."

Fatou was happy about her raise. So she decided to leave things as they were and take a break from the conversation with Fifi. She left the back room and headed for the front door of the salon, picking up flyers as she left.

Outside the A & C subway stop on 125th Street, Fatou greeted riders exiting the station with the words "hair braiding" while handing them flyers. Then she pointed in the direction of Sister Fifi's.

Although by now Fatou was somewhat fluent in English, she didn't want to engage in senseless conversation with any passersby. She merely wanted to watch the hours click away until it was time for her to take her appointments.

While passing out flyers, Fatou noticed Natali leaning on her car speaking to an attractive West Indian-looking girl.

"Hi, Natali," she said. "What are you still doing in this area?"

"Oh, hi, Fatou," she replied. "I'm out here recruiting for my internet business. It's been a good day for me. I've met a couple of women who are interested in becoming escorts. In fact, this is Chyna. We are discussing the possibility of her working for me as an escort."

"Hi, Fatou," Chyna said. "I have heard a lot about you. And Natali was right. You are very beautiful. I don't know why you won't work with her. You would make tons of money. Men would love to spend their time with a woman as beautiful as you."

"But I am hardly a woman," Fatou said.

"That makes it even better," Chyna replied. "With some men, the younger the woman, the better. You would be surprised how many men are looking for ripe young tenderloins. At a minimum, you should give it a try."

"But how does one try giving herself to a man?" Fatou asked.

"Either you let the man have you or not."

"Things are not always so crystal clear," Natali said.

"Sometimes on the internet I just wear sexy clothes—dresses, swimsuits. I don't go further than that unless the customers who are logged onto my pay site convince me to do so by paying a premium."

"Yes, but they have the internet in the motherland," Fatou said shyly. "I would never risk someone from home seeing me. That type of thing would be such an embarrassment to me."

"Well, they don't have to see you," Natali said. "And you don't have to be on the internet. If you were an escort just a couple of hours a week, you'd make much more than you're making at Fifi's."

"Yes, but then people will look at me as a whore," Fatou said, horrified.

"And who thinks such things of me?" Natali asked. "The answer is no one. I am very discreet and would help you to be the same way. Whatever you do in my home stays in my home. Besides, most of my clients are not in a position to be forthcoming about their wild sides. And those who have the ability to open their big mouths don't do it, because they fear I will no longer deal with them. It is a win-win situation."

"But how can you lay with someone you don't love?" Fatou asked.

"Honey, you have a lot to learn," Chyna said.

"Clearly," Natali agreed. "These men do whatever they damn well please and fool us to believe that we're sullied if we act as they do. You have to survive and care for yourself. Lama gives you nothing. You work for your room and board and buy your own food."

"Yes, but he paid La Dotte," Fatou said, interrupting.

"And what the hell did you get out of it?" Natali asked, becoming frustrated. "Your parents benefited from La Dotte and Lama benefitted. You, you got nothing. And you are still getting nothing. The time has come for you to make a better life for yourself. If you must use your body, then so be it."

"Besides," Natali continued, "look what Patra got using her body. She used to sleep with Lama for money. Now he takes care of her. You barely ever see him. His only purpose for checking up on you is to make sure that you don't become fond of someone else."

"That is not totally true," Fatou said. "Lama loves me. He only wants to spend time with his children."

"Yes, to buy them things and to give them real affection, something you have never gotten from him. The man thinks that he owns you. He does not have to be your first and your last. You could be missing out on the best sex ever without even knowing it."

"But love is so much more important than sex," Fatou said.

"My gosh, she is further gone than I thought," Chyna said, laughing.

"Yes. And she thinks she has it all figured out," Natali said. "If only her West African principles matched with North American realities. One can never get ahead in this land thinking that they should remain innocent."

"But I am far from innocent," Fatou conceded.

"Well, your mind may not be innocent," Natali said. "But your heart most certainly is. You need to live a little bit so you don't die of boredom. And while you're living, you may as well start making a decent amount of money. For that, I can help you."

"Yes," Chyna chimed in. "At least just give it a try."

"Yes, at least." Natali agreed.

Fatou checked her watch and noticed that she had about an hour and a half before she had to return to Sister Fifi's.

"OK. I am game," she said. "Besides, you only live once. I will only offer a man companionship, not my body. And I must be back at Fifi's by 1:30. I do not want Fifi telling Lama anything."

"I guarantee it," Natali said.

"She is still foolish in love but at least she is waking up a bit," Chyna added.

"Well, we must hurry," Natali said with excitement. "I am about to introduce you to a very lucrative and entertaining new world. You are about to forget all about your boring life."

Natali introduced Fatou to a very prominent-looking older white man. Fatou learned that he was a congressman who made very important political and policy decisions in America.

"She will spend time with you today," Natali said. "But she will not lay with you. For that you must pick another girl," she added.

"But the other girls aren't as beautiful as she is," he protested. "Can't she at least dance for me?" he asked.

"Well, I am very fond of dancing," Fatou replied innocently.

"Hush, child," Natali chided "He does not speak of the type of dancing you are referring to. He wants you to dance for him while you are undressing. Then he wants you to dance even more."

"That is very odd," Fatou said.

"But it's also very sexy," he said.

"If she weren't so young, it would be sexy," Natali said. "But since she is young, it is merely perverse."

"That's why I'll pay even more," he said nonchalantly. "I'll pay $200 for her time and another $500 if she dances for me."

"You will spend all of your riches just to look at me?" Fatou asked. "And this is even with knowing that I will not touch you and you will not touch me?"

The congressman looked at Natali oddly, so she explained to Fatou what he expected. "The point of exotic dancing is that you must touch him to excite him. But he cannot touch you, and there will be no sex."

"But what does he get out of it if he can't touch me back?" Fatou asked foolishly.

"What the fuck do you care?" Natali said, becoming upset. "Are you going to dance for the man or not?"

"I do not know how I am to tease a man into excitement," Fatou confessed. "That sounds as if it is not easy."

"Well, I will show you," Natali said. "But you still haven't told me if you agree to do it."

"If it is easy enough, I will do it," Fatou said.

"Good," Natali said as she walked over to her stereo system, turning it on. "But you must give me 20 percent for my labor, and this is in addition to the 20 percent that I get for organizing everything."

Fatou didn't comment. She stared at Natali curiously as she wound her body to R Kelly's remake of the song "Bump and Grind."

Fatou was amazed at how excited the congressman looked as Natali removed her bra and bounced her breasts in his face. Natali's breasts were perky but nowhere near as large as Fatou's. Natali turned around and bent all the way over in front of the congressman, grabbing her ankles. Then she rubbed her buttocks against his erection before lifting herself up to rub his erection with her hand.

She looked at Fatou and said, "OK, child, you can take over from here. I am not getting paid to dance with him the entire time."

Fatou felt bashful but knew she was much more limber than Natali. And she knew that her body was more voluptuous.

She eased toward the congressman and teased him like Natali had teased him. She stood in from of him and lifted her leg straight above her head. Then she allowed her leg, still straight, to fall upon his shoulder while rubbing her womanhood on his erection. He was amazed at her flexibility.

Fatou slowly kicked her leg out to the side, removing it from the congressman's shoulder, then she simultaneously turned herself around on his lap. She casually and erotically rubbed her buttocks against his erection while leaning back into his chest, feeling his heart beat rapidly against her back.

Impressed with herself, she lifted up slightly and began to rub the congressman's erection with her hand, careful to have hold of more of him than his khaki pants. Then she shot up and removed her undergarments to give him full view of her nakedness.

"Gosh, I have to you!" the congressman said shakily.

"That is not part of our deal," Fatou said. "But I will allow you to touch me if you'd like."

The congressman eagerly obliged when she straddled his lap by taking her breasts into his mouth one by one and sucking them. She closed her eyes and enjoyed the sensation. *God, I wish this were Lama,* she thought to herself as the congressman grabbed her buttocks.

Fatou mentally escaped to the brownstone and imagined that it was Lama's fingers, not the congressman's, that she placed in her mouth. After sucking them, she inserted them inside of her, again imagining that it was Lama. As the congressman played inside of her with his fingers, she gyrated on his lap as if she were making love to Lama.

Suddenly, Fatou felt something that she had never felt before. It seemed as if she were floating in the clouds and her body became hypersensitive. Each stroke of the congressman's tongue on her breasts and each invasion of her womanhood with his fingers sent Fatou chills. She momentarily became breathless and everything around her went blank as her body released fluids onto the congressman's hands.

"Let me taste your juices!" he shouted. "Please! You must let me taste your juices!"

Fatou was lost in her first orgasm and didn't feel the congressman slide underneath her and bury his face in her womanhood. He licked at her madly, increasing her tingling sensations. As the congressman's tongue lurked inside of her, Fatou could not contain herself. Before long, she was experiencing her second orgasm, followed shortly by her third.

"My God," the congressman shouted, startled. "She is multiorgasmic. What must I do to have her?"

Natali, who was finally able to gather her own composure after being aroused by the recent happenings, told the congressman that he had already reached the limit of his entertainment.

"I have already allowed you to touch and taste her," she said. "We both know that wasn't part of the deal."

"But I'm on fire!" he pleaded. "You can't leave me this way. I'm begging you."

"Alright," Natali answered. "But it will be me, not her, who satisfies you. And for that you will have to pay more."

"Are you sure?" he asked, looking at Fatou. "You have the opportunity to make much more money."

Coming down off her orgasms, Fatou was barely able to utter

between breaths, "Natali is the expert. Let her take care of you."

Fatou pulled herself off of the congressman and leaned her naked body back on Natali's plush carpet. Her breasts rose and fell heavily as she tried hard to catch her breath.

Natali approached the congressman and rubbed his erection through his pants. "What's your pleasure?" she asked. "You realize that you already owe me $700."

"You know that I love your tongue," he said. "If I can't have her, I must have your tongue."

"Well that will be an even thousand," Natali said. "Are you sure that's OK?"

He pulled out his credit card, so she took that to mean yes.

Natali rubbed on the congressman's erection through his pants. Then she stuck her tongue out, revealing the black pearl that pierced it. She waved it suggestively in the air, antagonizing the congressman with desire for what she was about to do.

Natali paused her torment of the congressman to push a button on her desk. When the door cracked open, she waved Chyna into the room and whispered something into her ear while handing her the congressman's credit card.

Chyna punched a thousand dollars into the credit card terminal, then slid the card through. When the authorization appeared, she signaled to Natali with her eyes that everything was OK. Natali cut her eyes at her letting her know that she could leave the room. So Chyna placed the card and receipt on the desk before leaving.

Natali slithered over to the congressman and knelt in front of him. She started rubbing him on his belly before grabbing at his belt to unbuckle it. Next, she pulled his zipper down with her teeth and stared up into his eyes.

Natali tore at his belt loops, pulling them harshly as he stood up. His pants slid off and his erection was released into the air. Natali licked all around the congressman's inner thigh, then placed his scrotum in her mouth while rubbing up and down the length of his erection. The congressman looked as if he were about to have a heart attack. Fatou watched curiously, taking in everything Natali was showing her.

Natali took her tongue and flicked the tip all around the congressman's erection, carefully ensuring that he felt her pearl touching his manhood. Then she took all of him inside of her mouth and slowly moved her head up and down.

Almost instantly, the congressman started to shudder while grabbing Natali's hair, then released his juices inside of her mouth. She squeezed her jaws tightly around his manhood to ensure that he received the full effect of his pleasure. Once he relaxed and released her hair, she got up and walked into the bathroom, spit the congressman's semen into the toilet, flushed it, and turned on her faucet.

After brushing her teeth and washing her face, Natali returned to the room. She looked at Fatou laying on the floor, amused that she had yet to recover from her orgasms.

"You must hurry, child," Natali said, "if I am to get you back to Fifi's on time."

"Where can I refresh myself?" Fatou asked, her body still trembling slightly from what the congressman had done to her.

Natali threw her a wash rag and told her that there was soap in the bathroom.

While washing herself, Fatou shivered when she placed the cloth between her legs. *I certainly do not know what I am feeling,* she thought as she tried to hurry.

When she left the bathroom, the congressman was gone. Natali handed her an envelope containing $420 and told her, "We must go."

Back at Sister Fifi's, Fatou learned that her customer had been waiting for ten minutes.

"You really need an attitude adjustment," Fifi screamed while Natali looked on.

"It's only ten minutes," the customer said. "You're making a big deal out of nothing."

"Yes. You have no idea how frustrating it is to handle the prying eyes of those men as they leave the MTA."

Fifi rolled her eyes and stomped out of the salon. Fatou turned toward her client, waving her to the hair wash station.

After washing her client's hair, Fatou sat her underneath a dryer. Then she asked Natali to come with her to the back room so that they could speak.

In the back room, Fatou took the envelope out of her back pocket and counted. Amazed, she asked, "I can really make so much money to feel as delightful as I did today?"

"Yes. And there's a whole lot more money where that came from," Natali replied.

"Well, it is settled then." Fatou said assuredly. "I will tell Fifi that I will come in every day at noon. Most of my appointments are after that anyway, so I can spend a couple of hours with you first. Will that work for you?"

"Yes, of course," Natali said. "But are you certain that Lama will be OK with that? Fifi will surely tell him."

"As you said, I have to start making a better life for myself. Lama isn't helping, so who is he to complain? My biggest problem will be learning what to do with myself once I make all the extra money."

Natali smiled at Fatou and embraced her. Then she told her she must go. "I'll see you in the morning," she said happily.

Fatou returned to her client and checked to see if her hair was completely dry. It was and she braided it immaculately. Her client tipped her $50 and left the salon beaming. Fatou was happy that Fifi was not around to witness her receiving the tip.

CHAPTER TEN

Good While It Lasted

Fifi returned to the salon very late and was surprised to see that Fatou was still there.

"I must speak with you," Fatou said flatly, without raising her eyes to meet Fifi's.

"What is it now, child?" Fifi asked.

"I am becoming very tired working so many hours," Fatou said. "Most of my customers do not arrive until after lunchtime. I wish to come in at noon from now on. I do not want to feel like I am forty before I even turn eighteen."

Fifi stared at Fatou wearily and said, "I cannot understand for the life of me why you are so unhappy. You have opportunities that people in your country dream of."

"Why do you speak of my unhappiness?" Fatou asked. "I am merely speaking of maintaining my youth. I do not think that I will be as irritable as I have been lately if I am allowed to get more rest."

"Well, I do not feel like debating with you tonight, child," Fifi answered. "But your attitude had better improve drastically once you start coming here at noon."

"Thank you, Sister Fifi," Fatou said, smiling.

"But wait," Fifi said. "On weekends and holidays you must still be here by eight. Noon will be too late on those days."

"That is understandable," Fatou said as she turned to leave the salon.

I am so grateful to Natali, Fatou said to herself. *She has shown me that I have much more power than I believed.*

For three weeks, Fatou danced in Natali's house with different elderly white men every morning between eight and eleven.

As her reward, she averaged $500 a day. Natali told her that she could triple her earnings if she went further with the customers. Yet she refused to. She clung to some perverse sense of loyalty to Lama.

While at Natali's one morning, Fatou was surprised to see the congressman who was her first customer nervously come calling.

She learned that he was in trouble because of the charge made he made on his credit card.

"We must come up with a reasonable explanation," he said frantically. "The Republican Congress is on a witch hunt and will do anything to destroy a Democrat."

"Relax," Natali said. "We'll come up with something. Just give me time to think."

"Well, be careful," he said, grabbing at the doorknob. "You don't know how low politicians will sink."

The next morning as Fatou approached Natali's house, she noticed several police cars parked outside. She paused, not knowing what to do next. As she stood there, Natali was escorted out of her house by several officers. She noticed Fatou but ignored her. The cops lowered her into their car and drove off with her. Fatou remained standing there for nearly ten minutes with tears forming in her eyes.

At last she walked away. With over three hours to kill, she didn't know what to do.

While walking, she noticed a newspaper machine and bought a New York Times. She decided to head to Starbucks to read it while enjoying a French vanilla latte.

Flipping through the paper, Fatou noticed an advertisement for a place that taught foreigners English and also helped them receive their GED or Adult High School Diploma. She became very excited.

"This is what I will now do with my mornings," she said to herself as she fumbled in her purse to find the change to call the number on the ad.

Fatou learned that she could start her schooling the next day. She also learned that in exchange for the school keeping quiet about the illegal aliens it taught, she would be required to pay an $800 fee.

Fatou mentally counted the money she had made over the last three weeks and was certain that she could afford the school. She headed to Fifi's, excited that the next day she would finally be able to do what she originally thought she'd be doing in the US.

The next day, Fatou scored very highly on each part of her screening exam except for US history and vocabulary.

"It should take you very little time to sharpen your skills," the counselor told her.

Fatou made arrangements to be tutored each morning between 8 and 10:30. For the service, she was to pay $20 a day on top of the $800 fee. But she went unruffled by the terms. She had close to $4,000 in savings.

After two weeks, Fatou did superbly on a practice test. Her counselor believed that she would pass the actual test he would be administering in just a few days. "But I must tell you," he said, "If you fail the test, you will have to pay an additional $200 to retake it."

Confident in her abilities, Fatou decided to take the test. A month later, she learned that she had passed and would be receiving her Adult High School Diploma at a ceremony held at her school in two days. She could barely contain herself and dressed up adorably for the affair.

"Mati," she said, prior to leaving the brownstone, "I have some very good news to share with you. But you must not tell anyone."

"What is it?" Mati asked, smiling heartily at Fatou.

"Today I will receive my Adult High School Diploma," Fatou announced proudly. "I have secretly been attending school in the mornings. Now I have finally succeeded at what I came here to do."

"That is excellent news," Mati said happily. "And you will receive it just months before your seventeenth birthday. What could you have asked for as a better present?"

"I owe it all to you," Fatou said tearfully. "I never could have come this far if you hadn't taken me under your wing. I love you dearly, Mati."

"Oh, bless you, child," Mati replied. "I only wish that I could have protected you more. What I've given you is just a small fragment of what you deserve. With your diploma and demeanor, I am certain that you will be chosen in the lottery. In a short time, you will be able to stay in the US even without Lama. I am so proud of you. You have gotten through a bad situation and earned all of the accolades you are about to receive."

"Thank you, Mati," Fatou said. "But I really must go. I will return later as a graduate."

When Fatou reached the school, oddly, the side door she normally used to enter the building was closed. Fatou peered inside into darkness. She walked around to the front.

She saw several signs taped to the front door and moved in closer to read them. They all said the same thing. *This institution has been ordered closed by the federal government of the United States of America. To receive your GED or diploma, contact the Immigration and Naturalization Service or INS.*

Fatou didn't care to write down the address or phone number. Crushed, she walked slowly down the street, kicking each rock she encountered.

What am I to do now? She thought. *What am I to do now?*

CHAPTER ELEVEN

Teenage Madam

Fatou received a letter from Natali at Sister Fifi's that made her very happy.

Natali was being held by the INS at a detention center in Miami, Florida, many miles from Fatou.

In her letter, Natali asked Fatou to take charge of her escorts so that she could send her financial assistance. She had arranged a place of business for Fatou and included in her letter a phone number where Chyna could be contacted. Everything else, she added, could be accomplished by Fatou with Chyna's assistance.

Fatou contemplated taking Natali up on her offer. Yet her biggest fear was to be captured and deported. "If I am to do this, I have to come up with a way where I do not put my freedom in jeopardy," she said to herself.

Fatou called Chyna and arranged a meeting at Starbucks on 125th Street. At the meeting, Chyna was very pleased to see Fatou and greeted her with a tight hug. They sat at one of the few empty tables and waited for their French vanilla lattes and danishes before they got down to business.

"So when will you be resuming operations?" Chyna asked while sipping her latte.

"You are moving rather hastily," Fatou replied. "I have yet to decide if I will be doing this or not. It is very dangerous."

"But you won't be burdened with many risks," Chyna said, smiling. "You will have to spend very little time at the location. I will basically be conducting most of the affairs."

"So what do you need me for?" Fatou asked.

"Well, first of all, everyone loves you," Chyna said. "Just knowing that you are associated with the business will bring customers in. And of course we'll need your financial backing. But whatever money you invest will be recouped right away. The big fish in this city have had no place to go since Natali has been picked up."

"I am certain that you've made a lot more money than I have," Fatou commented. "Whatever you get from me will be small potatoes compared to your share. I can't see how that would be acceptable to you."

"Well, things aren't as they seem," Chyna said. "I have sent a lot of money and materials to Natali. That has taken a big bite out of what I had put away. Now I only have a couple thousand to invest. It will take between five and six thousand to reinvent the service. Surely you'll be able to meet me halfway."

"But where will the business be?" Fatou asked. "And how safe is the location? We don't want to be found out like Natali was."

"That was just an accident," Chyna said. "Natali and I have come up with a way to get around the problems created by credit cards. We will make all customers pay with American Express traveler's checks. Our business will be a check cashing establishment. This will be our front of the house business. In the back, we'll keep our escorts. We won't be found out."

"That's very elaborate," Fatou said. "For that we will probably need much more money than we have. Are you sure we can afford this?"

"I am positive," Chyna replied. "But since you have a little time before you have to go to Fifi's, you should come with me to see the place. It won't take very long."

Chyna and Fatou finished their lattes and danishes and left Starbucks poised to begin what they hoped would be a lucrative venture.

The girls exited the C train at the 110th Street. Fatou followed Chyna two blocks west to a large building that had a For Lease sign on it. The windows were uncovered, and they were able to look inside. They walked around the building's perimeter, pausing from time to time making comments.

"I have already spoken to the management company in charge of this building," Chyna said. "They tell me that we can lease it for $1,000 a month plus utilities. We should be able to cover that expense easily after we are up and running. The difficulty comes from the two months up front rent they are asking for. That would leave us very little money to buy the materials we need for the check cashing front. And to make things look more appealing in the back rooms, we'll need to fix them up. That'll cost even more. But we can do it."

"Wow. It is all very scary to me," Fatou said. "If anything goes wrong, we might lose everything."

"But we can put ourselves in a position to benefit significantly also," Chyna replied. "All we need is to bust our asses and keep a positive attitude."

"Do you really think that we can pull it off?" Fatou asked. "What makes us any smarter than Natali?"

"We don't have to be smarter," Chyna said. "All we have to do is learn from Natali's mistakes."

"So how long will it take to get everything started?" Fatou asked.

"Not long," Chyna said.

"It sounds like you have everything all figured out," Fatou replied.

"All the necessary arrangements have been made. All I'm waiting for is you," Chyna replied with a smile.

They peered inside the building a little longer before walking down Cathedral Parkway to the catch the train.

"Let us meet again tomorrow," Fatou said after hugging her good bye. "We can finalize everything then."

At Sister Fifi's, Fatou was barely cognizant of the jealousy the other stylists threw her way. She was only thinking of making enough money for herself to escape her current situation in Harlem.

Harlem isn't so bad, she thought. *It's just that everyone affiliated with Lama and Fifi give me problems.*

Fatou greeted Mati at Lama's house and assured her for the umpteenth time that her heart was not broken by what had happened to her at the school. But Mati knew Fatou was lying.

"Maybe you can do a little digging and find another school that will let you take the examination for your diploma," Mati said. "You already know that you will pass the test. You should not be worried about what happened before. Just prepare yourself for a brighter tomorrow."

"I will," Fatou promised. "I just need a little time to get my head

83

together first. But I am not what Americans would call depressed. I am just a bit drained and need to rest up."

Fatou returned to her room to rest her weary body. Everything she had endured had taken a toll on her, so she planned to sleep the entire night away. She gathered her shower bag and headed for the bathroom, excited about having the water massage her thighs and lower back.

"Yes," she moaned to herself once the water temperature adjusted perfectly to her liking.

Fatou was pleased that Nefara had yet to come home. She would be able to let the water soothe her a little longer than usual. She lathered shea butter body wash all over herself and enjoyed its relaxing fragrance.

She began to feel so tranquil that she thought she'd hurt herself by falling asleep in the shower. So Fatou turned off the water and dragged herself onto the floor mat. Then she dried off and smoothed oil all over her body. After putting on the silk Frederick's of Hollywood pajama set given to her as a gift nearly a year ago, she exited the bathroom and prepared to hit the bed harder than she had in a very long time.

Fatou was asleep within five minutes. Not once did she toss or turn. Her body enjoyed the most peaceful sleep she'd had in years.

As Fatou slept, Lama entered the room and pulled the sheets off his wife so to get a good look at her. Her face was as angelic to him in America as it had been in West Africa. "I love to see you without the makeup I force you to wear to hide your youth," Lama said softly to himself. "You are is so beautiful."

He softly ran his hands through her hair and marveled at its softness. Then he touched her face lightly with the back of his hand.

Lama leaned forward and pecked Fatou on her forehead, keeping his face close to hers so that he could feel her breath touch his skin. Her mouth smelled of peppermint sticks.

Before long, Lama kissed her softly on her lips, initially trying not to awake her. "What am I thinking," he said to himself. "I am the man of the house. It's my job to decide when she's able to sleep."

Lama's soft kisses became harsh and were a precursor to his rough fondling of her breast and digging his hand down her pajama bottoms.

Fatou stirred and said, "Baby, please let me sleep. I am very tired. Please allow me to satisfy you early in the morning."

"I want it when I want it," Lama said harshly while fumbling with her buttons. When they seemed too complicated to figure out, he ripped them open.

"Wait, you beast!," Fatou shouted before gathering the two buttons he ripped off. She finished removing her pajama bottoms herself.

"Now I am naked," she said, lying on her back with her legs open. "Please try not to wake me again," she whispered to him before closing her eyes and pretending to sleep.

Lama was unmoved by the knowledge that Fatou wouldn't be participating. More often than not, their sexual escapades consisted of him doing whatever he wanted without Fatou contributing.

In her mind, she didn't have to pretend to enjoy Lama's treatment of her. Her only desire was to withstand his tirade until she could pay him the money he had paid for La Dotte and be free of him.

Lama ravished Fatou's breasts as if he were a starving child. He'd been focusing so much time on Patra that he'd forgotten how wonderful it was to be with Fatou.

"God, she tastes so heavenly," Lama mumbled to himself as he took in her scent.

He thumped his head on Fatou's chest clumsily and dragged it lower, scratching her with his raggedy beard and leaving trails of spit on her body.

Ouch! Fatou thought. *You have no idea how fragile a woman's body is.*

As Lama bent his face into her womanhood, she thought, *You have no idea how to please one either.*

Lama pulled himself up from Fatou's love box, leaving her clitoris throbbing in pain because of his carelessness. Then he jabbed himself inside of her, pounding without rhythm or poise.

Minutes later, Fatou felt Lama getting excited and pulled herself away from him right before his fluids drenched her stomach.

"Are you happy now?" she asked as she got up and returned to the bathroom to clean herself.

"I am neglecting my wife," Lama whispered to himself before falling asleep, totally unaware that the love Fatou once had had for him had withered away.

"I will get myself out of this mess," Fatou asserted to herself while wiping Lama's fluids off with a tissue, flushing both them and thoughts of the false facade of her marriage down the toilet. Tears flowed freely down her face.

She tiptoed into the bedroom to retrieve her pajamas only to hear Lama's snores echoing in the air.

After covering herself, she put a blanket on the floor and took refuge there, hoping that Lama would get the hint in the morning.

"I want out of this mess," she said to God or to anyone who might hear. Then she fell back to sleep, peacefully floating away from the brownstone she had once thought would be the hub of a perfect life.

CHAPTER TWELVE

Eye-opening Truths

Several months later, Fatou sat at a desk at her escort service and wrote to her parents. It was her first contact with them in the almost five years since.

In her letter, she spoke of her harsh life in America and how she couldn't believe that they were behind her suffering. "Yet I don't hate you anymore," she wrote. "I've learned to forgive and know that Allah will bless me for not wishing ill will upon my parents."

She continued by telling her parents that she'd saved enough money to return La Dotte and wanted their assistance in getting out of her arranged marriage. "I am nearing the legal age for marriage in the US and fear that I will be tied to a monster forever if I do not get away from Lama soon."

Binta was overcome with tears as she read her daughter's letter. She looked at Alpha pleadingly.

"Baby, we must do something about this," she pleaded. "We cannot leave our daughter in harm's way so far from her loved ones."

Alpha paced around the tent before finally coming up with an idea. "I will go speak to an elder," he said. "Hopefully his counsel will give us a way to get Fatou out of this. Besides, she is willing to return La Dotte."

Binta squeezed her husband tightly as he headed to greet Kouadio for a ride to an elder.

"Hello, Alpha," Kouadio said to him as he approached his car. "It has been many moons since I've seen you."

"Yes, it has, my friend," Alpha replied. "I hope everything has been well with you."

"Of course. Of course," Kouadio said. "But I should be asking you that. I drove Fatou La Princesse to the airport years ago to go the Americas. I am certain that she has yet to revisit her homeland."

"You are correct," Alpha said. "She has yet to visit. But hopefully that will be changing soon."

"I must commend you on living up to your pledge to Daleba," Kouadio said. "I was certain you wouldn't follow through once he and his wife visited America to hide her pregnancy. Still you allowed Lama to take Fatou's hand."

"What is this you speak of?" Alpha asked Kouadio. "Fatou is the first daughter born of either myself or Daleba. I am sure of it."

"No," Kouadio said assuredly. "I am certain that Daleba left his daughter Patra in America to be raised by his cousin Fifi. Patra is only three or four years Fatou's senior. I took Daleba and Nasara to the airport myself."

Alpha pondered this new information and immediately felt a rush of anger. "You must take me to an elder at once," he shouted.

The elder was very displeased by Alpha's story. He was also concerned that Lama had defiled tradition by not waiting a little longer to take Fatou's hand. "She was merely a baby," the elder said. "Now

I am certain that Lama has sullied her. Her innocence is gone forever."

The elder sat quietly for several minutes before finally speaking.

"For their deception, Daleba 's family is forever in your debt. You are to contact Lama and tell him that the elders no longer sanction his union with Fatou. Make sure that he knows that he has forfeited La Dotte."

"Oh, bless you," Alpha said to the elder. "I do not know how to thank you."

"That is unnecessary," the elder replied. "I regret that your family has been wounded."

Alpha remained in the developed portion of his village so that he could ring Lama. When he reached him, he didn't waste any time.

"Lama," Alpha shouted. "You must give Fatou her freedom at once. It has been sanctioned by the elders."

"What do you mean?" Lama asked. "Where is all of this coming from so suddenly?"

"For one, Daleba wasn't honest," Alpha said. "He fathered a daughter before me and hid her in the Americas. Now our daughter has lost her innocence based upon your father's deception. She is scarred for life, and it is all his fault. Your family owes me the world. But the elders say that you will repay me by forfeiting La Dotte and setting Fatou free."

"Nonsense," Lama said, slamming down the phone. "I will never let her go. Fatou is mine forever."

Lama decided to go question Fifi. He was glad that no one in America knew the full story of his ancestry. All they knew was that he was from the same village.

Lama greeted Fifi and got right down to business. "Fifi, what is the story of Daleba leaving the village to visit you and sticking you with a child to raise in America?" he asked, surprising Fifi.

"How do you know of this?" she inquired. "What you speak of is a secret that Daleba said I must take with me to my grave."

"Well, I must know the truth," Lama pleaded. "I have some important business to settle that is tied to this matter of Daleba and his child. You must tell me the truth."

Fifi sensed Lama's desperation and decided to come clean.

"OK, Lama," she said. "But you must promise never to mention this to anyone."

He shook his head in agreement, so she proceeded. "Patra is Daleba 's daughter. Daleba left her with me after Nasara died delivering her. It was very tragic for him."

Lama walked off without commenting, looking like he'd seen a ghost. *I've been frolicking with my own sister,* he thought. *I am a horrible person.*

Patra sensed his despair and followed him outside of Sister Fifi's. "Why do you walk off without addressing me?" she asked. "What have I done to upset you?"

"It is not you, it is me," Lama said. "I just need a moment to clear my head of some things."

"I know how to help clear your head," Patra said coyly. "Come back inside with me, and I will help you clear your head."

"Now is not a good time," Lama responded.

"Why is this not a good time?" Patra asked. "When is it not a good time for you? You are always ready. You're insatiable."

Lama didn't comment and allowed Patra to take his hand and lead him into the back room. She made passionate love to Lama while he was torn between lust and guilt.

I must make this the last time, Lama thought. *This absolutely has to be the last time.*

Three days later, Lama's naked body slept beside Patra's. Moments earlier, he had broken his promise to himself and shared a torrid love-making session with his sister.

Fatou was sound asleep in the brownstone and dreamed that her life would soon be better. When she awakened, she prepared herself to leave by gathering up her things. Once inside the C station, she pulled out her cell phone to call Chyna.

"Chyna, I will not be in today," she said. "I need to do a few things."

"OK," Chyna replied. "I'll hold down the fort."

Fatou decided to stop at Starbucks for a latte before going to Sister Fifi's. She felt that she had been neglecting her clients and planned to go into the salon early.

Fatou learned that she had an hour before any clients were scheduled, so she grabbed a stack of flyers and headed to the subway station.

"Hair braiding," she shouted at every passerby, handing each a flyer in the process.

Without looking up, Fatou nonchalantly attempted to pass a Jamaican man a flyer. Yet rather than take it, he grabbed her hand.

She glanced up into the face of a Sean Paul look-alike. He had long braids that were woven into a nice design, but Fatou saw that it was time for them to be redone. His caramel skin was flawless, and his Harlem Globetrotters throwback jersey revealed a brick-like chest.

Fatou thought that he was scrumptious.

"Hi. I'm David," he said. "So will you be braiding my hair?" he asked in a Jamaican accent

Fatou shook her head. Instead, he handed him a business card for her check cashing business and continued to hand out the flyers.

"What is this?" David asked.

"It is a card for my other business," Fatou said "I can braid your hair there later, about 8:30. Do not be late."

David smiled at her and said, "You sure are bossy. I like that. But before I come, tell me if it'll be worth my while."

"Eight-thirty," Fatou said, smiling, and walked off a few steps, tossing the remainder of the flyers in a trash can.

David watched Fatou's plump backside as she switched away. But out of the corner of his eye, he noticed a police officer uniform and quickly turned toward his Lincoln Navigator. He was double parked. The overweight black officer was writing him a ticket. He snapped.

"What the blood clot? You fat fuck! Why are you writing a ticket when you see that I'm right here?"

The officer ignored him and placed the ticket underneath his windshield wipers and walked off.

David's voice trailed behind him. "I don't give a shit about your ticket," he hollered "This little bit of money doesn't mean shit to me. Fuck you! Go harass someone else."

Fatou was amused by David and laughed quietly to herself as she walked away. *He is an interesting character,* she thought.

Back at Sister Fifi's, the hours didn't move fast enough for Fatou. But her customers were happy to see her around a little earlier than usual.

"I'm so glad that you're here!" exclaimed a customer named Renée.

"Me, too," added a customer named Susan. "I've heard how angelic your hands are. I'm tired of my head hurting for days after getting my hair braided. Then it still comes out a lot sooner than the girls you braid. Everybody here should be taking lessons from you."

Fatou glanced around the shop and saw the other stylists glaring at her with contempt in their eyes, but she didn't care. Still, she tried to help the other stylists save face so she wouldn't be stuck in the shop longer than she wanted to be.

"I am not that special," Fatou said modestly. "I merely try to give you whatever it is you want."

"Don't be humble with me, young lady," Susan said matter-of-factly. "Just hurry up with Donna's hair so you can start working on mine."

"Hold up, Ms. Bitch," Renée sassed. "I know you don't think that you're going before me."

"Hell, yeah," Susan spit back. "I was here long before you, and I know you don't have an appointment. Besides, I'm tired of leaving here with a headache. I need the royal treatment today."

"No, what you need to do is carry your ass back over there to Patra like you always do," Renée hissed.

"For what?" Susan asked. "So she can try to pull my scalp out rushing to go back there and fuck that old ass nigga?"

Renée glanced at Fatou and back at Susan indicating that she may have touched a nerve.

"I'm sorry, sweetie," Susan said calmly. "But the truth is the truth. Her no-good ass ain't up here now, and where is she? She's in the back fucking your so-called husband. I'd slap the dog shit out of her, but I guess I can understand why you don't bother. I wouldn't want his crusty ass either."

"Susan, do you even know how to calm the hell down?" Renée asked. "Fatou doesn't need to hear your BS."

"She needs to hear all of it and then some," Susan said smoothly. "Maybe if she didn't have to worry about those two, we'd see her around here more often and my head wouldn't be aching every time I got it done."

"OK, we understand you," Renée said, relenting. "Maybe I will let you go first so you can get your ghetto ass out of here."

"Bitch! You as ghetto as me," Susan said, popping her gum. "We grew up on the same street, Adam Clayton Powell, not far from the Black Fashion Museum. Or have you forgotten?"

"Please don't remind me," Renée said jokingly. "I need to take your ass outside so we can puff on this spliff. Maybe that will calm your ass down." She turned to Fatou. "Let us know when you're done with Donna, sweetie, so no one tries to jump us."

Susan and Renée exited the shop and all the stylists started whispering about Fatou. Even Fifi glared at her harshly. Finally, Fifi struck up an argument. "Fatou, you need to handle your clients so that they aren't in here disrespecting everyone else."

"My clients?" Fatou said inquisitively. "Those two have been coming here for years before I ever heard of this salon."

"That doesn't mean anything," Fifi said. "If they are at your station today, they are your clients today."

"She wouldn't have to worry about stuff like that if she wasn't always trying to steal everyone else's clients," a stylist named

Ramonda added.

"Oh, please," Donna snapped from Fatou's chair. "If y'all knew how to do fucking hair, bitches would be in your seats. Don't get mad at her because she knows what she's doing and you don't."

"Whatever!" Ramonda snapped.

"That's enough," Fifi said. "I'd like to have a peaceful day in the shop for once."

Ramonda rolled her eyes toward Fatou. Fatou snickered lightly to herself before turning her thoughts to what was going on between Patra and Lama in the back room. She despised Lama now and couldn't figure out for the life of her why she was upset that he was with Patra when she didn't want him anymore.

While Fatou was thinking of Lama, he was in the back room of Sister Fifi's once again frolicking with Patra. The two siblings were embracing each other passionately, unaware that Patra was nearly a month pregnant with their fourth child.

Lama finished making love to Patra and rushed out of the room. He tried to kiss Fatou, but she pulled her head away.

"Don't even think about it," she said before her thoughts wandered off to her appointment later with David.

"Don't forget," Lama whispered to Fifi. "If Fatou receives any letters from the motherland, you are to give them to me, just as you've done in the past. But now it is of the utmost importance."

"I already know this, Lama," Fifi hissed, frustrated. "Be gone now. I have too much work to do before closing. It's bad enough that your little wife has brought chaos into my shop today."

"I'm doing you a favor being here, not the other way around," Fatou snapped. "You need me, remember?"

"Mind your manners," Lama sneered at Fatou, staring a while before he walked out.

Fatou smirked at him and thought, *My money is saved, so I won't be stuck with you much longer. Pretty soon I will be all on my own.*

CHAPTER THIRTEEN

A Whole New World

Fatou rushed to the C train after leaving Fifi's and for once embraced all of the sights and sounds of Harlem. She smiled at the African women approaching Fifi's who routinely visited to sell African food. She marveled at their happiness despite the fact that they only made about $100 a day.

After greeting them on the street, she smiled and paid a street vendor a dollar for some pineapple on a stick. She was happy that she had beat the police who raided the vendor's stand just minutes after she bought her treat.

Fatou shook her head and thought, *What a shame,* and continued to the subway station.

Once on the C train, she was happy to be entertained by two gentlemen playing a drumbeat that resembled her homeland's. While they played, she thought back to other entertainment she'd experienced on the train. One time, two little boys jumped over each other and twisted their bodies as if they were oblivious to the tight space within the subway car. Another tim, another young boy did what Americans called the electric boogie. His routine consisted of spinning on his head, jumping through his legs, and making windmills on his back. Fatou had never really paid much attention before.

The rhythm of the drums took over her senses, and Fatou rose and started twisting her body as if she was back home in West Africa. Riders cheered Fatou and the drummers as if they'd practiced their impromptu routine forever. It was customary for a few of the riders to give train performers small monetary tokens. But with Fatou's help, nearly everyone on the train handed out money. No one reached for change. Fatou earned herself and the drummers close to two hundred dollars for a couple of minutes work on a train. She left feeling alive and invigorated.

Fatou was turning into a Harlem child.

Rather than go straight to her business, Fatou decided to walk along Central Park West on Frederick Douglas Boulevard. She walked four blocks south and decided to turn west on Duke Ellington. She had heard much about the great musician who played jazz many years before she was born. As she approached Amsterdam Avenue, she paused at the Jewish Hospital to think about the Holocaust.

So many people died gruesome and oppressive deaths in other countries, she thought. *And so many Africans have had their own holocaust coming over to this country from the motherland. This country has so much history.*

Not wanting to be taken out of her happy state, Fatou turned north on Amsterdam and walked back toward Cathedral Parkway. While walking up to her check cashing place, she found it ironic that her business fostered jezebel-type activities despite being so close to the Cathedral of St. John the Divine.

"Well, I have to eat," she said to herself as she placed the key in the door and unlocked it. She was eagerly awaiting David's arrival.

"Hello," Chyna said as she walked from the back after hearing Fatou come in. "Is everything OK with you, partner?"

"Of course it is," Fatou replied. "I have had a fabulous day. It is so great to be surrounded by so much history. I was looking at a map today, and did you know that Lenox Avenue has portions named for the great Malcolm X, since he spent so much time there helping black Americans in the sixties? And did you know that even on 125th Street they've given another great leader, Martin Luther King, Jr., the same honor?"

"I know all of that," Chyna said curiously. "But what has gotten into you today that would make you so interested?"

"Oh, nothing," she replied "I'm just noticing parts of Harlem that are considered sacred ground. The culture is very rich here."

"If you say so," Chyna asserted bewilderedly. "Can you make sure the girls stay in line? I need some fresh air. I've been in here all day."

"Yes, of course," Fatou answered, wishing that Chyna had more appreciation for the little things in life.

As Chyna walked toward the door, David turned the knob and walked in. "May I help you?" Chyna asked, annoyed that someone would just walk in.

Noticing Fatou in the background, David said, "That's OK. I'm about to get this beautiful specimen right here to braid my hair if you don't mind."

Chyna shrugged her shoulders and exited as if she didn't care. But she was upset. For whatever reason, Fatou had left the door unlocked and that was a definite no no.

"Hello, beautiful," David said, smiling at Fatou. "I hope I haven't upset your friend."

"No. She's probably just having a bad day," Fatou replied. "I had to spend a lot of time at my other job, so she didn't have any help."

"Well, if that's what you think it is, you run with it," David said cheerfully. "But shorty has a problem with you. One day you'll realize that what I'm saying is true."

"You meet Chyna for less than a minute, and you're telling me that she has a problem with me?" Fatou hissed playfully. "What makes you so knowledgeable?"

"When you've survived these streets as long as I have, it's only because you know things. It's my business to know what a person has on their mind before they ever say a word."

"Oh, really," Fatou said, laughing. "And are you supposed to be some type of mind doctor or something?"

"Well, I do hit people off with something that takes away their problems for a second. But I don't claim to be a doctor. I've never been to college. All of my schooling has been done on these streets."

"So you don't know any more than I do," Fatou said sarcastically.

"Negative," David replied. "I know a helluva lot, and you don't know squat. And I know that girl has it in for you, so you best be careful. Now are you gonna dispense with the small talk and braid my hair? We have shit we need to do."

"Oh, really?" Fatou asked. "I said that I'd braid your hair and nothing else. Besides, I have to get home to my husband."

"You're not fucking married! What kind of man wouldn't put a ring on the finger of a woman like you? Stop tryna play me."

"I'm not playing with you," Fatou said, defending herself. "I am married. I've been married for five years."

"Yeah, right. And that would mean you were about thirteen or fourteen when you got married. You can't be much older than nineteen."

"Actually, I'm about to turn seventeen," Fatou replied. "But what does that have to do with anything? I'm still married. In a month I'll be seventeen, and in two months, I will have been married for five years."

"What kind of sick fuck would marry a twelve-year-old?" David asked.

"Well, my marriage was arranged in my village so that I could escape poverty and have a better life in America," Fatou said. "I am married to the type of man that gave my family La Dotte and allowed us to overcome a very hard time."

"Spare me," David hissed. "Those old-time ways should have been buried with the old timers. That dowry don't mean anything here. You're in America now. And I'm certain that the only reason you don't have a ring on your finger is your perverted-ass husband knows that he'd be shipped off with the rest of the pedophiles. I'm just glad that I didn't run up in you not knowing that you're not legal yet."

"And what makes you think I would do anything with you, Mr. Overconfident?"

"Cuz I'm a rude boy, and you know your body wants me," David replied confidently.

"Spare me," Fatou said, laughing despite knowing that David was right.

They continued talking while Fatou braided David's hair, and they found out a lot about each other. David learned of Fatou's marriage to Lama, her pregnancy, her prehistoric abortion, her stepchildren that were mothered by Patra, and the deplorable working conditions and wages at Fifi's.

Fatou learned that David was in business for himself supplying all of New York and parts of Jersey with what he called product. She also learned that she could make $500 a day working for him for only traveling back and forth on the subway. She declined.

"I cannot leave Fifi," she said, frightened. "Lama would kill me if he found out that I wasn't under the watchful eye of Fifi. He wants to know about my every move."

"Fuck Lama and fuck Fifi," David hollered. "I'm about to put you on some real stuff. Don't you know who I am? Let me school you on who I am."

Fatou and David sat quietly for a few minutes after he chirped someone on his Nextel. Eventually, a knock was heard on the door, so Fatou peeked out.

"Yo, Ma, where's David at?" the young Jamaican at the door asked.

"I guess someone wants you," Fatou said, turning to David.

"Well, let his ass in," David replied.

Fatou stared at David as if she thought he had nerve to be telling her what to be doing inside her own business.

"Look, the whole world is mine," David said while getting up to open the door.

Fatou stood dumbfounded as the two men greeted each other.

"What's up, God?" the young Jamaican said. "You're looking real blingy."

"What is this blingy?" Fatou asked while closing the door.

"I mean he's freezing. He's icy. His ass is subzero." The young Jamaican could tell that Fatou was confused, so he looked at David.

"What's up with Ma? She's fine as hell, but she's a lost puppy."

"Mind your manners, Ace," David said. "This is Fatou. She is the owner of this establishment and doesn't speak very much slang."

"Well, what up, shorty?" Ace said, lifting her hand as if he were going to kiss it.

David smacked his hand off of Fatou's before Ace could bring it to his lips and said, "There won't be any of that. She's not even eighteen yet. And when she does become eighteen, she's mine."

"My bad," Ace said as Fatou looked at David, admiring his audacity.

"Anyway, Fatou," David said, "Blingy is short for bling-bling. Sometimes people say someone is icy or anything relating to cold. All that it means is that someone is wearing a lot of platinum and diamonds."

When David put his arm out, Fatou noticed the platinum-faced Rolex with a diamond bezel. She also noticed the huge platinum bracelets that adorned his wrist.

"How can you afford such things?" Fatou asked.

"David's serving up all of New York," Ace said, bragging for his home boy. "He's the man. If you don't know, you'd better ask somebody."

David smiled, loving his ego being stroked. Satisfied, he dismissed Ace and continued his conversation with Fatou.

"Now, Fatou," he said, "Are you still going to worry yourself with trivial things like Lama and Fifi, or are you gonna join my team?"

"I know you don't believe me, but Lama is a violent man," Fatou confessed. "There are only so many hours in the day, so I'm uncertain how I can work with you while still working at Fifi's and running my business here. I will not risk Lama hurting me."

David noticed that Fatou was very upset while she was speaking of Lama, so he backed off. But he told himself that his plan for finding a new mule to carry his drugs was not foiled. It was merely put on hold.

Fatou and David stole many moments together over the next month. It was among the happiest times Fatou had had since coming to America.

For her seventeenth birthday, David threw her a big party at the check cashing place, introducing her to all of his lieutenants. Fatou met Donny from the Bronx. He stood about six feet two inches tall, weighed about two hundred sixty pounds, and probably had not an ounce of body fat on him. With his smooth bald head, he looked like a gladiator. Donny was a very intimidating sight to see.

Donny pulled in about $ 50,000 a week selling what he called his big three—crack cocaine, purple haze, and wet weed dipped in embalming fluid.

Redd, who handled Jamaica, Queens, was very charismatic. With the exception of a body frame that was similar to Iron Mike Tyson's in his prime, Redd was the spitting image of the LA Lakers' Rick Fox. Redd's pretty-boy face and wavy hair helped him be very successful with the ladies. Yet his financial prosperity from moving about $50,000 worth of product a week throughout Jamaica, Queens, didn't seem to hurt his mack game either.

On a typical week, Redd took in between $80,000 to $100,000, most of it through his powdered cocaine sales, but he also dabbled in crack and weed.

Joe-Joe seemed to be as gullible as they came. But he held down

Brooklyn to the fullest. He was a five foot five powerhouse with a very daunting fight game. In Rahway prison, it was rumored that he took out an entire cell block by himself. Then he turned his vengeance on his squad for not helping him after he got out of the hole. Supposedly, they all covered up and took their licks as best as they could. No one wanted to square up one on one against Joe-Joe. Joe-Joe grossed between $50,000 to $60,000 a week. Like Donny, his biggest sellers were crack cocaine, purple haze and wet.

Ken, who took to Fatou right away, controlled about one hundred sixteen blocks in downtown Queens. He was a very muscular Nigerian immigrant with a sleek frame. But what he lacked in brawn, he made up with an itchy trigger finger. He had a Desert Eagle 44 Magnum, a 9- millimeter Glock, and a night vision Uzi with an infrared scope and red sensor beam that locked onto any target. Ken called them Bird, Nina, and Bloodbath. respectively. Normally, he made about $70,000 a week selling crack and wet. He used to sell regular weed but he said he got tired of chicks trying to smoke for free.

Running things in Harlem was a mixed breed, half Italian, half Black named Ricco. All the homies showed him love by calling him Suave. His features reminded them of the Rock from the WWF, except he was a little taller and he wore a ponytail. Rumor had it that Suave was the illegitimate son of one of New York's true wise guys, Tony "The Butcher" Mizzonelli. And judging from the way Ricco sliced up his rivals after taking them out, that rumor probably held a lot of truth.

Ricco made money hand over fist. His slow week of about $120,000 surpassed all the other lieutenants. And in a good week he could make as much as two hundred grand. His success was due to variety of product. He sold powder and crack cocaine, heroin, weed and purple haze.

Sarge and Rottweiler were twin brothers who were holding down Newark, Elizabeth and Jersey City. Sarge handled Newark; Rottweiler controlled Elizabeth. They alternated every few days in Jersey City. The brothers sported wild Don King afros, diamond-laced patches that they called their third eyes, and humongous six-foot snakes that they each kept wrapped around their necks. Were it not for Rottweiler's love for the six dogs that held down the fort in his section of the brothers' million dollar home in Teaneck, you wouldn't be able to tell where one brother ended and the other began.

The twins had North Jersey on lock, bringing in close to $100,000 a week. They sold everything that Ricco sold plus they sold wet. Aside from the lieutenants, there was a horde of young boys. All them were loud-talking and gave predictions about which one of them would move up the ranks the fastest. In total, there were about twenty-five hustlers crowded into Fatou's business who ranged from small-time yes-men to big-time ballers. And they all came bearing gifts for Fatou. Chyna was beside herself.

"Fatou, may I talk to you for a minute?" Chyna asked. Once Fatou walked over to the side, Chyna hit her with, "Do you really it is wise having all of these felons in here? You know that we'll have some law enforcement customers showing up for appointments pretty soon."

"It'll be fine. I'll keep them up here and I'll try to stop them from making too much noise. But with what our customers come here for, I doubt they care about noise."

"OK. But I hope you're right."

"Don't worry," Fatou said assuredly. "Maybe you can have some of the girls mingle out here to find new clients. There's a lot of money in here."

"Ooh, can't you do it? I'll be busy taking care of things in the back."

"I can't let David see me being a madam. He knows that we are partners, but he thinks that you handle that half of the business."

"So it's OK for you to share the profits, but you don't want any part of the stigma attached to what we do?" Chyna hissed.

"Relax," Fatou said calmly. "It's my birthday. Remember? Don't get your panties all in a bunch."

Fatou walked off, and although David didn't hear the conversation, he sensed that there was some tension involved. He walked up behind her, hugged her and kissed her on the cheek.

Whispering in her ear, he said, "I told you that shorty has a problem with you."

He patted her on the butt and released her to go mingle. Fatou started to wonder if there was any truth to what David believed.

CHAPTER FOURTEEN

Independence Day

Fatou woke up happy the morning after her birthday party. She was peacefully reclining in a chair with David's muscular arms wrapped snugly around her.

She was amazed that he had kept his promise not have sex with her before she turned eighteen. *It feels so good, so innocent, to just be held,* she thought to herself. *I wasn't sure that a man could control his hormones around me. Even my own father took me, pretending that he was teaching me a lesson about marriage. David is the only man who truly cares about me.*

Fatou gently pulled herself away from David's arms and walked to the bathroom. She had a couple of hours before she had to go to Fifi's, so she grabbed her cell phone out of the outlet next to the recliner and called in to find out the time of her first appointment.

"Hello, Fifi."

"Child, how come you don't come home last night?" Fifi's voice blared through the phone. "Lama has been here acting like a madman, keeping me up most of the night."

"Some friends threw me a birthday party."

"You have no friends but us!" Fifi shouted.

"Sure I do," Fatou answered sarcastically. "Lama will just have to get used to the fact that I wasn't home being bored on my birthday. He should be happy knowing that I wasn't alone and lonely while he was out all night spending time with his real family."

"Don't let your tongue get your hind parts into a lashing," Fifi warned "Lama is very upset. You'd better be extra nice to him when you see him today. I'm to call him as soon as you get here."

"Speaking of that, what time is my first appointment?"

"Never you mind that, girl!" Fifi hollered. "You need to just get here as fast as you can."

"No. I'm tired. I don't want to come any earlier than I have to. Check the book for me, please."

"You are really pushing your luck, child," Fifi warned "The longer you put it off, the worse Lama is gonna be. Your first appointment is at twelve thirty, but if I were you, I'd get here right away."

"Thanks for the advice," Fatou said snidely before hanging up the phone.

"That didn't sound good," David said hoarsely to Fatou after she hung up her phone.

"Lama's gonna kick my ass for staying out all night," Fatou said, trying to sound unconcerned. "The one night in five years I decide not to come home, and it's the only time he's looking for me."

"Don't worry your pretty head about Lama," David said confidently. "I can handle him if you'd like."

"Somebody's gonna have to handle him. I hate to go to Fifi's knowing he's gonna go in there acting like a fool."

"Well, I have an idea."

"What?" Fatou asked. "Right now I'm about game for anything."

"You told me how Lama is always screwing Patra in the back room for money."

"Yeah, that he does," Fatou agreed.

"And you also said that Fifi is money hungry."

"Definitely."

"Well, why don't I go there pretending to try to pay for you."

"That won't work," Fatou said, cutting David off. "Fifi knows that I won't sell myself to anyone."

"Yeah, but I will make her an offer she won't refuse."

"What type of an offer," Fatou asked.

"I will offer her $500 if she lets me take you off the premises to braid my hair. Then I'll tell her that I'll only give you a bonus if you earn it. She won't care about you once I put the money in her hand."

"But she knows that I won't agree to any foul play," Fatou said hesitantly despite warming up to the idea.

"That's why I'll tease her with the money but won't put it in her hands until she makes you agree to say out of your own mouth that you'll go with me. Now, do you really think that Fifi is gonna allow you to make her lose out on $500?"

"I have to be honest," Fatou said. "Fifi is the last person I'd expect to let that much money slip away from." She paused. "But then what? After I leave with you, then what's supposed to happen?"

"You leave with me and that's the last time Lama or Fifi will see you. I'll make it seem like I kidnapped you."

Fatou digested David's words for a few minutes, then smiled.

"That may work," she said.

"It will work."

"You think so?"

"I know so."

"Then we'll do it," she said. "But on one condition."

"What's that?"

"You have to go with me to say goodbye to Mati. I cannot disappear without at least saying goodbye to Mati."

"You trust her?"

"Yes, with my life."

"True. True. Well, we can holla at her then. Is there anything else?"

"Let me think," she said

Fatou raised her eyebrows, concentrating, as if she were in deep thought.

"I know," she said. "How am I supposed to get in touch with my customers? I'll have to braid hair here from now on."

"Ma, you'll be making $500 a day on my team until you get up to speed, then you'll make even more than that. You won't need to be braiding no hair."

"I know that I won't need to do it, but I want to do it. I don't want to lose my skills. I'm gonna open my own salon one day."

"Well, suit yourself," David said.

Fatou pulled David up from the recliner so that she could hug him.

"David, don't be like that," she said "Don't lose interest in me because I say something you don't agree with. I've had more than my fair share of that with Lama."

"You're right, Ma," he said. "I'll help you out."

"Good," Fatou said, sitting down on the recliner and closing her eyes. "That will help me rest a lot easier. I asked Chyna to wake me up at eleven. Come lie down with me for a few more minutes."

"No, Ma," David said, pulling at Fatou's arm. "Get that ass up. You have work to do."

"What?" Fatou asked lazily.

"You have to call all of your best customers right now, but only the ones you can trust. Have them meet you at Fifi's so you can give them a card. But you have to find a way for nobody to see you. Just let them know that if they want their hair done, they'll have to check you out here."

"That's a good plan. But what if Fifi finds out about where I am? I'm sure she'll tell immigration on me."

"That's why I told you to only tell customers that you can trust. If it seems like they're gonna run their mouths, don't say shit to them. Let their heads get jacked up by them other bitches at the shop."

"I'm sure they'd be happy to see me leave anyway," Fatou replied. "But I don't want to put this business in jeopardy for Chyna. She is my partner, and I don't want anything with Lama and Fifi coming back to damage her."

"I like that," David said, extremely impressed. "I wish some of my lieutenants and young boys thought like you. You're more ready for this game than you think."

David started pulling at Fatou's arm again. "Ma, get that ass up. I got an idea, but we have to hurry."

"What?" Fatou whined.

"I'll tell you when you get dressed."

Fatou finally relented and dragged herself off the recliner.

While she dressed David called in a rush order for business cards at Kev's Copies in Harlem. "Make sure to put Fatou's African American Hair Braiding and the number that I gave you on the cards. And

I need them in about an hour."

The salesperson from Kev's Copies started to complain on the other end of the line.

"Look, man, I got you," David said assuredly. "There's a big tip in it for you as long as they're done on time. That's my word."

"Bet. I got you," said the salesman.

They hung up, and David went to the bathroom so he could continue to rush Fatou.

Fatou was drying herself off with a towel when David opened the door.

"Oh, shit," he said when he saw Fatou naked. She blushed but didn't cover herself up.

"You're working with a full house," David said. "Padonkadonk ain't the word, goddamn! Hurry that ass up so we can be out," he said, backing out of the door, trying not to look.

"Are you sure you want to leave?," Fatou asked.

"I ain't fucking with you like that, Ma. Just wait until your ass turns eighteen. Umm, umm, umm."

Mati was very sad to hear that Fatou would be leaving. But, she was glad for her at the same time.

"No one should have to put up with what you've put up with from Lama," Mati said. "You have been nothing but an angel since you've been here. I will miss you dearly."

"When I get myself together, I'll find a way to get in touch with you."

"Please do, child," Mati said tearfully. "I definitely want to know that you are OK."

"I'll be OK, Mati," Fatou assured her while grabbing her and giving her a heartfelt hug. "Don't you worry about me. As long as I'm away from Lama and Fifi, I'm sure I'll be fine."

The two women embraced for what seemed an eternity before Fatou finally let go.

"I have to go, Mati."

"I know," Mati said, crying. "Please don't forget me, child."

"I won't," Fatou assured her while pulling away. "I'll never forget everything you did for me."

Fatou walked off sniffling and was crying wholeheartedly by the time she rejoined David in the car.

"She saved my life, David."

David looked at her with a concerned expression but didn't respond.

"If it wasn't for Mati, I would be dead."

Fatou paused to let out a loud outburst of sobs.

"Mati is the only person who has always been there for me since I came to America."

"Now I'll take good care of you," David said. "And we'll make sure that Mati is well off. That's my word."

Fatou grabbed David's hand but didn't speak. She closed her eyes and tried to sob quietly as David steered the car to Kev's Copies.

CHAPTER FIFTEEN

Natali's Letter

Fatou composed herself as she and David left Kev's Copies, and she told him to take her to the subway stop at 125th Street.

"I told my clients to meet me there. I'll be handing out business cards so that no one in the shop will know."

"Now that's what I'm talking about," David said. "You're impressing me more and more by the second. That's how to use your brain."

Fatou smiled. She was happy that a man liked something about her other than her body.

He may really be the one for me, she thought.

At the subway stop, one by one, Fatou's clients showed up, offering their congratulations and telling her that she should have gone out on her own a long time ago.

The business card she gave them had a two-way pager number on it so that Fatou's clients could leave her messages or emails at my2way.com. Both David and Fatou were very careful to set things up in a way that Lama or Fifi could never just show up at a business address shown on the card and surprise her.

Fatou's check cashing business was never mentioned.

After all of her clients showed up, Fatou headed to Sister Fifi's for part two of her plan. She was sure that since she was early, Fifi would send her back to the subway stop to hand out flyers. And then she would see David and bring him back to the shop, pretending she had just met him for the first time.

David parked his SUV down the block from Fifi's and gave Fatou a few words of encouragement before she got out. "If Lama is in there wildin', let me come deal with his ass. You can't continue to be afraid of these fools."

"I'll be OK," Fatou said, even though she was uncertain how things were about to go down.

"Alright, I'll be waiting for you near the subway."

Fatou went to Fifi's and was met by a chorus of leering eyes and whispers.

"I'm glad you have come to your senses," Fifi said. "I thought you'd gone plum mad."

Fatou smiled but didn't comment. She started preparing her station, sneakily putting small items that she didn't want to leave behind into her oversized Coach bag.

As soon as she sat in her chair for a rest and after she had successfully packed up everything she wanted to take with her, Fifi glanced her way and proceeded to play right into her hands.

"Fatou, why don't you grab some flyers and go to the subway stop to bring some new customers in here. You have some free time before your first client arrives."

"OK, Fifi," Fatou replied, smiling to herself. *Everything is working out perfectly,* she thought.

Fatou walked over to the subway stop. David saw her but didn't acknowledge her right away. They had decided earlier to play it cool just in case someone decided to follow Fatou or, even worse, if Lama had one of his cabbie buddies spying on her. They wanted to be extra careful.

I don't know why Fatou has me playing like a bitch, David thought to himself. *I can easily deal with that nigga Mafioso with a Cuban necktie, slicing his throat from ear to ear. But if she wants me to chill, I'll chill. But if that nigga ever walks up on her, it's over.*

After about half an hour, thinking it had been long enough, David walked up to Fatou as if he were striking up a conversation with her for the first time. If you didn't know them, you would have really believed that they were strangers.

Fatou acted bashful with David and tentatively agreed to let him follow her to Fifi's. He even walked a few steps behind her after she told him she wouldn't want her husband getting the wrong idea if he caught them walking together.

"My husband has a very bad temper," she said, as if David didn't already know who Lama was and the cowardly violent acts he was capable of.

Walking into Fifi's, Fatou said, "Fifi, this gentleman wants his hair braided. You have to negotiate with him a price. He says that men don't pay as much for their hair as women. I have never braided a man's hair before."

Fifi gestured for David to come to her, so he walked up to her as if he were a regular guy, not one of the kings of New York.

"How do you want your hair?" she asked. "That will determine how much of her time you take up and how much money you have to pay."

"I want a really hot design," David replied.

"Can you be more specific?"

"You know, something fly. Your girl can use her imagination. I've heard that she's very good at braiding hair." David moved in closer to Fifi and started whispering. "And I've also heard some other things about your shop. I'd like to find out what else she is good at."

"Fatou is as quiet and fidgety as a church mouse," Fifi replied, catching his drift. "Why don't you enjoy the company of some other girl? You have many to choose from."

"No. I want her. Whatever it takes, I'm willing to pay. But it definitely has to be her."

"Well, what are you willing to pay?" Fifi asked, knowing that Lama would kill her if he knew what she was contemplating. "It will at least have to be a couple hundred."

"I'll put $500 from my hands to yours. But on one condition."

"What condition?"

"She has to braid my hair outside of the shop. If she treats me well, I'll give her a nice tip for herself. You don't even have to share your $500 with her. I'll take care of her myself."

"I am trying to tell you that Fatou doesn't participate in extra curricula activities," Fifi warned.

"Well that would be my loss," David said. "But why should you care? You'll have your money, so whatever happens with us shouldn't matter to you. Maybe I'll just get my hair braided, and she'll walk away with nothing. Or maybe she'll make me happy and walk away with a very big tip. Either way, you'll be the first person to be compensated."

"Wait over here," Fifi said while walking up to Fatou and pulling her arm. "Come with me to the back. I have to talk to you."

Fatou followed Fifi, pretending as if she didn't know what was going on. Fifi didn't waste any time once in the back room.

"You must go with the gentleman. He has something to do elsewhere so he can't sit here long enough to have his hair braided."

"Fifi! Lama would not approve of such things," Fatou said, feigning that she cared. "He is already very upset with me because of last night."

"I will deal with Lama."

"But how?"

"Don't worry about it."

"But I can't get in any more trouble."

"Stop interrupting me, child," Fifi hissed. "I told you that I would deal with Lama."

"I won't do it," Fatou said matter-of-factly. "Have you forgotten that I am a married woman?"

"And what does marriage have to do with you braiding the man's hair, child?" Fifi asked.

"Do not pretend you don't see the way he looks at me. He wants more than his hair braided."

"Look," Fifi snapped. "I am tired of playing games with you. I am not about to negotiate in my own shop. You will go with him. That's final! If I were you, I'd be nice. Maybe you will get a very good tip out of the deal."

"Just like that?" Fatou asked.

"Just like that."

With that, Fifi walked out the back room door and paused so Fatou could follow her.

"It is settled," Fifi said. "She will go with you, but you must pay your bill up front."

"Wait," David said. "I want her to tell me herself that she is going before I pay you. What if she backs down?"

"Tell him," Fifi commanded anxiously, glaring at Fatou.

Fatou sat quietly.

"Tell him," Fifi snapped again.

"I will go," Fatou whispered.

"What was that?" David asked.

"Louder!" Fifi shouted.

"I said, I will go," Fatou said, visibly shaken. She grabbed her Coach bag and stomped out the door. David paid Fifi and followed Fatou.

"Nice doing business with you," Fifi said. "I hope that you will be happy."

"Oh, I will be," David whispered to himself. "I will be."

Back at the check cashing place, Fatou saw the mailman outside. "Hi, Thomas," she said. "I haven't seen you in a while."

"That's because Chyna always collects the mail," he replied. "You are looking lovely today."

"Your damned right she is, government boy," David hissed. "Now be gone and stop holding up people's mail."

"David, where are your manners?" Fatou said bashfully before addressing Thomas. "I apologize, Thomas. I don't know what in the world has gotten into David today."

Thomas walked off without commenting, and David followed Fatou into the check cashing place. Fatou greeted her two workers, then turned to David.

"I don't know why you felt the need to embarrass me."

"Cuz niggas ain't slick," he replied. "He did the right thing, though. He knew he'd better get it on before he got shitted on."

"Men! Your testosterone makes you do the silliest things."

"Whatever."

Fatou skimmed through the envelopes and was shocked but very pleased to have received a letter from Natali.

"Oh, boy!" she said excitedly as she tore open the letter and sat down at her desk to read it.

November 19, 1999

Hi Fatou,

First things first. Happy birthday! I don't know why you haven't contacted me or returned any of my letters, but I won't ruin your birthday with such things. I was rather upset, though, that you didn't reach out to me this year or last year on my birthday.

We are fellow Scorpions.

I guess you and Chyna are still in business since your letters have never been returned to me for having an improper address. But I don't know what I did to you to make you stop thinking about me or helping me out. It is so tough in this detention center without having the things I need. Still, I thank you both for the two times you did send me $100. That money was very useful.

I told you and Chyna that I needed about two grand for a lawyer to help me prevent deportation, and I'm mad you haven't helped me. But everything happens for a reason, and it's not your fault that I'm in the predicament I'm in. Yet, I do think of you as a dear friend and thought you felt the same. Yes, I've had my reservations about Chyna, but thought that with you around, her deceitfulness could be controlled. If it makes you feel any better, I do have money stashed away and will repay every dime you give me once things change for the better. I guess this is my last effort plea. If you don't send some help soon, I will be leaving America for good.

I want you to know that I love you dearly, and even if you choose not to help me out, I still cherish you as a friend. Irregardless of everything, return this letter so that I will know that it is safe to write you with the information of where my money is stashed if they do decide to deport me. You can have it, all of it, as long as I know that you are still my friend.

Love you dearly,
Natali

Puzzled, Fatou held the letter in one hand, gently smacking it against the other. Finally she said, "This is very odd."

"What's that, Ma?" David asked.

"I told you about my friend Natali. Well, I haven't heard from her in almost two years. Now she writes me saying that she thinks I'm mad at her. Why would I be mad at her? And why would she say that me and Chyna have only sent her $100 twice when we've been sending her at least $300 a week since we opened this place? Natali must be confused."

"You're the only one who's confused," he said. "I smell a rat, and her name is Chyna. I told you about that bitch."

"You never liked her."

"Because I know the bitch is slimy as hell. She's a fucking trick. You can never trust a fucking trick."

"So what do you think of me?"

"You're not a fucking trick. But that bitch, Chyna. She's nothing but a damn ho. She may be an expensive ho. But she's still a ho."

"Yes, she sells her body," Fatou conceded, "but that has nothing to do with the things that Natali is saying in her letter."

"Let me see that," David said, grabbing the letter out of her hand. He read it intently, with a deliberate expression on his face. He shook his head once he finished.

"I told you that bitch wasn't shit. She's been playing you out the whole time," David snapped.

"Playing me out how?"

"How much money have you been giving her?"

"One, two hundred dollars a week. She matches it and sends it to Natali. But I did give her $2,500 before so that she could send Natali $5,000 for a lawyer."

"I'd take every dime out that bitch's hide!"

"You think she's been stealing from me?"

"Hello!"

"She can't be stealing from me. I trust her."

"I told you that you can't trust no fucking body. Especially another bitch that's always acting like she's jealous of you. I go through that shit every day with other niggas."

"I'll just ask her. There has to be some explanation."

"Don't be a fool all of your life."

"David, don't talk to me like that."

"Well, open your eyes then."

Fatou grabbed David's hands and looked him straight in the eyes. "No. No matter what is going on with me and my business affairs and no matter what you think, don't talk to me like that."

"I wish you stood up for yourself with other mothafuckas as much as you try to stand up to me."

Fatou didn't back down.

"All right. I'm sorry, boo. But you do act soft when it comes to other mothafuckas. You need to handle your shit."

"Maybe I do. Maybe I will."

"Fuck maybe. You need to deal with this right now."

"And do what?"

"Kick that fucking bone out on her ass."

"But what if there's some reasonable explanation? What if someone has been stealing the money we've been sending?"

"The eyes don't lie," David said.

"What's that supposed to mean?"

"Call her in here. Let her read the letter in your presence and watch her reaction. Then watch her try to squirm her way out of it and lie to you."

"You never liked her."

"And with good reason. But don't listen to me. Do what I suggest and see for yourself."

"Alright. Let me finish what I'm doing, then I'll deal with this."

"Boo," David said softly while grabbing Fatou and looking into her eyes. "I know this is your people, but you got to handle this shit. It's not gonna just go away. She's played you and you have to deal with it. Never let the streets talk about someone playing you and you not handling it. The every Tom, Dick and Harry out there is gonna step on you."

"You're right," Fatou agreed. "I'm just not used to all of this deception. We don't treat each other this way in my country."

"Well, welcome to America."

Fatou sighed, then gave David a tight hug. "I don't know what I would do without you," she said.

"That doesn't matter," he said. "I got your back for life. That's my word. Stick with me though, and you'll be as ruthless as these streets force you to be. You can't be soft in New York. Remember, nice guys always finish last. Only the lion survives in this jungle."

"You are right."

Fatou reluctantly released David and walked to the door that adjoined the check cashing place to the escort service. She opened the door, stuck her head in the back, and told Chyna she had to show her something.

"Remember, don't say shit," David whispered. "Act like everything is OK."

Fatou shook her head agreeably as Chyna walked through the door.

"What's up, partner?" Chyna asked.

"I need some help with this," Fatou said, handing her the letter.

Chyna started reading the letter and her guilt became obvious. It was written all over her face.

"Let me explain," Chyna said.

"You'd do this to me? I gave you my trust."

"Let me explain."

"I told you how fucked up things were for me."

"Let me explain, Fatou, please."

"I told you that I almost had enough money saved up to give Lama his money back and you still took my money."

"But..."

"You didn't give a shit about what I was going through."

David saw the situation escalating, so he walked up to the door and locked it, turning the "Open For Business" sign around to "Closed." Then he walked over to the cashiers and told them to take a fifteen-minute break. When they ignored him, he lifted up his shirt, revealing his chrome-plated 45. The cashiers rushed out, stumbling over each other, and David walked back to the two ladies. Fatou was grilling Chyna.

"How could you take my kindness for weakness?"

"But..."

"You disgust me!"

"I'll give it back."

"I don't want shit from you! Just leave!"

"But..."

"Bitch, I said just leave!"

Chyna stared at Fatou sadly for a second, then turned to leave.

"OK. If you feel like that, then fuck you!"

Fatou lunged at Chyna and pushed her. She fell. As Chyna got up and started heading for Fatou, David grabbed her by her hair and started yelling at her.

"I can't believe you tried to play Fatou out like that as much as she had your back. I told her that you ain't shit. You're just a slimy little bitch."

"Let me go, motherfucker!" Chyna yelled. "You're just a pussy anyway for putting your hands on a woman."

"Bitch, fuck you!" he snapped.

"You ain't got enough money, motherfucker," Chyna replied angrily.

"That's right, you're just a fucking trick," he yelled. "Stinking bitch."

David pulled Chyna's hair as if he were trying to yank it out of her head as he led her toward Fatou. When he reached Fatou, he shoved Chyna hard. Her knee crashed into the floor and she immediately started stroking it, trying to coax the pain away.

"You fucking pussy," Chyna yelled. "That's why them Jakes are gonna come see your ass. I know what you're into. They'd love to hear all the shit I got to tell them."

Chyna paused briefly to tend to her aching knee before continuing to bicker at David.

"Let's see how fucking tough you are when your ass is locked the fuck up."

David pulled his 45 out of his pants and stuck it in Chyna's mouth.

"Bitch, I'll body your ass right now," David spit angrily.

"You ain't gon' do shit, pussy," Chyna choked out. "With your fucking lame ass."

BANG

"Tell that shit to your friends in hell," David said after he shot her dead.

Fatou gasped, then David turned to her, finally remembering that she was also in the room.

"Don't look at me like that. She had that shit coming with all that fucking mouth. Plus she was talking about snitching, knowing she shoulda just kept her fucking mouth shut. Niggas ain't playin' games no more. If someone plays you out, you go straight to gun clappin'. That's how you handle drama on the streets."

"Is she dead?" Fatou asked.

"Hell, yeah. And good riddance."

"But you did that so easily, without any hesitation."

"With any luck, you'll be acting as fast one day. Now give me some plastic bags so we can get rid of this bitch. Make sure they're the thick black ones."

Fatou walked to the back and grabbed the trash bags. She was still shaken after seeing her first murder. She didn't know yet that she would witness many more.

David tried to calm her nerves as they carried Chyna out to his SUV.

"You had to do this, Boo," he said. "She wasn't thinking about you when she was robbing you, so why should you think about her?"

Fatou didn't comment. She walked silently with David until they reached his truck. Then she helped him guide Chyna's body onto the floor of the back seat.

"I'll be back," he said.

"Hurry," she replied, still shaken.

"No doubt."

He got in the car and drove toward the Brooklyn Bridge so he could dump the body.

When he arrived, he put his hazard lights on and lifted his hood, acting like he had a problem with his vehicle. Once the coast was clear, he opened the door closest to the side of the bridge, then pulled Chyna out. He kicked her until she fell over the side, then he spit out behind her.

"Ashes to ashes and dust to dust, you thieving bitch," David hissed before getting back in the SUV and driving off.

CHAPTER SIXTEEN

The Search Is On

Lama had been calling Fifi repeatedly for two days since Fatou disappeared, so often that she was barely able to do her clients' hair. She turned off her cell phone.

"Lama, Fifi cannot get to the phone," a co-worker said when Lama called. "She is very, very busy right now."

"Bitch, put her on the phone at once," Lama screamed.

She hung up on him.

"I am so tired of these bitches!" Lama hissed to himself as he steered his cab toward Sister Fifi's.

"Why are you avoiding me?" he yelled when he reached Sister Fifi's, busting in the door.

"Lama, this is my place of business," Fifi pleaded, trying to calm him down.

"I don't give a shit!" he snapped. "Your place of business is the reason why Fatou has disappeared."

"You must calm down," Fifi snapped back.

"Fuck you. Tell me where Fatou is."

"Let me take care of this," Fifi said to her client, Margaret, while touching her lightly on the shoulder.

"Go handle your business," Margaret replied.

Fifi went to the back room, and Lama stomped behind her.

He slammed the door shut once they were both inside.

"I am tired of playing games with you, Fifi!" he shouted.

"I told you that I don't know where she is, Lama!"

"You are a liar."

"I am telling the truth."

Lama grabbed Fifi hard by the shoulders and looked at her crazily.

"I will fucking kill you if you keep lying to me," he shouted wildly.

"Lama, take your hands off of me."

"You haven't seen a thing yet! Tell me the truth, you bitch. Tell me the truth."

He grabbed her neck and started choking her. Fifi feared for her life and flailed her arms wildly before trying to pry Lama's hands from her neck. When she failed to free herself, she squealed hoarsely to Lama between gasps for air her broken confession.

"OK, Lama. I will tell you."

"And you'd better hurry, you bitch!" he snapped insanely.

"She is at the juvenile hall," Fifi said, lying. "I was scared to tell you that they came and took her away. I tried to get my lawyer friend to get her released, but he has had trouble. She doesn't have any paperwork to prove she is an American. You are probably the only one who can have her released."

"Well, why didn't you tell me?" he asked, relaxing just a little. "I must find her. Which juvenile hall is she in?"

"I do not know," Fifi said, continuing the lie.

"Well, I will find out," Lama snapped.

He rushed out of Sister Fifi's and headed back to his cab.

For over a month, Lama visited different juvenile halls, but never saw Fatou. During that time, he lost twenty pounds and looked physically sick. His appetite and will to function normally appeared to be gone.

Haphazardly, he steered his cab up the West Side Highway, paying no attention to the picturesque view of Lower Manhattan or the stunning waterfront.

As his fare talked to someone on his cell phone, Lama turned onto West 23rd Street, following it until he passed Gramercy.

He maneuvered his way across the FDR Drive, oblivious to the beauty that surrounded him, Manhattan's skyscrapers on one side, the Wallabout Bay of the East River on another, and the Brooklyn and Queens skylines off in the distance.

"Make sure you get two packs of vinegar with my salad," Lama's thuggish passenger named Joe-Joe said charismatically.

"And tell Shorty not to put extra shit in my salad. Leave it like it is. Just hurry it up," Joe-Joe spit back. "I don't have time to stop to eat. Just do what I asked you. I'm out. One."

Joe-Joe's slang signaled Bee-Bop to have their drug connect meet him near Vinegar Hill to drop off two kilos of crack cocaine. He had Lama let him out of the cab on Tillary Street, then jumped into his Range Rover.

"Put two packs of vinegar on that salad," Bee-Bop said after chirping his connect. "It'll be ready in five minutes…that's what's up."

Bee-Bop grabbed his heater and stuffed it in his pants before leaving his grandmother's brownstone on Prince Street, located just above Flatbush Avenue in what is now called the DUMBO section of Brooklyn (Down Under the Manhattan Bridge Overpass), not far from downtown Brooklyn's Vinegar Hill area.

Bee-Bop continuously looked back to make sure that no one from the Faragut Housing Projects planned to ambush him for the backpack filled with Joe-Joe's cheddar that he'd switch with his connect at the drop spot on Hudson Street. He strutted down Concord Street after turning off Prince and paused to take out his mix CD blasting M.O.P.'s "Ante Up" and put in his Stillmatic CD to listen to Nas tear into Jay Z on "Ether." Though it was always about Queens Bridge niggas with Bee-Bop, listening to "Ante Up" didn't make him feel any better about carrying all of Joe-Joe's cash.

Bee-Bop laughed as he turned up Hudson, thinking about how Nas was right to dis Jay Z for wearing Hawaiian shirts.

"Don't no real niggas wear no bullshit like that," he said to himself.

While Bee-Bop was heading up Hudson, Joe-Joe was turning off of Tillary onto Flatbush, where he would turn right on Prospect and park his Range Rover on Bridge Street, trading it for his Kawasaki Ninja 1100 GPZ motorcycle. Joe-Joe wanted to cruise his motorcycle along the square Bridge, York, Hudson, and Concord streets made to watch Bee-Bop make his drop. He'd heard rumors about him and wanted to see if it was just other niggas hating on him or if he really had a reason to take Bee-Bop out the game for good.

As Joe-Joe mounted his motorcycle on Bridge, and Bee-Bop continued up Hudson, Lama turned his cab onto Hudson, passing Bee-Bop in the process. Lama was picking up some coffee from one of his favorite shops to help keep him awake. He hadn't gotten much sleep over the past month.

Bee-Bop's connect exited the York Street subway station and walked toward Hudson while Lama sipped his coffee and conversed with the proprietor of the shop.

Joe-Joe was on his motorcycle, riding along the four-block square. Bee-Bop's connect was wearing a brown, black and yellow three-piece outfit with a Dashiki blouse, Sokoto pants, and matching head scarf. On her feet she wore comfortable black leather Hush Puppy walking shoes. Slung around her waist was a black leather pouch that held her money and a small 22-caliber pistol.

Placing her thumbs underneath the straps of her backpack, Bee-Bop's connect looked around to make sure she fit into the crowd of pedestrians walking on the street as she continued toward Hudson. She did. She looked like any other student attending nearby Long Island University.

Bee-Bop's connection turned onto Hudson before he reached the drop spot. So while she lingered outside of a grocery store, she decided to buy a bottled water. Not wanting anyone to see her 22, she glanced around quickly before unzipping her pouch. Satisfied that no one was paying her any attention, she reached into the pouch to pull out some bills. Her lipstick fell to the ground, and she bent down to pick it up.

Several stores down, Lama exited the coffee shop and noticed an African woman bending down. He stared at her rudely, wondering what she looked like underneath the loose clothing.

As she stood up, their eyes met. He saw her gray eyes, eyes that he would recognize anywhere.

"Fatou, La Princesse!" he shouted.

Startled, she backed up a few steps before turning the corner onto York Street and darted in the direction she'd just come from.

Lama threw his coffee into the street and urged his old bones to run after Fatou.

Half a block away, Bee-Bop noticed the confusion and started running as well.

Fatou's heart was racing as she turned down Bridge Street. In the distance, Lama followed her, repeatedly yelling her name.

"Fatou, come back! Why do you run from me?"

Bee-Bop chirped Joe-Joe and let him know that Fatou was being chased down Bridge Street by an older African man. He also told him between breaths that he hoped she didn't drop his salad.

Joe-Joe screeched his Ninja to a halt on Concord and quickly turned in the opposite direction.

"Where the fuck is she?" Joe-Joe yelled through his Nextel.

"She's about to reach Concord," Bee-Bop chirped back.

Joe-Joe hopped off his bike right before Concord and Bridge just as Fatou ran by him.

"Come back!" Lama yelled.

He and Joe-Joe reached the intersection at the same time. Joe-Joe's lethal left hook connected with Lama's jaw and knocked him backwards. Lama landed like a sack of potatoes on the concrete.

"Damn! You got knocked the fuck out!" Bee-Bop hollered as he stood over Lama.

"Nigga, stop fucking playing and handle your B.I.," Joe-Joe snapped as he hopped back on his motorcycle and sped off.

"Fatou, it's OK," he chirped. "I said it's OK. Can you hear me?"

Fatou slowed down, looked behind her and noticed that Lama was no longer chasing her.

She stopped to pull her Nextel out of her pouch and answered Joe-Joe, "Yes, I hear you."

"Walk your ass up Flatbush, then," he shouted. "Do that shit under the bridge."

"Did you catch that shit, Bee-Bop?"

"I got you," Bee-Bop replied.

"All right, bet. Baby girl, let me holla at you before you get back on the train."

Fatou didn't comment. Seeing Lama had shaken her badly.

"Why the fuck ain't you blast his ass?" Joe-Joe asked Fatou after the drop went off without a hitch, and she returned to the train station.

"I froze," she admitted. "Besides, it was broad daylight!"

"That shit don't matter. And who the fuck was that herb-ass nigga anyway?"

"That's my husband. I left him a month ago. He's a fucking monster. He's the last person I ever expected to see in Brooklyn. I'm sure he'll be searching all over Brooklyn for me now. What happened to him?"

"I made his ass take a nap on Bridge Street. But yo...don't be bringing your Harlem pussy bullshit to BK. We don't play that around here. If a nigga want wreck, you give his ass wreck."

"I'm sorry," Fatou said shyly.

"Just don't let that shit happen again. Now go take the money to David before I have to deal with his bullshit."

Fatou walked off to get on the train while Joe-Joe watched her, shaking his head. When she went out of view, he used his Nextel to chirp David.

"Yo, pay phone," he said.

"All right, one," David replied.

They both walked to their designated pay phones, then David pulled out a prepaid phone card from his back pocket.

"That's the bullshit," Joe-Joe hissed into the phone after snatching it off the hook on the first ring.

"What's up," David asked.

"Your peoples needs to get a backbone."

"I said what's up, nigga."

"Let me find out you're using some married piece to do you a solid knowing her husband's on some domestic violence shit."

"What happened?"

"Some oldhead African was chasing Shorty down the street while she was carrying two birds. That's not a good look, man. That's not a good look."

"So, where's he at?"

"Stretched the fuck out on Bridge Street. We all got out of dodge after I stretched him. We couldn't fucking hang around being dirty. And I ain't want to be tied to your peoples, so I rolled out too."

"I wish I was there. I woulda blasted his ass."

"She shoulda blasted his ass. What's the purpose of her having heat if she ain't gonna use it?"

"True."

"On some real shit, we coulda been fucked up over this. You need to handle that, nigga."

"Yo, Joe-Joe."

"Yo?"

"You vented? You got your shit off your chest?"

"Yeah. Pretty much."

"Well don't forget who's the general and who's the lieutenant. I don't need no nigga telling me how to handle mine's."

"I was just saying."

"You ain't got to be saying shit. Good looking on how you handled the situation though."

David hung up the phone and headed back to his house. *I need to school this girl on being ruthless. The game ain't got no use for a soft ass. Her ass is about to get real hard.*

A few minutes later Lama woke up on Bridge Street, feeling the effects of Joe-Joe's attack, but even more upset at losing Fatou.

Woozily, he picked himself up from the ground and gingerly touched the huge lump on his head. He stumbled his first few steps as onlookers checked him out curiously.

"Fatou La Princesse...where have you gone?" he asked out loud to no one. "Where has my baby gone?" he whispered.

Disoriented, Lama looked around until he remembered the direction he'd run from just a few minutes earlier. He started walking slowly back up Bridge Street toward York, groggy from his ordeal.

Ten minutes later, Lama reached his cab on Hudson and was glad to find that he only had a parking ticket for an expired meter.

"Allah, bless you," he said, looking up to the skies. "My cab could have been vandalized or towed. It is only you that is the most benevolent, the most merciful."

Lama leaned against his cab for strength as he took his keys out of his pocket, then carefully inched himself inside, dropping hard against the seat. He leaned all the way back and rested his head, closing his eyes, trying to gather himself together. Before long, he fell into a deep sleep.

Twenty minutes later, the ringing of his cell phone jarred him out of his sleep.

"Lama, where have you been?" asked Thomas the base dispatcher. "I've been calling you for over an hour."

"I have seen her," Lama replied.

"Whatever that means. Why haven't you answered the radio either?"

"You are not listening. I have seen her. Today…I saw her. Fatou La Princesse."

"Well, where is she?" Thomas asked.

"I do not know. She is gone. But I will find her. I have to find her."

"But you said you just saw her."

"I did see her, but…but, I don't know what happened. I was chasing her then the next thing I remember I was pulling myself up off the ground on Bridge Street. That is it! She must be living somewhere in Brooklyn."

"Well, if she is, we will help you find her."

"Good. I will offer a reward."

"That is not necessary."

"No. I have to make sure that everyone is searching for Fatou in every crevice in Brooklyn."

Lama paused to collect his thoughts.

"I will give a thousand dollars to anyone who brings Fatou back to me. Let all the cabbies in Brooklyn know."

"Well, tell them," Thomas said. "Broadcast it yourself over your radio."

Lama picked up his radio and pushed the button, but didn't get a sound. He fumbled with it for a while then remembered that he had turned it off when he went into the coffee shop.

After turning it back on, he signaled Thomas to double-check himself. "Thomas, do you read me?" Lama asked, pushing the button.

"Loud and clear," Thomas replied.

Hoarsely, Lama made his announcement over the radio.

"I will give any cabbie from Brooklyn who runs across Fatou La Princesse one thousand dollars when you return her to me unharmed. I must get her back in my home at once. This is not a joke; it is very serious and very important. Hopefully, one of you will help me."

Lama ended his announcement by repeating his phone number over the air so that anyone with information could contact him. Then he closed his eyes to think some more.

Moments later, he hailed Thomas again on the radio.

"Thomas, I won't be taking any more calls today. I am too shaken. I must go home and try to get myself together."

"I understand, my brother," Thomas said. "Call me if you need anything."

Lama turned his radio off and headed back to Harlem, totally distressed. Despite seeing her, he knew that he was no closer to having her back in his life than he had been when the day began.

CHAPTER SEVENTEEN

That's Miss Bitch

It was December 31, 1999, New Year's Eve of a new millennium.

Fatou was pleased that she was about to give up her business and enjoy herself. David hadn't allowed her to be a mule again for him since the debacle in Brooklyn. Instead, he had created for her a crash course that would turn her into someone who was ruthless.

Although Fatou loved braiding hair, she missed the excitement of exploring New York City via the subways, something she used to do several hours every day.

But now, instead of traveling to meetings with David's lieutenants at places like the Bronx Zoo or Coney Island, Fatou cuddled on her loveseat and watched movies like *Set It Off*, *Coffy*, and *Cleopatra Jones* over and over and over.

Although she could repeat almost every word of those movies, she'd rather look at them than watch the repeats of the soap opera *All My Children* that David had special-ordered for her. But more than anything, she dreaded reading the microfiche that David had printed out regarding the case of fifteen-year-old Daphne Abdela, the rich white Upper West Side resident who, along with boyfriend Christo-

Proudly Present
at the

NEWARK SYMPHONY HALL

TERRACE BALLROOM

**1020 Broad St.
Newark, N.J.**

**Tickets $40
in advance
$45 at the door
$20 after 8:30PM
(dancing only)**

**Information
908-301-9496
www.teatrosi.com**

12 Magical Nights A Year!

An authentic monthly
Tango Argentino
dance lessons
experience!

Beginner &
Intermediate

Partner not necessary!

Dance to the
live sounds of
Tango musicians!

Fabulous Dessert Bar!

Full service bar available

**Purchase tickets at
NSH box office
1030 Broad St.
Newark, N.J.
Info. 973-643-8009**
www.newarksymphonyhall.org

THIRD TUESDAY OF EACH MONTH
7 to 10 PM
Doors open at 6:30 PM

A TASTE OF TANGO

With Your Host
Carolina Jaurena
& Her Special
Guest Artists

NEWARK SYMPHONY HALL
TERRACE BALLROOM
1020 BROAD STREET, NEWARK, N.J.

pher Vasquez, had murdered Matthew McMorrow.

The police theorized that Daphne encouraged Christopher to slash McMorrow's throat from ear to ear, then gut him. David felt she was a prime example of a bitch that was 'bout it', the underlying theme of all of Fatou's studies.

She looked on the bed at the escort service she'd just closed for the evening and saw tens of thousands of dollars worth of clothing that David had bought for her laid out on the bed. It looked like a warehouse for exclusive designer fashions.

Fatou finally selected to wear a bone-colored leather two-piece set, made exclusively for her, with matching full-shaft boots with 3.5" heels. She accessorized with a specially ordered eighteen karat gold watch with a lizard skin band and full-length lizard trenchcoat, both from Coach.

Fatou lay down on the bed pulling up her size five pants. She was easily a size seven, and her voluptuous thighs and plump butt didn't make her task any less daunting. She wondered which David would be more upset about—the tight pants or the small V sewn into the top rear, revealing a good deal of butt cleavage.

She smiled, knowing that he'd probably be most upset about how her low-cut top showed off her 34 Ds.

After zipping her pants, Fatou grabbed the clear plastic makeup bag she'd copped from the Mac counter at Macy's and headed for the bathroom. In the mirror, she applied a hint of blush and eyeliner, then topped off her look with a sparkling copper lipstick.

"Perfect," she said after puckering her lips and directing a small kiss at her reflection.

Fatou was a sight for sore eyes, and David told her as much when he came to pick her up in the Bentley he'd rented for New Year's Eve.

He walked around Fatou slowly and was taken a back by her beauty. David didn't know how he was going to manage to wait another year to have her.

"You are beautiful," he said. "But why do you show so much of yourself?"

"I do it for you," she said, walking close to him. "Are you telling me that you don't like how I look?"

"I love how you look. I just don't want everyone seeing as much as I get to see. Don't you want to tone it down a little?"

"Relax," she said while hugging him. "It's cold outside, so I'll have on a long coat. No one will be able to see anything. No one, that is, but you."

"Good."

"I'll never disrespect you, David," she said, looking him straight in the eyes. "But I do have to go overboard every now and then to make sure you know I exist. I want you to want me, that's all."

"I do want you."

"Oh, I can tell," she said, laughing, feeling his manhood stiffen on her leg. "But you never act like it."

"It's not time yet," David said, backing away.

"But when will it be time?" Fatou asked. Her young loins had totally taken her over.

"Soon."

"A year is not soon enough."

"Be patient."

"No."

"You have to be."

"But why?"

"I won't sleep with a minor."

"I'm seventeen. I've been reading. That's the age of consent in this country."

"You're still not legal."

"What is wrong with you?" she shouted. "Everybody in your squad drools over me, but you cower. Are you gay, David? I've read a lot about American men living double lives."

"I'm not American. I'm pure Jamaican. And I'm certainly not a fag boy. Anyway, it's time to be out. I can't let you be all dressed up with no place to go. You look too hot not to show off."

"I don't care about going out. The only person I want to impress is you," Fatou said, walking in closer to David as he continued to back away.

David had no place to go and fell backward onto the recliner. Fatou straddled him, then kissed him passionately. He kissed her back at first, then he pulled away.

"Look, Fatou, we can't do this, OK? Goddamn. I understand why niggas like R Kelly get hemmed up. Y'all young girls don't know how to take no for an answer. We try to do the right thing, but y'all throw the pussy at us. Damn!"

"Well, fine," Fatou snapped, getting up and stomping away. "Bitch ass nigga!"

"Watch your fucking mouth," David shouted back, amused, although he liked the way his training regiment changing Fatou. "I just hope she keeps that shit up when I test her tonight," he whispered to himself.

145

David drove the Bentley to the Ritz Carlton Hotel where he'd rented a room for the evening and pulled up to valet parking. He handed the driver a $50 tip and told him, "Don't scratch my shit."

Hand in hand, David and Fatou walked to Times Square for the big celebration. They waited on 47th Street between Broadway and Seventh for his three lieutenants.

"Yo, where you at?" David asked, chirping Ricco, Donny, and Joe-Joe one after the other.

"I'm on Seventh, not far from you," said Donny from the Bronx.

"I'm walking down Broadway," Joe-Joe from Brooklyn answered.

"Yo, baby. I'm chillin' right behind you," said Ricco from Harlem. "I told you you'd better get better at watching your back."

David turned and saw Ricco smiling at him, walking in his direction. They embraced when he reached him.

"What's up, baby?" Ricco asked with a smile.

"It's you, my nig," David replied. "You know Fatou."

"Looking gorgeous as ever," Ricco said, hugging her gently.

"So, where's everyone else?" he asked.

"On CP time. Though they claim they're real close to us."

"Is Ken coming?" Ricco asked. "You know it's his year."

"Nah. I came up with some bullshit reason to keep his ass in Queens. I don't need his ass clapping tonight."

"Good," Ricco said, comforted. "We don't need any shit to go down tonight with all the extra cops around here for that Year 2000 crap. That nigga's a walking time bomb."

"Well, he'll just have to go off at a celebration on Jamaica Avenue. I hope not, though. We're making too much cheddar in Queens."

"His cheddar's no sweeter than mine is in Harlem," Ricco bragged.

"No doubt. You're holding shit down," David agreed with Ricco, giving him some dap. "But what's up with you? Being the player that you are, I can't believe you ain't got a couple chicks on your arm."

"Oh, you're doubting my skills?" Ricco asked before whistling.

Three women were walking in their direction. The first was an Italian-looking brunette about five eight, wearing a tan sheepskin coat with bone-colored Bruno Magli mules. She was gorgeous, but by the looks of things, she'd pass out if she had another drink.

The second appeared to be Thai. She had very full lips and gorgeous facial features, including a beauty mark on her left cheek. She was about five six and wearing four inch Manolo Blahnik heels to make herself seem taller. Her look was accentuated by a black patent leather full-length raincoat.

And the third lady was exotic-looking and undoubtedly Greek. She was a thick, five seven, wearing a two-piece suede skirt set that appeared to be painted on. Her 36DD breasts seemed to be having all types of problems with her too-small bra, and her thick thighs were accentuated in suede Bruno Magli Mustiola boots that rose just below her knees.

"David and Fatou, this is Karmela, Imisha, and Pretti," Ricco said as introduction.

"Hello," David and Fatou said in unison.

"I love your jacket," Pretti said to Fatou. "Where did you get it?"

"Actually, I called the company directly. Would you like their number?" Fatou replied smugly.

"No, not really," Pretti answered.

"Good. Because they never have sales like the one Bruno Magli just had. When you go with Coach, you can always expect to pay full price."

"Meow," David and Ricco whispered to each other, laughing.

"OK, enough," David said as Donny and Joe-Joe walked up almost simultaneously.

Joe-Joe had a militant-looking female walking with him who was either a tomboy or a carpet muncher. She sized up Fatou the moment she saw her.

"Why are y'all niggas always late?" David asked while handing out press passes to everyone.

"What the fuck is this?" Joe-Joe asked.

"Nigga, ain't you see how Five 0 had niggas hemmed up in those wooden pens? With these passes on, we can walk around freely."

"Nigga, who's gonna believe we're reporters? We're straight gangsters."

"Be that as it may," David said, "we don't have the time to be harassed tonight by the boys in blue. I paid a pretty penny for these passes, so let's just go and have a good time."

"No doubt," Donny said, agreeing with David.

"All right," Joe-Joe said, relenting.

"So Joe-Joe has his woman," Fatou whispered to David. "That means Ricco planned to hook you and Donny up with two of his hookers and keep one for himself. You know I have an escort service, so it doesn't have to go down like that. Or better yet, you can fuck me."

"You're crazy," David whispered.

"Like a fox," Fatou snapped.

"Well, can you just stop tripping?" he asked as they reached the Viacom building on 44th Street, right across from One Times Square.

"That depends," she said.

"On what?"

"How these bitches act. Y'all niggas ain't slick."

"What is up with your mouth?" he asked. "Let me find out you're finally getting gully on me."

"Let one of these bitches disrespect me, and you'll find out everything you need to know."

The group found an area and started to drink Hennessey out of flasks that Ricco pulled from his coat.

"This is it," Ricco said. "It'll have your shit rock hard all night."

"True," David agreed, laughing.

"How would you know?" Fatou asked. "You're terrified of me."

"Whatever," David snapped.

"Damn, is this the same scared little ass that was running from an old head not even a month ago?" Joe-Joe asked.

"Why is this pencil dick talking to me?" Fatou asked David. Then to Joe-Joe, "Are you not taking steroids or something? I hear that men with all of those muscles can't do shit in the bedroom."

"You better back the fuck off my man," hissed Joe-Joe's friend.

"Chill, Brittany," Joe-Joe said. "I can handle her light ass. Ain't nobody catching feelings here."

"Well, she just better check herself," Brittany said snidely.

"Or what?" Fatou asked.

"Or I may have to teach you some respect," Brittany said.

"Well, you need to teach yourself some respect by fixing that busted-ass weave before you come out...on New Year's Eve, no less."

"Fuck you," Brittany hissed.

"You wish."

"Chill," David said finally. "If y'all can't control your liquor, y'all can stop drinking."

"We're not drunk," Fatou said before pointing at a twenty-some-thing-year-old white man stumbling in their direction. "That's drunk."

"Damn," Joe-Joe said. "That mothafucka ain't feeling no pain."

"Yeah, he's probably about to puke!" Brittany added.

When the white man reached the group a few seconds later, the countdown for the approach of the millennium was at about two minutes.

"Happy New Year," he slurred loudly, well before the countdown was over.

"Can you back the fuck up?" Fatou yelled, wiping her face as if the man was spitting.

"We...we're all just hav...hav...having a good time, dude," he replied. "Woooooh-weeeeeeeeeee."

As the crowd started counting down "twenty, nineteen, eighteen," Fatou looked angrily at the man and responded.

"Well, how about you have a good time somewhere else?"

"Fuck you, bitch," the man hollered.

"Happy New Year," the crowd yelled in unison as thousands of fireworks went off.

Fatou took off her boot and smacked the man in the head with it. The heel stuck inside his forehead.

"That's Miss Bitch to you!" Fatou hissed as everyone stared at her in disbelief.

David grabbed her and led her away, followed by his entourage, before anyone in the crowd could figure out what has just happened.

"Damn, Fatou!" David snapped. "You're gonna do that now with all this heat here on New Year's?"

"He should have watched his mouth."

"But he was just a drunk."

"That's no excuse."

"Be happy for her," Joe-Joe said. "She's sticking up for herself."

"A and B, man, A and B," David hissed in Joe-Joe's direction.

"Does this mean that the party's over?" Ricco asked.

"I hope not," Donny said. "I'm tryna hang with you. What are you about to get into?" he asked, turning to David.

"Not a damned thing!l," Fatou snapped.

"I'm a grown-ass man," David said. "I can speak for myself."

"Man, take that girl home before she gets us all arrested," Ricco said. "Her temper's as bad as Ken's."

"She can stay if she wants to stay," Brittany said. "She was just defending herself."

"It ain't gonna happen, Brittany, so it don't matter if we leave or stay," David said

"What are you talking about?" Brittany asked.

"Whatever," David replied. "Just know that you ain't slick."

David turned to Fatou and said, "I need to holla at Joe-Joe real fast. I'm not going anywhere."

"OK," she said.

"Well, hurry up, nigga, damn," Donny shouted impatiently.

"Nigga, just control your dick," David said. "That pussy ain't going nowhere."

The fellas laughed and Ricco's women friends looked on as if they didn't know what time it was. Joe-Joe, Brittany and David walked off a little to the side.

"Yo, I'm glad that shit happened with the white boy and not you, Brittany," David said "I may be trying too hard to turn her ass into a gangster's."

"I'm glad, too," Brittany said. "I would have hated to have to kick her ass."

"Don't you mean lick her ass," David said, laughing.

"You did put that shit out there, boo," Joe-Joe added. "You ain't even try to hide how much you want her ass."

"Whatever," Brittany snapped.

"I'm mad I pushed you to toughen her up," Joe-Joe confessed. "We may have another Ken on our hands."

"She'll be fine," David said. "The decision to turn her into a gangster bitch was mine. When I put her back on the streets, she'll mellow out. I think she's just frustrated about being bored."

"No, what you need to do is give her some dick," Brittany said snidely. "All that pent-up frustration is what's stressing her out."

"And I guess you're volunteering to help her release some of that frustration?" David asked.

"I'm always down for the team," Brittany replied.

"Bitch, you're always down to munch on some carpets," Joe-Joe said, laughing. "Don't worry, you can munch on this dick tonight."

"Whatever," she said.

"So what's the situation in Brooklyn?" David asked. "Are the Gypsy cabbies still asking questions?"

"True that," Joe-Joe said.

"I may keep the mule you now have in Brooklyn until this situation dies down."

"That's smart," Joe-Joe said.

"I know, nigga," David replied sarcastically. "That's why I'm in charge....Well, I'm about to be out."

"Make sure you take care of her tonight," Brittany said.

"Mind yours," David replied.

"Aiight! You won't be happy until she kills somebody!" Brittany said, knowingly. "A bitch in heat is a moody bitch. You already saw her mood swings turn violent."

"I can handle her," David snapped. "I don't know what makes you two think that you have to be offering up so much advice. I got this. Me, the five star general."

"I hear you, brainiac," Brittany said. "I guess you never heard that generals stop at four stars."

David looked at her coldly and walked away.

"I'm back, baby," David said to Fatou, hugging her and kissing the back of her neck.

"Now that's what I'm talking about," Brittany whispered.

"Mind your business," Joe-Joe said underneath his breath.

David gave his squad dap, then he and Fatou walked off, leaving everyone else together intoxicated and feeling frisky as if they were about to celebrate the new year with a bang.

CHAPTER EIGHTEEN

School Is In Session

David walked Fatou back to the Ritz Carlton. He could tell that she was a little drunk because she was slurring her words, a lot of words, too many words, each time she opened her mouth.

"I like these fucking boots, David. Can we go get my shoes back? Please, baby, I want my goddamned boots."

"Relax, boo-boo. We're almost back at the hotel."

"Fuck the hotel! It's not like anything is gonna happen there! I want my damned boots."

"Fatou, shut up! Damn!"

"Wait, David. You're gonna respect me. Do you hear me? Your gon' damn well respect me."

"Fatou, can you chill, please? You're making a spectacle of yourself. Remind me not to let you drink anymore."

"I'm not a drunk. I'm a sociable drinker."

"Whatever. You're fucking drunk."

"Am not."

"You are too."

"Am not."

"I'm not gonna play this fucking game with you, Fatou. Let's just go up in here and relax."

"I love you, David," Fatou said calmly. "But you are going to respect me."

"I love you too, wild one," David said, laughing. "And I do respect you. I just don't know if I can handle you drunk."

"You can't handle me if all I have to drink is water," Fatou said while putting her tongue in David's ear.

"You wouldn't be tripping like you do if I put it on your ass."

"Well, please do."

"I'm twenty-seven and you're seventeen. So what does that make me?"

"Someone who's scared to death of my love box."

"You need your rest, Fatou. We have a very busy day tomorrow."

"I need some tonight. Lama was a stiff in bed but at least he'd give it to me sometimes."

"Fuck Lama."

"No. Why don't you fuck me?"

David stared at Fatou coldly and was glad when his cell phone rang.

"Yo," he said. "What happened?"

"I'm not stupid," Fatou said in the background.

"Is our squad intact?" David asked.

"You think you're going to chill with Ricco's hos, but it's not happening," Fatou said.

"Bet, I'll holla at y'all niggas tomorrow," David said, ending his phone call.

He turned to Fatou and said, "You know, you're really trippin'. Just like you ain't been gettin' no dick, I ain't been gettin' no ass."

"That's not my fault," Fatou said. "I've been trying to give it to you."

"You know…"

"Wait," Fatou interrupted. "You're the strangest hustler I've ever heard of. You know the type of business I run, and I know for a fact that men will fuck anybody—especially hustlers. You can't save my innocence, baby. It's already been lost. How can you want me to act like a beast on the one hand but treat me like a prissy little girl on the other? I need love in my life. I need your arms wrapped around me to let me know that everything is OK. I need to know that you want me the same as I want you."

"You know I want you."

"Well, take me, David. That's all you have to do is take me. I'm right here. And if it makes you feel any better, girls in my country are given away to families when they're just fifteen or sixteen. And they are expected to act as women, especially in their husbands' beds. Tomorrow, you plan to take me under your wing and show me everything. I can see it in your eyes. You've taken me from a scared little girl and made me queen bitch. And I understand that to the world outside, I have to have a heart of stone. But when it's you and me, I can put all that down. I can relax and enjoy quiet time with my man—special time. I want you inside of me, David. I want you to help take away all the pain I've experienced since I've been in this country. I want to feel real love, true love that can only be shared by two people who care about each other as we do. Outside of these walls, it's me and you against the world. But inside, I want to see your tenderness. I want to know that I can take you there. Make me feel special,

David. Otherwise, all I am to you is business. I'm just another pawn in your game."

"Don't say that," he said.

"It seems like that's the truth."

"Well, it isn't. I love you, baby. You're more than just a part of the game to me."

"Well, don't tell me, David. Show me. I want you to show me."

Fatou walked into David's arms and caressed his face with the back of her hand. They kissed softly at first, then very passionately. David sucked on Fatou's neck before slowly removing her top, revealing her breasts. He licked around her aureole tenderly, then moved his tongue to her nipples, alternating back and forth. Fatou cradled his head with her arm while softly caressing him and playing with his hair.

David lowered himself and traced a trail down Fatou's body with his tongue, pausing momentarily at her belly button while he undid her pants, fighting to pull them down.

David caressed Fatou's thighs and legs warmly before removing her stockings, massaging and kissing each foot in the process. Then he resumed exploring her body with his tongue, this time starting at her ankles and working his way up.

David paused in his journey at the most warm and fleshy portion of Fatou's inner thighs so that he could suck passionately on her as if she wasn't already overcome by anticipation.

Next he steadied himself on his knees, placed his hands firmly on Fatou's buttocks, and pulled her close to him.

David then took the tip of his tongue and lightly flicked it on Fatou's lovebox, then looked up at her.

"More," she demanded.

He smiled confidently before barely touching her with the tip of his tongue several times. Fatou pushed David's head down forcefully. She'd had enough of his teasing.

David finally rocked the little man in the boat back and forth with his tongue, then took it in his mouth, being careful not to apply too much pressure. Fatou wiggled about underneath him.

She was a volcano about to explode.

Once she did release her juices, David savored them with his tongue, loving her flavor. Then he eased himself on top of her, slowly placing his manhood inside of her.

"Yes, David, yes," Fatou moaned. "Finally."

She loved the way David felt inside of her as he gyrated himself in a circular motion while caressing her hair. He pulled her face closer, then locked her tongue with his, kissing her passionately with every stroke.

Their two bodies existed as one for what seemed an eternity until they finally climaxed together. Drained, David collapsed on top of Fatou, and she held on to to him for dear life.

They fell asleep in each other's arms.

In the morning, David woke to the smell of coffee brewing inside of their suite. Fatou was sitting at the tip of the bed, sipping on a cup while lovingly looking him in his eyes.

"Good morning, sleepyhead," she said.

David acknowledged her with a yawn.

"I didn't know I wore you out so much."

"Yeah, right," David said, laughing. "I did all the work."

"And you were wonderful, baby. Would you like some coffee?"

"Nah. But I could use a Philly right about now. Are you hungry?"

"Only for more of you."

David laughed, then said, "I can't give you too much of this good thing. I don't want you to start trippin' too hard."

"You're too late for that. Your shot is the bomb."

"No one says that anymore, baby."

"Who cares? Are you gonna take me back to heaven or not?"

"Maybe. But don't think that because you're fucking me you can start playing mind games and shit. I'm still the man."

"You've always been the man to me. That's something that won't ever change."

"True that," he said. "Now let me give you a little bit more so we can get down to business."

They made love again and Fatou couldn't believe how good she felt. She hadn't thought she would find happiness in America, but she was glad that she had. David had given her everything, and she knew that she would even kill for him. Even worse, she'd give her life for his.

"Go take a shower, baby," David said, snapping Fatou out of her thoughts.

"You're not coming with me?" she asked.

"We're in too much heat for each other right now," he said. "We'll fuck around and never get shit poppin' off today. I'll jump in the shower when you're done."

"Well, that's your loss," Fatou said. She kissed David passionately on the mouth before walking off to the shower, thankful that he didn't follow. Her legs were burning, and she knew she needed a break.

After they'd both showered and gotten dressed, David wanted

them to check out. He didn't feel comfortable discussing business in the hotel.

In the car, he got right down to it. "Today I'm gonna introduce you to some real important players in my organization. You have to remember everyone's name and number without writing anything down. I want to make sure you know what to do in case anything happens to me."

"Nothing is gonna happen to you."

"Babe, this is serious. Stay focused. Pay attention to everything I'm telling you."

"Sorry."

"No need. Now first I'm gonna introduce you to his old head named Eric. He's gonna be your driver when you don't take the train. He drove for a couple New York mayors so he knows more secrets and shortcuts than anyone else I can think of. Pay attention to him when he speaks. He's kind of strange, but he knows his shit."

"You know I didn't bring a change of clothes. Are you sure it's a good idea for me to be dressed like this in front of him?"

"Eric is about his business. That shit don't matter. Are you sure you're ready for this? You say the dumbest shit at the wrong time."

"I'm just saying."

"Fatou, chill. Stop gettin' the game fucked up. I can't be worried about niggas checkin' you out. I'd never get shit done if I was stressed out about that. So we're gonna use that shit to our advantage. When we're on these streets, it's all about gettin' paper and making it home alive. Let's keep that relationship shit behind closed doors."

"You're so smart."

"And so are you. So stop acting dumb."

Fatou looked at David sideways but didn't comment. She knew he was right. If her training regimen hadn't done anything else, it showed her how not controlling her emotions could get her killed on the streets.

"So what's next after meeting this guy Eric?" she asked.

"Then we're gonna meet my OEM (Office of Emergency Management) connect. I call him Underground, like the mall in Atlanta."

"Why do you call him that?"

"He helps me do business in emergency shelters. A lot of people don't know this, but there's a whole tunnel system underneath the streets of New York. They're set up so the government can function if the shit ever hits the fan."

"And what will this Underground do?"

"Supply you with keys to the entrances, just like me. But he won't do it until he trusts you. And even though you have keys, all of the doors are double locked. I always have to contact Underground to unlock one lock on every entrance before I can visit the shelters. No one is supposed to have keys to both sets of locks. I don't know how Underground pulled that off."

"What do I need the keys for?"

"Are you paying attention? I told you that you have to be ready in case anything happens to me. Just ride with me and think about what's going on when things go down. I can't tell you everything. You have to live it."

"OK."

"After Underground, you'll meet my private chef, Poncho."

"Poncho?"

"Poncho is a fifty-year-old Indian. His tribe's land was stolen by the government. We can relate to each other's struggles. That's why I put him on. I showed him how to cook up the product, and he's gonna show you. You should always know how to cook the shit up so you can check the weights before and after. Poncho hasn't tried to cheat me yet, but don't trust no one in this game. If a nigga knows that you can double check his ass, he won't try to skim a few ounces from you off the top. That adds up, and you're in this business to make money, not give it away."

"Well, why don't you just cook it yourself."

"You don't want to be caught with all that paraphernalia where you lay your head down. You pay someone else well to take that risk. You just make sure that person's loyal, so they don't turn on you if they get knocked."

"Knocked?"

"Arrested. Niggas are always trying to make deals for their freedom when cops run down on them. You don't want no snitches in your camp. But no matter how hard you try to make niggas come clean, you can never really tell whose gonna sell you out in the long run. That's just part of the risk of staying in this game. Niggas are always coming at your neck. And everyone wants what you have. They'll set you up in a heartbeat for a come up."

"This all seems so deceitful."

"Welcome to America, baby. I'm glad you finally joined us."

David took Fatou around and introduced her to everyone he wanted her to meet, taking full advantage of some of the city's brass taking the holiday off. Fatou met people that David's lieutenants would die a thousand deaths to meet. But he wanted no one except Fatou to wield the power he had. She was the only person he trusted, and he prayed he hadn't made a mistake in trusting her.

He schooled her on why it was important to pay off city officials.

"You can never have too many people on your team," he said.

Judges, cops, firemen, POs (parole officers), and politicians were all on David's payroll. If any type of sting, investigation or hostile takeover was being planned, David was the first to know.

"Never forget that lawyers are the scum of the earth," he said. "Like everyone else, they want your money. They are not your friends. Keep it professional with them and don't get too close."

"Your life sounds so emotionless," Fatou said.

"I do what I have to do to survive. I never forget to love my own ass more than I love anyone else's."

"Including mine?"

"You said it, not me."

The two sat quietly as David drove the Long Island Expressway into Queens, merging onto the Grand Central Parkway and stopping near the USTA's National Tennis Center. They exited the car and walked toward Shea Stadium, turning down a small street.

David's downtown Queens lieutenant, Ken, was standing on a miniature scooter in the middle of the street. Ken rode over toward them, smiling.

"What up, dun?" he said.

"Holla at me," David said. "Exactly what happened?"

Ken looked at David as if he didn't want to say the wrong thing in front of Fatou.

"It's cool," David said. "She's one of us."

Still not totally comfortable, Ken proceeded none-the-less.

"Little Man chirped me and said he ain't like how certain niggas was acting near this squatter. I got on my scooter and started riding over to him to check it out. His cousins Trey and Rob had his back, so at least he wasn't alone."

"Them niggas ain't warriors," David said.

"I know. That's why I wanted to get there with quick. Anyway, by the time I turned the corner, they were jumping out the squatter trying to ambush Little Man. I whipped out and started blasting, but they got Little Man first. It was just a flesh wound, though."

"Did you get any of them?"

"Yeah, I bodied two of them niggas. But two of them got away."

"What did you use?"

"Bloodbath?"

"You had on your gloves?"

"Nah, the shit happened so fast."

"That don't mean shit, man. Remember, you have to stay focused."

"Nobody saw me, though."

"Get rid of it," David demanded.

"Damn. That's my favorite heat."

"Ballistics."

"True, true."

"Don't worry. You can buy another one like it."

"You think I ain't."

"I know you, nigga. That's a done deal. But not yet. I want you to get it and let Fatou get her feet wet before you get rid of it."

Ken looked at him curiously.

"I know you ain't think that last night was the end of it, did you, nigga?"

"Nah, but you're a little early to be bringing wreck in the street. It won't even start getting dark for another hour."

"Fuck that. We ain't no coward-ass niggas. If someone comes at us, we're gonna handle ours in broad daylight. Then niggas will know we ain't playing and go fuck with some other sets. They'll leave our shit alone."

"Alright, I'll go get my heat."

"Well, you ain't got to make a speech, nigga," David said, mimicking a scene from *Cooley High*.

"Get my feet wet?" Fatou said when Ken left.

"Yeah. You're about to put in some work too. You ain't think this was all fun and games, did you?"

"But this is so sudden."

"Damned right. And you're 'bout it or you ain't."

"I'm with you, baby, you know that."

"This ain't about that love shit. But since you mentioned it, Ken called me last night to let me know some shit went down. You're on some bullshit about someone trying to cheat on you while some poo butt niggas are tryna ambush our team."

"I guess I was wrong."

"You guess?" David asked.

"Well, last night I was wrong, but today...today I'm 'bout it."

"Your ass better be."

Ken returned with the heat and told David where his nemeses from last night were hanging out. They were about two blocks away.

David told Ken to pass off the heat to Fatou and wait for his chirp. His plan was for him and Fatou to walk near the spot, then chirp Ken so he could ride up on the scooter. The three of them would pull off the ambush when Ken got there.

"Are you straight with Nina?" David asked Ken.

"As long as I got steel in my hands, I'm gon' always be straight."

"No doubt."

"Are you ready, baby?" David asked, turning to Fatou.

She shook her head yes.

"I'll chirp you," David said before hugging Fatou closely and walking down the street with her like they were simply a happy couple in love, not two people seeking revenge.

As they walked, Fatou thought about the expression on Pam Grier's face in the movie *Coffy*. It was a symbol of pure hatred and of staunch determination to get back something that was taken away. Fatou had become one with the emotions she'd witnessed in Pam Grier's eyes and allowed the passion to push her over the edge. She knew that, like Foxy Brown, she had a score to settle, and she felt the lioness inside her simmering, about to boil over.

As Ken appeared to be approaching almost a block away, and before David knew what was happening, everything inside of Fatou impelled her to force the action. She started yelling, preparing to seal Ken's enemies' fates.

Rat-a-tat-tat went the sound of gunplay in the air. It was the only sound that could be heard for blocks around. It even drowned out Fatou's high-pitched yelling that lasted the duration of her assault. By the time her trigger finger released the pressure, not a bird flapped its wings in the air. Not a mosquito buzzed in anyone's ears. Time stood still.

When the dust settled, Ken rode by David and Fatou so that no one could tie the three of them together. David heard police sirens in the distance, so he grabbed Fatou and took her into an alleyway. She wondered why he chose to go in that direction when they needed to escape. He could see the confusion in her eyes.

"Relax," he said before reaching into his pocket and grabbing his keys for the tunnels. He unlocked a manhole cover and they descended into New York's underworld just as they heard the cops turning into the alley.

"They went that way," said an unknown witness.

"I don't have time for fucking fun and games," the cop yelled after seeing that the alleyway was empty. "There was just a massacre right here."

"I'm sure I saw them run that way," the witness said.

"Just like New York," the cop said. "No one ever sees shit or knows shit. We're out of here."

The alleyway cleared out and David breathed a sigh of relief.

"Welcome to the tunnels," he said. "Now you know their importance. It's your job to learn each and every one of them like the back of your hand. Any mistakes can mean your life."

David started walking away, and Fatou followed. She was very impressed with what she'd learned so far. It seemed as if everything David did was well thought out. It was starting to become apparent why David had enjoyed his success on the streets while so many others had failed.

I have to be as tight as him, Fatou thought. *No. My shit will be even tighter.*

They exited the tunnels in a small alley not far from the USTA, amidst the shadows of Shea Stadium. Everything that had seemed like senseless pieces in some abstract painting was starting to come together for Fatou. She couldn't wait to soak up more of David's knowledge of the game.

He didn't disappoint her.

They returned to David's home in Jamaica, Queens. He was still in teacher mode.

"Staying on top of the game," David said, "means that you have to always stay one step ahead of everyone else. But before I move on, I want to give you the tour of my home—our home."

Fatou smiled, glad that David finally trusted her enough to show her where he laid his head every night. Going from room to room, she soaked up the ambiance.

The living room had fine, solid oak floors that shone brighter than polished silver. Sitting on the floor, taking up nearly two corners of the room, was a massive leather sectional sofa. Its cream color was in perfect contrast to the brown of the oak floor.

On either side of the couch were end tables with brass bases and sparkling crystal tops. To the right of the couch and first end table was a love seat that boasted the same plush, butter-soft leather as the couch. To the left of the couch and second end table, there was a matching recliner twice as marvelous as Fatou's favorite chair.

"Sit here," David said. Fatou quickly obliged.

She sank into soft leather and couldn't imagine being more comfortable. Then David flicked two buttons, and the recliner heated up, removing all traces of the outside chill Fatou had brought in with her. And her whole body tingled as a massager vibrated underneath her, making her feel as if twelve skilled hands were working feverishly to relieve her stress.

"I can stay in this chair for hours," she cooed.

"Maybe," David said. "But not today. Come on. Let me finish showing you around."

David directed Fatou's attention to the sixty-inch color television and surround sound system that sat directly across from the couch in an entertainment center that was to die for. Its base was solid brass like the end tables, and the different levels shared the same thick crystal shelves.

Built into the corner of the room opposite the big screen television was the largest fish tank that Fatou had ever seen. It was about four feet high and five feet wide, set in an auburn marble base and secured with lizard skin fasteners.

The tank had three compartments. One held an array of jack dempseys, oscars, algae eaters and piranhas. The second was a refuge for two African lizards, and the third housed an octopus that was busy devouring a defenseless toad. The tank in its entirety looked like if it would cost two years' mortgages.

The kitchen had a Sub Zero refrigerator with an automatic ice maker that spit out crushed ice or cubes or chilled water and held enough food to feed a king's army. Every appliance imaginable lined the marble countertops, including a microwave oven big and powerful enough to cook a thirty-pound turkey in just a couple of hours. There were so many juicers, food processors and choppers Fatou wondered how many of the gadgets were actually used.

Outside the kitchen was the backyard with an immaculate deck surrounding an indoor/outdoor pool. The part of the pool that was covered by the manmade shelter was only about four feet deep, with a heated Jacuzzi. The uncovered portion of the pool was eight feet deep and had a diving board. Around the circumference of the pool sat little African statues that were pulling double duty, some as lamps, some holding large candles.

Back inside the house, David led Fatou up a spiraling staircase. The staircase in itself was miraculous, boasting shiny fine wood and a heavy brass railing. At the top of the stairs was the first sign of carpeting in the house, a plush, velvety choice that was softer than most pillows.

David's master bedroom was huge. The king size bed with its matching dressers and headboard looked small in the space. Across from the foot of the bed was another big screen television and surround sound system that rivaled the design of the one in the living room. Scattered throughout the room were brass and wooden African statues that added a regal air.

Fatou entered the walk-in closet. Solid brass stanchions protruded from the top of the wall with hangers on their ends to hold fine Italian suits, and from the bottom of the wall to hold exotic skinned shoes and a wide variety of Iversons, G Unit, S Dot Carters and Air Jordan athletic shoes. All of the suits hung in neat columns and, just as in the rest of the house, there wasn't a thing out of order.

Finalizing the decor was a pure crystal mirror that spanned about four feet wide and covered the entire height of the closet. There wasn't a smudge or piece of dust anywhere on the mirror, or in the entire house for that matter.

David's guest bedroom was a bigger version of his walk-in closet. Designer clothing hung from stanchions throughout the room in neatly aligned columns. The room looked like the workroom for designers showing off their wares to audiences at the Magic Show.

Back downstairs, Fatou was in awe of what she had just seen. She plopped down on the couch and said, "I could die in this house. I would have to work three lifetimes to afford all this."

"You got that right," David replied. "With all the furniture and added features, this spot cost close to two mill, and there's another house not far from here that's the exact duplicate. From the swimming pool to the appliances to the furniture, nothing except the clothing that fills the closets is different. I bought it just for you."

"You're kidding me," she said.

"No, I'm not."

"Well, you need to chill, David," Fatou pleaded. "You spend a couple of million dollars on a house, thousands of dollars for just me and you at restaurants, buy up the bar when we go out for drinks. You even tip the car wash guys a hundred dollars apiece for taking care of your ride. You need to tone it down, boo. You're a robbery waiting to happen. Now you bought another house! I appreciate all you do, but your flashy ass might get me killed in that house."

"Don't worry about it. No one but you and I know about it. It's the safe house we'll use if anything happens. And it's a lot more. One of my three safes is there. Well, I actually have four if you count the decoy here. Yes, a decoy. I'll show it to you. It's in the attic."

Fatou started walking toward the stairs.

"Fatou, why are you fucking around when this is serious shit?" David asked.

"I'm just going to the attic," she said.

"Follow me," he said, then led her to the kitchen, giving her yet another lecture.

"Sometimes deception is all you have," David said. "You have to drill something into someone's head until that's all they have to go on. You do whatever you have to do to make people believe what you want them to believe."

"What does all of that mean?" Fatou asked.

"Just know that I have mastered the art of deception," David said as he slid pieces of wall paneling in the kitchen. When he finished, he revealed what appeared to be a solid steel wall.

"Wait. I forgot the remote," he said.

Fatou looked at David curiously when he returned to the kitchen holding a large remote control in his hand. It had many buttons. He placed it in front of the steel wall and pressed one of them. Seconds later, a slight rumbling noise was heard, and the steel wall opened up. David stepped inside an elevator, motioning for Fatou to follow.

"This is the entrance to the elevator. You can reach the attic only this way. No one even knows there's an attic in this house."

The elevator stopped and David pushed several buttons on the inside wall and several buttons on the remote.

"I hope you were paying attention to what I just did, because if anyone ever found this elevator, they still couldn't get to the attic without entering the proper sequence of codes into panels on the elevator and the buttons on the remote. You have to memorize everything I show you."

When the elevator doors opened, they walked into a room wall to wall with steel. Fatou assumed David kept the attic cool to ensure that nothing happened to the expensive computer equipment that seemed to cover every available inch of space. In all, she counted thirty monitors and thirty CPUs.

David sensed Fatou's confusion as he walked her around the attic, and pointed out the small details she would never have noticed. Then he paused and turned to her.

"If anyone does make it in here," he said. "At first glance, this room appears to be a monitoring station to scrutinize everything that happens in a two-block radius of this house. But this room is so much more."

David pressed some buttons on the remote. Images on the monitors came to life, showing interior and exterior views of every tunnel in the city.

"This is how I know what is going on outside this house. This is how I protect the fruits of my labor. Somewhere inside of the tunnels, there's a safe that holds a quarter of the money I've saved these past eight years. I own a yacht. My lieutenants think I rent it. But I don't. In the yacht's hold is another safe with twenty percent of what I've saved. In the safe house, there's a safe similar to what I'm about to show you that holds fifty percent of what I've stashed away. If anything ever happens to me, you will have everything. I have saved more money than thirty kings of small nations could spend in twenty lifetimes."

"And how much is that?" Fatou asked.

"Enough to make sure that you will always be OK," he said vaguely. "But pay attention. This is very important."

David aimed the remote control into the air, then stepped back fifteen paces. After a clamoring, a huge steel box started moving slowly down toward the floor from the ceiling.

"This is my decoy safe," David said. "There's always several million in here, but never more than five. Still in all, that's a huge come up for any stick up boy or petty hustler in the game."

David pushed the remote control buttons, and when the safe door opened, Fatou saw what millions of dollars looked like.

"I hope we can live forever enjoying this," he said. "But if that's not possible, it'll make me happy knowing that you are OK."

"Listen, David," she said. "I have lived a hard life and hated being poor. But money is not the reason why I love you. I would take you alone, even if you were penniless. I love you, David, not your money."

David gave Fatou a hug but didn't speak. He pushed the buttons again on the remote control, shutting the safe door and causing it to again disappear into the eaves. He grabbed Fatou's hand and casually walked with her back onto the elevator.

David didn't say another word on the ride back down to the kitchen. Nor did he speak when they exited the elevator. He purposefully started placing the wood paneling back over the elevator door, hiding it.

Fatou was lost in a daydream, thinking about everything she'd endured since she arrived in America. She never imagined that her fortunes would have turned out so magically.

Although her life now was extremely dangerous, she was living the life of a princess.

David noticed that Fatou wasn't watching what he was doing and got very upset at her.

"Fatou, what the hell are you thinking," he yelled. "You have to pay attention! This shit may save your life one day."

"I'm sorry," Fatou whispered.

"Don't be sorry. Be alert. Do you know that if you are trying to escape to the attic and someone gets too close, the elevator will not go up? It takes about four minutes for this paneling to replace itself once you are on the elevator. If you don't know how to do this, you're screwed. You'd be playing games with your life."

"Baby, I said that I apologize," Fatou said softly. "I know how much you love me. And I know that you are only trying to protect me. I will never, ever, do anything to let you down."

"Just keep my dream alive, baby," he said. "No matter what happens, I need to know that you will keep my dream alive. Soak up everything I tell you, and you'll keep me happy, be it in life or in death. And one more thing."

"What is it?" Fatou asked.

"I want you to have my seed," he said.

Fatou's expression changed from overwhelming joy to intense pain.

"Patra, the abortion, my insides…David you know that I cannot have children," she said tearfully.

"I've been speaking to a specialist who believes he can help you," David said confidently. "That's why I'm doing everything I can do to make sure that you are covered if anything happens to me. The specialist feels confident that you were young enough when the incident happened for your internal organs to have repaired themselves. You will have my child."

"I love you so much, David," she said. "But I am so angry. I'm angry at the world. But only you can have every ounce of tenderness inside of me. I will love you as long as God allows me to. I will fight for you. I will ride with you. And I will die for you."

"No, you won't," David said. "You will live and raise my child. My entire empire is yours. And when you're running things, no one will be able to tell that it's not me. I'm sure you'll make me proud."

Fatou didn't comment, but she knew in her heart that she would die for David. Of course she wanted to have his child, but if anyone came at David the wrong way, they would have hell to pay.

After everything she'd been through, Fatou was now a trained and ruthless executioner, ready to dish out her form of street justice. She felt that she owed David everything. And with her loyalty, she was anxious to pay her dues.

CHAPTER NINETEEN

The Jump Off

Fatou spent the next six months being driven around by Eric several days a week and spending as much time as she could with Poncho and Underground. She understood why David was always so drained, since she'd also been supervising the lieutenants more than he had. Yet her main concern had been putting herself in the position to run the entire operation if anything happened to David. To that end, it had been about a month since Underground trusted her enough to provide her with her own set of keys for the tunnels. At least once a week she traveled alone in the tunnels on her scooter—even though she knew David would kill her if he knew she kept a scooter down there.

The lieutenants finally trusted Fatou. Even Joe-Joe respected her gangsta. He told her that he'd never seen someone change so quickly into a beast.

Aside from Ken, he was her biggest ally.

Still, Fatou had mixed feelings about both of them. She paid attention to how Joe-Joe was always second-guessing David. And she believed Ken was too overbearing, especially with her. She felt that he treated her too delicately, like a strung-out nigga treats his wifey.

But to maintain peace within her squad, she didn't mention anything to David. She handled things as best as she could on her own.

Fatou left Eric feeling particularly good about herself. He tested her again on her knowledge of the different tunnels, and she passed with flying colors. She knew the entrances and exits for all of the tunnels and was also able to tell Eric why it was better to choose one tunnel over another.

Fatou felt today would be a happy day despite knowing that she would have to deal with Ken and his blatant flirting. Even he couldn't take her out of her good spirits.

She exited the C train on 116th Street and headed to the drop-off location. As usual, Ken was on CP time, and would take away all of Fatou's free time. Ken was lucky that she didn't really have any plans for him to ruin. Otherwise, she would have been all up in his face when he arrived.

From her hideout location in the alley, Fatou heard footsteps. She peeked out to make sure it was Ken.

"Mothafuckas are gonna start being penalized if they keep up this nigga bullshit," she said when she recognized him.

"Something came up, Ma," he said. "You ain't gotta bite my head off."

"Save it," she said. "Let's get this fucking show on the road." She removed the backpack containing two keys from her shoulders and handed it to Ken, waiting for him to pass her his backpack. When he attempted to open it, she smacked his hand.

"Stop bullshittin', nigga…You know we do business on an honor system."

"My bad," he said before handing her the bag. "Let's get something to eat."

"Business first, nigga. Shit!" she hissed. "You acting like you're fucking new or something."

"Nah...I mean that we can get something after we take care of what we need to take care of."

"Listen, we're both dirty," Fatou said. "Let's get the fuck out of dodge with this shit and talk later. Just chirp me."

Fatou wondered why she left things up in the air with Ken. She drove off on the scooter, perplexed. *It probably would have been better to just shut him down,* she thought. But she saw no harm in an innocent lunch.

After Ken disappeared into the alleyway, Fatou listened intently to ensure that no one else was coming. When all was silent, she took out her key and stuck it in the manhole, unlocked it and disappeared into the tunnel.

She knew that it was lunchtime, so she felt comfortable about stashing the money in the safe. She entered the combination and lost control for the umpteenth time when the open door to reveal tens of millions of dollars. But she didn't linger long.

She locked up and hid the safe before exiting the tunnels well ahead of schedule.

"I have some time to play with," she said to herself. "I guess I'll join Ken for lunch."

A couple of minutes later, Ken chirped Fatou, asking her if they were set to get some lunch.

"I know a nice African restaurant not far from where you are called Bao Bab," he said. "It's between Lenox and Seventh on 116th."

"OK," Fatou responded. "I am a little hungry. Meet me there in five minutes. I feel like walking."

Five minutes later, Ken pulled up in his Excursion, blasting a Capleton song, smiling from ear to ear.

"Nigga, how come you're always on time for some bullshit, but you can't seem to get it together when we're conducting business?" Fatou asked Ken when he hopped out of his SUV.

"Don't be aggravated," he said. "I just want us to have a nice lunch without any troubles."

"I'm gonna give your ass some trouble all right if you keep wastin' my time showing up late," Fatou said, rolling her eyes.

They walked into the restaurant, found a table in the corner, and exchanged small talk while waiting for their food.

Ken ordered them both a hunk of lamb, a lettuce, tomato, and onion salad with cucumber dressing, and a piece of maize bread.

"Let me ask you something," Fatou said. "Do you always order your boss's food, or do you think you know me or something?"

"I don't mean any harm, baby girl," he said "I just wanted you to try this. I knew it would make you think of your homeland."

"Well, that's the last thing that I want to think about," she said irritably. "Ken, there's something funny going on with the way you act around me."

"What do you mean by funny?" Ken asked.

"The funny way you look at me, the way you're always so attentive to my needs. Everything. It seems as if you are either auditioning for a show or trying to win my heart."

"You're my general's woman," Ken said.

"I'm glad you mentioned it before I did," Fatou said. "You're my favorite lieutenant, Ken, but you make me really uncomfortable. Fall back, OK? I'm very much in love with David."

Ken grabbed Fatou's hand and went to kiss it, but she pulled away, turning her face and body slightly. An African cabdriver who had been staring in their direction jumped up from his chair.

"Damn, baby girl," Ken said. "I was just gonna say, if you insist…"

"Fatou!" yelled the cabdriver named Adama. "It has been a very long time. Where have you been?"

"Adama, what are you doing here?" she asked.

"Never you mind," Adama said, sounding excited. "I am to take you to Lama at once."

"Do you see me fucking sitting here?" Ken snapped "She ain't goin' no fuckin' where wit' you. Matter fact, get the fuck out of our conversation."

"She is from my commune in Africa," Adama said. "I have known her since she was a baby. I have every right to speak to her."

"Fuck you and fuck Africa," Ken shouted. "We're in Harlem right now, on 116th. This is my world, where I rule shit…"

"Ken, let me handle this," Fatou said.

"Fatou, you must go with me," Adama said as he tugged at her arm.

"Nigga, you must be fuckin' crazy," Ken shouted, leaning over in his chair and smacking Adama's hand off Fatou. Out of nowhere, Adama punched Ken, and he fell backward in the chair.

"Fuck this!" Ken shouted while grabbing Nina out of his sock and shooting Adama dead.

All of the customers in the store started yelling and running. Ken put Nina away, then he and Fatou left in the confusion, driving off before anyone could point them out.

"Why the fuck didn't you let me handle that shit, Ken?" Fatou asked.

"That nigga disrespected me, that's why," Ken shouted

"Do you know who the fuck he was?"

"Another fucking statistic," Ken said sarcastically.

"No, he's not a statistic, Ken. He's the first casualty of the war that you just started."

"What war?"

"The war with Salu. Adama was the only family he had left in the world, and you just assassinated him"

"Salu has a squad," Ken said. "But we ain't scared of them niggas. If they want some, we can body their asses, too."

"So young and so naive," Fatou said.

"You're the young buck, not me."

"Your body may be older than mine," she said, "but your mind definitely has a long way to go. Get your mind right, Ken. You've put everybody in jeopardy with your bullshit. So just get your mind right."

Ken drove Fatou to Eighth Avenue so she could get on the D train to 34th Street. He looked at his watch and didn't want her to be late, so he tried to give her fifty dollars to catch a cab from Downtown Manhattan to Jamaica, Queens.

"Nigga, you work for me, remember?" Fatou hissed. "What the fuck do I need your money for?"

"I'm just trying to do the right thing, baby girl."

"No, what you're trying to do is piss me off," she said, interrupting him. "You better start thinking of me as a captain and not as some piece of ass."

Fatou walked off angrily, mad at Ken because he had jumped in her business with Adama and their family might now have a war on their hands.

Ordinarily, Fatou would check on her check cashing and escort business, but it was more important to inform David of what was going on. So rather than risk dealing with questionable traffic, she took the Long Island Railroad to Jamaica.

Fatou reached David's house much faster than she had anticipated. So fast in fact that she didn't have sufficient time to compose herself. From the minute he answered the door, David knew that something was wrong.

"What's up, baby?" he said. "Why do you look like someone kidnapped your best friend?"

"You think so?" she said vaguely.

"I know so. Why don't you just tell me what happened? Did you hook up with Joe-Joe?"

"Yeah, Joe-Joe's cool. I straightened him out earlier."

"What about Ken? Is he tight now?"

"Yeah, he's straight too."

"They both took care of you."

"Yeah."

"And you dropped everything off."

"Yeah, all the cheddar's in the fridge."

"Then I don't get it," David said. "What the fuck is wrong with you if everything went according to plan?"

"Can I ask you a question?" Fatou said.

"What?"

"Do you think that Ken would like Natali? She'll be out in a few weeks, and I think they might make a cute couple."

"What the hell do I care about Ken and whoever?"

"Cuz I think he's stressed," Fatou said. "Wouldn't he be better off if he had a woman to come home to?"

"Ken has more bitches than he can handle already."

"But ain't none of them wifey. Y'all niggas don't wanna admit it, but you know you love it when you have that one special woman to hold you down, someone you can depend on."

"What the hell does this have to do with anything?" David asked.

"I just think that Ken would be easier to deal with if he had a steady woman. That might slow him down a little bit, maybe even help him funnel some of that negative energy."

David bent over Fatou, who was now sitting in the recliner, and said softly in her ear, "I'm tired of playing games, baby. Tell me what the hell happened out there today."

"It was two small things or two big things, depending on how you choose to look at it."

"I'm listening," David said.

"What I think is a very big thing is that Ken is too damned attentive when he's dealing with me. That's your fucking job. It's flattering and all, but when it makes you start having piss poor judgment, that's where I draw the line."

"Did he push up on you?"

"No. Not exactly."

"So what's the problem?"

"He always wants to have lunch together. And it's always baby girl this, and baby girl that."

"Ken hits me up all the time for lunch."

"David, stop taking up for his ass. I ain't never spent a dime if I'm with Ken, so that dumb shit you said about you treating him to lunch is just that, dumb shit. Plus, he's opening doors, pulling out chairs, and today he stepped up to a nigga for saying something to me while I was with him."

"That's a respect thing."

"But I'm your woman, not his."

"That nigga who stepped up to you didn't know that."

"Nor did he care," Fatou said. "It was someone from my commune in Africa that came here years before I did. He's friends with Lama. His name is Adama. I mean, his name was Adama."

"What do you mean 'was'?"

"Ken bodied that nigga right in the middle of a crowded restaurant, with all types of witnesses in broad daylight."

"Just because he was tryna holla at you?"

"Pretty much, but that's not all of it. Adama grabbed my wrist and tried to take me with him. Ken smacked his hand off of me and then Adama stole his ass before he had a chance to get out his seat. Next thing you know, Ken is pulling Nina out, bustin' caps. Adama's dead, and Ken still doesn't get it."

"Get what?"

"For one, I'm a big girl and I can take care of myself."

"And?"

"And, two, if he would have let me take care of myself and stopped acting like my guardian angel, he wouldn't have killed Adama, the only family that Salu has left on this earth."

"Salu! Shit! This ain't good," David said grimly.

"David," Fatou said seriously. "We could be in a war with the number two team on the streets because Ken wanted to be someone's knight in fucking shining armor."

"Where's Ken now?"

"I guess back in Queens."

"Does anyone else know anything?"

"Outside of the thirty-something people in the restaurant, I don't think so."

"We gotta do damage control," David said.

"Who the fuck is we?" Fatou asked.

"I'm the general, you're the captain, so really, whatever I come up with should be passed down to you so you can tell the lieutenants."

"You're on your own with this one, baby," Fatou said.

"There's gonna come a time when you're the only one who's gonna be able to step up to the plate."

"Stop fucking saying that!" Fatou shouted. "If that shit has to happen, let it happen, but I don't wanna keep hearing about it! Besides, right now, you are here, and since you know that right now Ken makes me uncomfortable, I know that you're gonna deal with this before I have to be around him again."

"I guess you want me to do all the work around here."

"Only in the bedroom, baby," Fatou said tauntingly. "Only in the bedroom."

"This is not a laughing matter, Fatou," he said. "I need to round up the troops. If you ain't gonna be a part of this meeting, you gotta find something to do."

"Well, I need a drink," she said. "Give me a bottle from your bar."

"Make a damned drink. What the fuck are you gonna do with a whole bottle?"

"Stop being stingy, David. Damn. You got all typa shit and most of it's collecting dust anyway."

"My bar's always fully stocked, and I want it to stay fully stocked."

"Whatever," Fatou snapped. "I'm going out."

Fatou stomped out of the house, and David started calling his lieutenants for an emergency meeting. He wanted to be finished with his meeting before Fatou came back from wherever she went.

At the meeting, David let all his lieutenants know what had happened in Harlem between Fatou, Ken and Adama. He had Ken fill in the blanks as needed.

"So, everyone, hopefully the rampage that Fatou's been on for the last six months has softened our competition out there," David said. "Cuz y'all know we're about to be in the shit—at war with the second tightest clique out there."

"Yeah, but we're the tightest," Ricco said. "Ain't nobody out there fucking with us."

"Still, we used to be second best way back when, and the only thing that took us over the top was hunger. Who's to say that Salu's squad isn't hungrier than ours?" David asked.

"Well, them niggas better eat all they want somewhere else," Joe-Joe said.

"No doubt," Ken said. "Our squad is bringing the noise on all them wannabees."

"Hold that thought, Ken," David said. "I gotta handle something real quick."

David left the room and the lieutenants began to speak freely once they know he couldn't hear them.

"Damn, Ken," Donny said. "You got us all up in some shit cuz you're tryna impress your general's woman. What the fuck is up with that?"

"It ain't have shit to do with baby girl," Ken hissed. "That motha-fucka disrespected me, so he paid for it with his life."

"How'd he disrespect you when he was beefin' with her?" Donny asked.

"Yeah, and you ain't have to body 'im," Joe-Joe cut in. "You could'a just kicked his ass. Oh, my bad. Judging from your face, you tried that shit. I forgot your light ass don't be thinking about your fight game gettin' better. That nigga probably embarrassed you, and that's why you took him out."

"He ain't embarrass nobody," Ken snapped. "He was the one stretched out with blood gushing from his mouth."

"Yeah, but the nigga put blood in your mouth first," Joe-Joe said, laughing. "All because he saw you tryna get a piece of some ass that's off-limits."

"Nigga, I know you ain't talking," Ken said. "Like you and Brit-tany ain't try to get sumthin' poppin' off with baby girl. You're full of shit."

"I think everybody can admit that they'd knock that shit off quick-ly if they had the chance," Donny said, "but you're the only one who's going outta your way to try to make the shit happen."

"I ain't going outta my way for shit," Ken said, lying through his teeth.

"Bullshit!" Ricco said. "What other reason would you have to jump up in her business when she's been on a six month spree stretchin' mothafuckas out? If any bitch can handle herself, you should know that she can."

"Like I said, it ain't have shit to do with that," Ken said, continuing his lie. "The only reason I busted a cap in his ass was that he disrespected me."

"Let's concentrate on that point," David said after walking back into the room. "What do you mean by he disrespected you?"

"A man doesn't come up talking shit to a woman when she's sittin' with another man—especially if he starts getting physical with her," Ken said. "That's blatant disrespect."

"True that," David said, moving closer to Ken. "But is that all of it, or do you have sumthin' else to tell me?"

"Sumthin' like what?" Ken asked.

David leaned over and started talking ominously in Ken's ear.

"Come on, Ken," David said, "Keep it real, nigga. I see how you stare at Fatou's ass when she's walking away. I can't front. It's plumper than a mothafucka."

"What are you talking about?" Ken said, laughing.

"And I know you always want her to go eat with you in the middle of her handlin' business for our squad."

"I be hungry," Ken started before being interrupted.

"Let me finish," David hissed. "You're pulling out chairs, opening doors. Be honest, nigga. You got sumthin' you wanna tell me?"

"Nah, man," Ken said nervously.

"I mean, I ain't no hater," David said. "If you wanna fuck baby girl, then go for it."

"Nah, man..."

"Bullshit, nigga," David shouted. "That goes for any of y'all," David said, looking over his other lieutenants. "I sent Fatou out drinking so her soft titties and luscious ass wouldn't distract you. Go handle your business. If she gives you pussy, I can't get mad. But I'll tell you what, y'all niggas better get that shit out your system tonight. After that, Fatou is off limits, as if I should have to tell any of you mothafuckas! Now I gotta clear my head and figure out what the fuck to do with this situation. Y'all niggas can just chill for a second. I'm going upstairs. Don't drink up all my shit. But more importantly, don't act like I was just stuttering about Fatou when she comes back."

David walked off and all the lieutenants stared into space behind him for a few seconds. Finally, Ricco broke the silence. "You done fucked up now, Ken."

"Man, this is all just a big misunderstanding," Ken said.

"Lie to us all you want," Joe-Joe said. "But you better get your shit together. Whether you know it or not, that was a fucking warning."

"Pretty much," Ricco said, agreeing.

"Well, I love y'all niggas," Ken said. "Y'all the only family I got. I ain't doing nothing to fuck with that."

"I hope you mean that," Joe-Joe said, embracing Ken to show him some love.

All of the other lieutenants joined in the embrace.

"Let's drink to our loyalty," Ricco said. "We all rely on each other to protect our asses—especially now."

"True that," they all said in unison, pulling beers out from under the bar.

The tension in the air finally subsided, and it seemed like they were all squad. Yet Ken still tried to hide his nervousness. Deep inside, he knew how badly he wanted Fatou. He told himself that he had to do a better job of hiding his feelings.

Ken put his act to the test when David rejoined them after about an hour.

"Come here, my nig," Ken said, sponging while giving David a manly hug. "My bad man," he continued. "I got too familiar with Fatou, and that was way outta line."

"Later for that," David said, releasing Ken. "We gotta rap about some important shit right now."

David reminded his lieutentants that Salu's crew at Motherland Taxi had one big advantage over his crew—they were always mobile in their cabs.

And they all had radios in their taxis. Every Motherland driver was aware of where his homies were and if they were in trouble. The dispatcher could feed them new information by the second.

Although a lot of hustlers made anonymous phone calls to the police to get rid of their competition, David knew he didn't have that option. Motherland's scheme of picking up drug customers who pretended to need taxis shielded them from the police. And their back-up plan of having a few decoy cars without drugs had proven to be a valuable ploy when undercover detectives tried to catch them in he act of dealing. David's crew would be sitting ducks if they tried to snitch on Motherland. His people were on the streets. Salu's crew were mobile. It was much easier for cops to roll up on a corner than to chase a car.

So David came up with a plan to isolate Salu's drivers and set as many traps as possible. The more drivers they could ambush, the better.

"Main thing is," David said, "everyone gotta be on point. Don't get fucking sloppy and wind up getting your ass shot the hell up. We're gonna be the ones bringing the wreck, not them niggas. Like y'all said, we are the grimiest niggas on the streets. Salu's gonna have to find that shit out the hard way."

CHAPTER TWENTY

A Summer At War

A month had gone by, and there had been only a few small skirmish-es between David's and Salu's crews. A couple of small-time soldiers had become casualties in their conflict. No lieutenants had been lost.

David and Fatou were at his home, spending a rare moment of free time together. Fatou laughed at David as he drank Maalox straight from the bottle.

"Are you taking that shit for ulcers again?" she asked. "How can you be so affected by this? I thought this shit was in your blood."

"Beat it, you fucking New Jack," he said. "You're still wet behind the ears. You haven't had to worry about mothafuckas sneakin' up on you and hatin', tryna take you out the game, every day for years. I got stick up kids to dodge, ruthless soldiers and lieutenants tryna come up. What the fuck do you know about my stress?"

"Temper, temper," she said. "That's all part of the game. Remember? Don't worry, though. Mommy won't let nothing happen to your black ass."

"Oh, so you're protecting me now," he said, laughing. "What part of the fucking game is this?"

"The part where the young gun steps up in a way that no one ever dreamed of," she said. "Lucky thing for you the only thing I wanna do to you that you can't handle is give you this pussy. I don't think even you could deal with my wrath when it comes."

"Oh, now I can't handle you?" he asked.

"Now? What the fuck do you mean now? You could never handle this pussy—not since the first time I gave you some."

"Is that right?" David asked, kissing Fatou's neck. "I may have ulcers, but that ain't gonna stop me from hittin' that thing the way I'm supposed to."

"Mmm hmm," Fatou said.

They started kissing and rubbing on each other passionately until a piercing alarm went off.

"Oh, shit," David yelled, grabbing the remote control. "Follow me. Quick!"

Fatou was unsure of what was going on, but she knew that whatever it was, David would be able to find out.

David ran to his walk-in closet, and Fatou got confused. "Why don't you go downstairs to the elevator?" she asked.

"We probably don't have time for that," he said. "Just relax. I got this under control."

David pushed the remote in the direction of the mirror. Like in the kitchen, there was a quick noise, then the mirror slid to the side to reveal a large monitor. Then the monitor slowly receded into the closet, making room for them to squeeze in.

"Get in," David said.

Fatou was curious, but she didn't question him.

She followed David's lead and joined him in the hiding space.

Behind them, the mirrors closed quickly. In front of them, images on the monitor came to life. Several men were outside David's house, looking around frantically, occasionally peeping as if they were checking for witnesses and police. In the background, David noticed several empty taxis.

"That fucking Salu!" David shouted. "He's trying to bring the noise to my fucking house! Fuck that pussy."

David looked at Fatou and told her, "It's time that we had some fun, baby."

He studied the remote for a second, then held the volume button all the way down while pointing it at the monitor. He leaned in toward the microphone on the monitor and started screaming into it.

"Fuck you bitch asses! You can't get me! Your dumb asses will never take me. Fuck all y'all niggas."

The men on the the monitor started doing 360s, looking in every direction. Finally they headed to the door and paused. David pushed a button on the remote, and the door opened. They scattered but then inched forward cautiously.

Thinking they were safe, one by one the men slowly came inside the house, pulling firearms out of their waists. David and Fatou counted six in all.

"You stupid bitches," David yelled into the microphone. "You done fucked up now!"

They searched for David but to no avail. They jumped when David pushed a button on the remote and the front door slammed closed. He hit another button, and the doorknobs retracted into the steel door-frame. When he hit yet another button, steel mini-blinds encased the windows, sealing in the intruders.

It didn't take them long to realize they were trapped.

When David touched the remote control again, sprinkler-like spikes dropped from the ceiling, and Fatou saw a fine mist being released from them.

"Don't worry," David said, "the gas can't get to us. We're safe here. But those guys will be sleeping for a long time."

One by one, Salu's men dropped like flies. David pushed a button on the remote and conducted a scan of the premises. He saw no one else.

"We have to wait a few minutes for the gas to clear," David said.

"When were you gonna tell me about this?" Fatou asked.

"Some shit you just have to experience," he said.

"Experience, my ass. There's no way I would know what to do when the shit hit the fan with all those damn gadgets. I'd be fucked up in the game."

"Well, you're not," David said while pushing the button retracting the mirror and freeing them from the hiding space.

"Hurry up. We don't have a lot of time before they wake up." David ran down the stairs and went straight for the kitchen.

He grabbed a large trash bag and some duct tape.

"What in the hell are you doing?" Fatou asked.

"Shhh," David whispered. "Help me take their clothes off."

David and Fatou removed the clothes from the six members of Salu's squad. Then he duct taped them in three pairs, belly to back.

"These fuckin' queers can't holla at me," David said, laughing heartily. "I want everyone to see that they can't holla at me. Help me drag these niggas out so I can put them on top of their cars."

"Wait," Fatou said, chuckling to herself when it dawned on her how sinister David was being. She grabbed her purse and pulled out a digital camera. "When we're finished, we gonna put Salu's punk-ass squad on blast."

They pulled the three pairs of men outside and placed them on the hoods of the their three taxis. Then Fatou took pictures with her digital camera, making sure that she got the Motherland Taxi sign in the shots.

"That's enough," David said. "I gotta get back inside and check on my scanner to see what the hell Salu is up to."

Fatou followed David with a mischievous look on her face, knowing that they'd one-upped Salu. Yet as soon as she and David heard one of Salu's drivers mentioning his location on the radio, she changed her tune.

"He's not far from here," Fatou yelled.

"No shit. Let's get the fuck outta here."

They grabbed their heat and ran out the door. David opted to drive his Porsche instead of his SUV. He felt they could use the speed.

"Damn, baby, you have a Porsche?" Fatou said. "I guess there's a lot you haven't told me yet."

"Now's not the time, boo," David said, pulling the car out of the garage. "Fuck!" he yelled when he saw a Motherland taxi just turning the corner.

"Do you think he sees us?" Fatou asked.

"Definitely. Get your heat ready."

David knew his Porsche would overpower the taxi, but he wasn't sure how much traffic there would be. He hopped onto the Van Wyck Expressway so he could take the Jackie Robinson Parkway to Brooklyn. He knew it would be faster to take Atlantic Avenue when he exited Van Wyck, but he was not sure if he'd be able to take advantage of his Porsche's power if he got stuck in traffic.

The Porsche's engine roared as David weaved in and out of traffic.

The taxi was no match at all for the Porsche. But the driver had called for back-up and was trying to stay close.

As David merged onto the Jackie Robinson, two Motherland taxis were cruising in the right and center lanes, waiting for him. Since he was driving so fast, he didn't see them until the last possible moment and swerved onto the shoulder to avoid them. They rewarded him for not colliding into them by spraying a mass of bullets behind him with their Uzis. But David was driving much too fast and their efforts were futile.

They sped up and followed in hot pursuit. But the third taxi David had left in the dust on the Van Wyck crashed into the back of the second taxi, and the impact of the collision caused that taxi to veer into the first. Luckily, both taxis were totalled, but there was no explosion.

"He's getting away," yelled one of the drivers into the taxi radio. "He's driving a black Porsche south on the JR. He just left the Van Wyck. We crashed and can't follow. Do you copy? Someone has to follow him!"

David was smiling in his Porsche, but he didn't get too cocky.

He knew that he still had a bit more driving to do before he made it safely into Brooklyn.

"Joe-Joe," Fatou screamed into her Nextel, chirping her Brooklyn lieutenant.

"What up, Fatou?" he chirped back.

"We're headed your way," she said. "We're being ambushed by a bunch of Motherland taxis. Now we're on the JR about to go...wait.

David, which way are we going?"

"I'm taking Pennsylvania to the Belt Parkway to Flatbush," David yelled.

"Are you there, Joe-Joe?"

"Go ahead, Fatou."

"He's staying on the JR to Pennsylvania then following the Belt to Flatbush."

"Why the fuck don't he just take Linden from Pennsylvania?" Joe-Joe chirped back.

"Too much fucking traffic," David yelled. "Those niggas can't fuck wit me on the highway."

"Did you hear that?"

"Hell no, ma," Joe-Joe said "What the fuck did you say?"

"There's too much goddamned traffic to drive on the streets," Fatou yelled. "We'd be sitting ducks out here. Just make sure you have sumthin' real nice waitin' for their asses in Brooklyn."

"Hell, yeah," Joe-Joe hissed evilly.

"How much longer?" Fatou asked David.

"Not long. Just chill and enjoy the ride. You know I got this."

"If you say so."

"Shit, Fatou. Stop doubting me and make yourself useful. Grab that walkie-talkie out the glove."

Fatou took it out and went to hand it to David.

"Hold the fucking thing, goddamn. Push the button in so I can talk."

Fatou looked at David sideways, but considering the circumstances, she didn't object to his yelling.

"Mayday, mayday," David yelled. "Penn-Belt-Flat...clear me!"

Fatou looked curiously at David.

"Let go of the button, Fatou, so I can hear what he says."

"You and Flat," are the only words they heard coming across the radio when Fatou let go of the button.

"Hold it in so I can talk, then let it go," David screamed.

"OK."

"Repeat your last," David yelled.

"There's a bottleneck on the Belt. A cabbie's broke down and a couple others are helping. That's between Avenue U and Flat."

"Hold it in," David said.

Fatou held in the button.

"Out," David said into the radio. Then he turned to Fatou and told her to chirp Joe-Joe again.

"Change of plans...I'm taking Flatlands to Flatbush. We only have about seven minutes to get off the highway."

"What's up, ma?" Joe-Joe asked, responding to Fatou's chirp.

"In seven minutes we're taking Flatlands to Flatbush. We're not getting on the Belt. Repeat, you have only seven minutes to set sumthin' up."

"Got you, Fatou," Joe-Joe shouted before chirping as many soldiers and young boys as he could find.

"Listen," Joe-Joe yelled into his Nextel. "If you see any Motherland taxis headed in that direction, smoke their fucking asses and ask questions later. We ain't fucking playing games right now."

David's adrenaline was pumping as he turned onto Flatland, reducing his speed to 75 mph.

"Why are you slowing down?" Fatou asked.

"What the fuck is that up there?" David asked. "Never mind, the shit looks funny, so I'm turning on Ralph."

David turned onto Ralph Avenue, and Salu's crew jumped into their cabs in hot pursuit, pulling out from behind a school bus.

"I'm popping the trunk, so when I stop, grab that fucking bag and haul ass behind me," David yelled. "We'll meet Joe-Joe on foot at the other side of Flatbush soon as we come out the tunnels."

David stopped his car on Ralph right below Remsen Avenue and Kings Highway. He and Fatou escaped to the tunnels just before Salu's crew came and lit up his empty Porsche with gunfire.

"There's no one here!" a Motherland driver yelled. "Where the fuck could they have gone?"

CHAPTER TWENTY-ONE

Brooklyn Battlegrounds

Joe-Joe got a chirp from one of his soldiers that a couple of taxis were waiting on Utica had squealed down Flatland and turned north on to Ralph.

"Take a couple cars with you and bring the fucking noise," Joe-Joe yelled. "Have your heat drawn and ready."

Joe-Joe's soldiers followed his orders and within minutes, surrounded the taxis on Ralph Avenue. Every type of buckshot, bullet and shell imaginable rained down on the taxis from the surrounding rooftops, cars, scooters and bicycles. In less than a minute, all three of Salu's Motherland taxis were annihilated.

After carefully exiting the tunnel closest to Flatland and Flatbush, David chirped Joe-Joe to let him know that they were coming up from behind.

"How the fuck are y'all here when your Porsche is sprayed the fuck up on Ralph?" Joe-Joe asked when they walked up.

"That's why I'm running this shit," David said arrogantly. "But I couldn't do the damn thing like I do without thorough-ass lieutenants like yourself. I'd like to say that you handled yourself rather proper today, Joe-Joe. That's how you handle a soft-ass so-called threat."

"No doubt," Joe-Joe replied.

They laughed and gave each other pounds, but deep inside David was worried. He'd had too many close calls lately. Fatou, on the other hand, was still in the midst of the rush.

I'm definitely built for this shit, she thought to herself.

Suddenly Fatou remembered that Natali would be coming home today.

"David, we have to go to Harlem, or at least I do. Natali will be back in town today. I haven't seen her in years."

"That's the one you put down with Ken?"

Fatou shook her head yes.

"What ever happened with that?"

"I don't know," she said. "I guess I'll find out today."

"Well, I'll chill wit you for a minute before I go handle some business. I wanna meet this fuckin' Natali."

"That's cool, but don't get yourself fucked up today. Natali is kinda hot, so ya ass better not be droolin' over her."

"Let me find out you're acting jealous," David said, laughing.

"Hmm," Fatou responded. "I ain't got shit to be jealous of. I'm just lettin' you know that you'd best not disrespect me, especially with my best friend. Keep ya fuckin' eyeballs in your head and off of my girl. That's not too hard to understand, is it?"

"Whatever," David said, exasperated.

"No, don't make me show you what-the-fuck-ever," Fatou said sarcastically.

David ignored her and turned to Joe-Joe. "Dog, let me use one of your rides. We can drop it off later."

"No doubt," Joe-Joe said. "Hop in so we can swing past my house."

They got in the car with Joe-Joe and remained quiet the short distance to his house. They switched cars and David and Fatou left Joe-Joe's house, heading toward Harlem.

Since David was quiet for a while, Fatou started looking at him strangely, then asked, "What's wrong with you?"

"Nothin'," he said.

"Yes, there is."

"I said nothin'.

"David, what the fuck is wrong with you?"

"Ain't nothin' wrong with me. It's your disrespectful ass."

"What the fuck are you talking about, David?"

"I'm talking about you being fucking disrespectful."

"How, David? How am I disrespectful?"

"Maybe you forgot, but I'm the general and you're the fucking captain. I put you on to this shit, remember?"

"And what does that have to do with anything?"

"Don't ever fucking disrespect me again in front of my lieutenants."

"Ain't nobody disrespect you. I just told you don't be staring my girl up and down, that's all."

"Well, that's still disrespectful."

"On the one hand there's business shit. On the other hand there's relationship shit. Now if I ever come at you sideways about the business in front of a lieutenant, then you can say I disrespected you."

"Fuck that," David snapped. "You ain't gon' come at me sideways about shit in front of my peeps, relationship shit or not."

"You know what? Oh, never mind," Fatou said, heated. "If you feel like that, it's gonna be a long time before you get some. You can act like Mr. Big Man with someone else. You need a break anyway."

"You're the who wanted me to fuck you so bad. Remember?" David asked, laughing.

"Well, that was a long time ago," Fatou said sarcastically.

"Now all you can think about is gettin' a shot of this shit."

"You're funny," David said.

"And I'll be funny," Fatou said. "But your ass is gon' be hard up Mr. Big Man who says I can't check you about relationship shit in front of your peeps. We'll see about that."

"I guess we will," he said.

"Yeah, I guess we will."

They didn't speak again until they arrived at Fatou's spot in Harlem. Natali was standing outside, smoking a Black and Mild.

"That's her!" Fatou exclaimed before jumping out of the car to run to her girlfriend.

"Natali!"

"Fatou!"

They embraced until David walked up and finally broke it up.

"Oh, Natali, this is David," Fatou said. "I told you all about him in my letters."

"Hi, David," she said, extending her hand for him to shake it.

"Hello, Miss Natali," he said facetiously while kissing her hand and looking Fatou in the eyes. "Fatou said that you were very attractive, but she never said you were all like this."

"Did I miss something here?" Natali asked.

"My man is being an asshole right now," Fatou said. "But that's

OK, because he's about to catch a serious case of blue balls."

"Don't listen to her," David said.

"Umm, excuse me," Fatou said. "Can you go somewhere? We have a lot of catching up to do."

"Stop hatin'," he said. "Anyway, you're right. Ken's gonna really dig your girl."

"Oh, I forgot about Ken," Natali said. "Are we going to his barbecue at his people's house in Brooklyn?"

"What barbecue?" David asked.

"That's right," Natali said. "He never told y'all cuz he says y'all never hang out with him."

"Ken's full of shit," David said. "Let me chirp his ass."

"Yo, nigga," Ken said, responding to David's chirp.

"That's fucked up," David said. "How you having barbecues and shit and not be invitin' me, dog?"

"Man, you don't even fuck wit me like that," Ken said. "I ain't wanna waste my time telling you when I know you ain't coming."

"Well, I am coming, nigga. Where the fuck is the shit?"

"I know where it is," Natali said.

"Who was that?" Ken asked.

"Your people, man," David said. "She just got home."

"That's what's up," Ken said. "You comin' through, ma?"

"Yeah, she's coming," Fatou answered.

"True dat," Ken said.

Fatou and David put their Nextels away after Ken's last chirp, but Ken didn't. He called someone named Jesse and had a quick conversation.

"Yo. Guess who's coming through today?" Ken asked

"Who?" Jesse asked.

"David."

"Word," Jesse said. "David's gonna be in Brooklyn?"

"Yeah."

"What time?" Jesse asked. "I'll come through."

"Maybe in about an hour or two."

"True dat," Jesse said. "I'll holla at you then."

"You know what to bring, nigga."

"Yeah," Jesse said. "I got you."

About an hour later, Fatou was driving the new Land Cruiser that David had bought her. David was riding shotgun and Natali was in the back seat.

David decided to chirp Joe-Joe to see what was up with him. "Yo, nigga," Joe-Joe said.

"I didn't bring your car cuz I wasn't sure if you were coming to Ken's barbecue or not," David said.

"Well, where the fuck is it?" Joe-Joe asked.

"In Brooklyn."

"How that mothafucka gon' have some shit in my stompin' grounds and not tell me about it?"

"He ain't tell nobody," David said. "That nigga talkin' about he ain't tell us cuz we don't be fuckin' wit him like that."

"That's bullshit," Joe-Joe said. "We might not call his ghetto ass when we're goin' to nice shit, but that's because he don't be feelin' that typa shit. He knows we would come to his barbecue though."

"Bring your ass on then, nigga," David said. "That's your hood any fucking way."

"I'm gon' come though," Joe-Joe said. "I gotta do something real fast, but I can be there in about an hour. Where the fuck in Brooklyn is he having the shit at, though."

"It's on Utica, not far from Linden," Natali said.

"Yo, nigga. It's near where we had our little run-in today—on Utica, not far from Linden."

"Small fucking world," Joe-Joe said. "Anyway, I'll see y'all niggas in about an hour."

"All right. One," David said to Joe-Joe. "Damn. I forgot to tell that nigga not to be rolling up with a big ass posse like he always does," he said to no one in particular. "Oh, well. I just hope that nigga Ken has enough food."

"Yeah," Natali said. "After all the bullshit I've been eating for the last few years, I need some barbecue."

"Knowing Ken, though, we better hope that nigga don't cook fucking Cajun black meat on the grill," David said, laughing.

"Don't say that," Natali replied. "That would be fucked up considering I just left from eatin' bullshit."

"Well, if you're expecting some gourmet shit, you don't know Ken the way I do," David said.

"Why the fuck are you kicking your man's back in?" Fatou asked.

"Here the fuck you go," David said.

"Whatever," Fatou hissed. "You just better remember what I told you and stop showing off."

"Go ahead and get your shit off right now," David said. "But you better remember what the fuck I said when you get to the spot."

"Now y'all know y'all love each other too much for this petty bullshit," Natali said.

"You're right, I do love him," Fatou said. "But that don't mean I won't put my foot up his ass."

"You must think I ain't fucking sittin' here," David said.

Fatou sat at a stop sign longer than she had to so she could turn to David and look him in the eyes.

"I know you're just trying to be fucking funny, so stop. OK?" she said.

"What?" David said, trying to hold in his laugh.

"You're not funny, nigga," Fatou said. "But two can play that game."

"Whatever," David said.

"I know whatever," she said. "That's why you'll see what I mean when we get there."

Fatou pulled Natali aside when they got to Ken's cookout and told her about the argument she'd had earlier with David. She also let her know that she didn't mean any harm, yet she planned to flirt with Ken a little to teach David a lesson. Yet she didn't mention to Natali how she'd always felt that Ken was paying her too much attention. In fact, Fatou had never said a word to her best friend.

The two of them walked over to the crowd. Everyone was dancing. With DJ Red Alert mixing up the sounds from the radio, the crowded barbecue seemed like a mini block party.

David stared at Fatou like he'd finally shown her who was boss, but he had no idea about her intentions. He watched her converse with Natali with a look of triumph on his face.

When Ken walked up, he shook his hand and gave him a one shoulder hug, then directed Ken's attention to Natali.

"Oh, snap," Ken said. "What's up ma?"

"Ken, this is Natali," Fatou said. "I know that y'all have a lot to talk about, but you have all day to do that. I want to dance with you first, since this is your party."

Fatou grabbed Ken's hand and pulled him over to where everyone was dancing. Ken was dancing with Fatou respectfully, but she continuously moved up on him. Ken moved back and from side to side, trying to make sure that it didn't seem like he moving in on his general's woman.

Fatou turned her back to Ken and looked to where David was standing. She wanted to make sure he saw the show. Of course David's eyes were stuck on Fatou the entire time, so it didn't take long for her eyes to find his.

She smiled a devilish grin at him, then moved back until her butt was rubbing against Ken's groin. Ken tried to move back out of the way, but he couldn't go any further. There were too many people dancing. He was trapped.

Fatou seized the opportunity and ground her butt into Ken, making sure that he felt the full effect of its softness. When she felt Ken's erection, she smiled at David even harder.

David tried to regain his composure by striking up a conversation with Natali, but he was too distracted.

"David, I know that you're a strong and powerful man," Natali said, "but sometimes you just have to be the bigger man and apologize."

"I ain't apologizing for shit."

"You know Fatou loves the hell out of you, so why are you letting her disrespect you, herself and me by dancing with your peoples and the person I'm supposed to be getting to know?"

"I ain't got shit to do with her disrespecting herself," David said.

"Men are so fucking stupid," Natali said, walking away toward Fatou.

"Can I talk to you?" Natali whispered into Fatou's ear.

"Go ahead," Fatou said, still grinding her butt into Ken.

Still whispering in Fatou's ear, Natali said, "I know that you and David are beefin' right now, but you are dancing with the person I'm about to make my man real soon."

"I'm sorry," Fatou said, embracing Natali. "He's all yours."

Fatou grabbed Natali's hand and Ken's hand and placed them together so that they were holding hands.

"You should be dancing with him, girl, not me," Fatou said before walking away.

David casually strolled to where Fatou was standing and whispered in her ear.

"So you had to show the fuck off, didn't you...I guess you think that you're a fucking smart ass...you couldn't just chill the out, could you? You had to show your ass in front of company."

"David, I love you," Fatou said. "But you don't seem to get it. You are going to respect me when it comes to my friends, period. And I don't give a goddamn about generals, lieutenants, or anyone else. If you can't show me respect, you're gonna just have to see how it feels when the shoe's on the other foot. So, how did it feel, David?"

David didn't say anything. He just stared at her.

"I guess now you know that it doesn't feel good being disrespected by your mate with one of your friends. I hope we understand each other now," Fatou said, walking away from David and going to sit in her car.

David didn't follow Fatou. He stood in the same spot, wondering what he should do and how he should be feeling.

He started watching Ken dance with Natali, and was much calmer about the situation.

Natali started talking suggestively to Ken while they were dancing, and he was eating it up.

"I'm glad that you're ready for me," Natali said, rubbing his groin with her hand. "But I'm wondering if this is all for me or if you're still thinking about what Fatou was doing to you."

"This is for you, ma," Ken said, lying.

"Good," Natali said. "I've been cooped up for a long time, and I need for you to do some of the shit you talked about in those letters. But I don't want you to be fucking me and thinking about someone else."

"Nah, ma," Ken said. "It ain't gon' be no doubt who I'm giving this dick to when we do the damned thing."

"Well, what the fuck are you waiting for?" Natali asked.

"Shit, we can take this in the house," Ken said. "But it ain't my house, so we can't get too comfortable. And it'll have to be quick. I'll just give you a little sumthin' to let you know what's about to go down later."

Ken guided Natali to the upstairs bathroom, and they started ripping each other's clothes off. Ken was very pleased with Natali's body. Her previous size four shape had been transformed into an eight while she was locked up. Natali's dangerous curves had been further aided by the extra weight. And her breasts had increased from a 36B to a supple 36C. Ken couldn't wait to have her.

As Ken started sucking on Natali's breasts, he received a chirp on his Nextel from Jesse. He pressed the button to acknowledge the call but didn't say anything. He didn't want to be distracted from what he was doing with Natali.

"Ken, I can't make it, yo. I wanna make sure that it's cool for my peoples to come though."

"All right, Jesse," Ken said quickly before getting back to Natali.

"It'll be in about twenty minutes," Jesse said.

Ken didn't respond. He continued to kiss Natali all over her body as he removed the last of her clothes.

Once she was naked, Ken turned her around and started kissing her butt from behind. Knowing that he didn't have much time, Ken walked behind Natali and placed himself inside of her.

At first he ground slowly and Natali shivered, engulfed in a pleasure that she hadn't known in a long time. Then Ken started to increase his pace, and Natali loved it even more.

"Yes. Give me that shit, nigga," she said.

Ken obliged and pounded into Natali. Little did Natali know, though, that Ken's eyes were closed and he was imagining that he was with someone else.

When it started getting really good for Ken, he lost control of himself and started moaning.

"Give me that pussy, baby girl," he said. "Ooh shit, Fatou!"

"What the fuck did you just say?" Natali asked, turning around violently.

"Nothing."

"Bullshit," she said, smacking him in the face. "Thanks for the nut, but you can leave me the fuck alone. If you want my girl, you need to holla at her ass and stop pretending to be feeling me."

"I am feeling you," Ken said, as Natali got dressed. "I just made a mistake. That's all."

"Well, fuck you and your mistake," Natali said, walking out the bathroom.

She went outside and walked over to Fatou and David.

"Where the fuck have you been, ho?" Fatou said, laughing.

"Having a good time until dumb ass fucked it up," Natali replied.

"How did he fuck it up?"

"Don't ask," Natali said.

Ken came out of the house and David walked toward him. They started talking about Natali, but their conversation was cut short.

Pop. Pop. Pop.

Out of nowhere, gunshots rang out. Many of the guests at the barbecue were struck by bullets, but Ken and David were able to get low and crouch behind a table and chairs. When they peeked out, they noticed a group of Motherland taxis in the middle of the street.

As if he knew what his crew needed, Joe-Joe and his posse saw the taxis and sped up onto the scene. They blocked them in and started shooting at them. David and Ken moved from their hiding places when they saw Joe-Joe and started blasting.

When the gunshots finally subsided, all of the Motherland taxi drivers had been annihilated and half a dozen guests had been killed. Fatou and Natali emerged from where they were hiding and ran toward David and Ken. David was fine, but Ken had suffered a bullet wound to his shoulder.

"Joe-Joe, get one of your young boys to drop Ken off at the hospital," David said before turning to Fatou. "Let's get the fuck out of here."

Neither Fatou nor Natali responded immediately. Then they

snapped out of it and rushed back to the Land Cruiser.

"I wanna be with Ken," Natali said. "He's an asshole, but I still wanna make sure he's OK."

"Well, let me take David to get his truck, then I'll take you to the hospital," Fatou said. "I'm sure he wants his wheels."

"Tru dat," David said. "I need to make sure that my squad is tight. I'll holla at you later once all is good."

Everyone sat deep in thought. Fatou was wondering if she'd made a mistake and re-agitated the situation with Ken after it was squashed. She also wondered if David had learned his lesson, and if she had inadvertently created trouble with Natali in the process.

Natali was hoping that Ken's slip of the tongue was from a passing fantasy that would go away. She believed that she could forgive Ken, but she didn't want to be with him if he had the hots for her girl.

David was thinking that he had to show Fatou who was boss. But he was also wondering if he was going to have to call in some favors to deal with Salu and his crew. And Ken was pulling in a lot of cheddar in downtown Queens, and it would be a big blow to lose him.

When Fatou pulled up in front of David's house, he didn't budge. She sat there momentarily and then commented.

"David what are you doing?" she asked. "We're here."

"I'm waiting for you to give me some love before I get out," he said.

"And you think you deserve love?" she asked sarcastically.

"You did your shit, and I did mine. So it's over, right?" he asked.

"That depends," she said. "As long as you understand what I meant by disrespecting me, it can be over."

"Boo, we have a whole lotta important shit to deal with right now," he said.

"You're right," Fatou agreed. "I still love you even though you're an ass. Go handle your business."

She gave him a peck on the lips and he got out.

"Get up front," Fatou said to Natali.

"That asshole called out your name while we were fucking," Natali said calmly. "Is there anything that you need to tell me about you and Ken?"

"Fuck!" Fatou said.

"Does that mean yes or no?"

"We never did anything, if that's what you mean. But he did used to pay me too much attention until I straightened him out. He's cute, I can't front. But I'm in love with David. That's why I told you about him. I thought you would make a nice couple."

"That's fucked up, girl. You know that nigga wants you."

"Not anymore," Fatou said, hiding from the truth.

"He was in my pussy and calling out your name. What does that mean?"

"It means that I made a mistake. I shoulda never been rubbing my ass against his dick, trying to piss David off. That was wrong as far as you're concerned, so I'm sorry. Still, the fact that he was thinking about something that had just happened doesn't mean he wants me. I'm sure he wants you and just made a mistake."

"I see the way he looks at you though."

"He doesn't look at me any differently than David was looking at you. But that doesn't mean David wants you. He loves me and was just using you to prove a point to me—the same thing I was doing with Ken. I shoulda never put you in the middle of our shit, though."

"You're right about that, but it's over."

"Yeah. Ken's a good guy. You just have to keep his ass in check. Every bitch in Queens wants him."

"I know I have to get used to that shit, and I will...as long as I don't have to worry about you wanting his ass too."

"I would never do you like that, Natali, and you know it. Niggas come and go, but friends are forever."

Fatou sat at a stop sign and hugged Natali. They both were teary-eyed.

CHAPTER TWENTY-TWO

Connections

It was July 5th, and because it was a Friday, most of the city and state offices were closed. David was in his bed thinking about the day before in Brooklyn.

Ken was going be okay, so David didn't have him to worry about. But the many close calls he'd experienced lately had his stomach pulsating more often than usual. Before he was just speculating, but now he was sure he had an ulcer.

I'm gonna have to get some help with this, David thought to himself before grabbing his Palm Pilot and scrolling through his long list of influential contacts in the city's government.

Since Underground had always been the most loyal city official he dealt with, David decided to call him first. He wanted Underground's opinion on which L & I (license and inspection) and police department connections he should sic on Motherland Taxi.

Underground advised David to call Captain Ramirez of the city's Drug Task Force and Brian Nedley at L & I.

"Why do I have to call them?" David asked. "I've never dealt with either of those two before."

"They're the big players now," Underground said. "Nobody can get things moving faster than them."

"But they're gonna have to be wondering why I'm calling them," David retorted. "Don't you think we know enough people? Wouldn't it be better if you made the requests, considering that Motherland Taxi has been involved in several violent outbreaks within the five boroughs? No one would find your interest unreasonable or suspicious. If I called them, I'm sure they'd think something was fishy."

"You may have a point there," Underground said.

"I have a big point. I'm not asking you to do anything that would draw attention to yourself. I just want you to give a couple of people a wake-up call to do their damn job. Salu's squad will be weakened in the process."

"I'll rattle a few cages," Underground said.

"That's what's up. I'll holla at you later, man."

David hung up the phone feeling a little better about the situation. Since Underground was gonna make calls to the city officials, David had a little free time to handle some other things. He decided to call Fatou.

"Hello," she said.

"You stay away from me all night and don't fucking call? Now that's a first," David hissed sarcastically.

"Oh, I'm doing fine, sweetheart, and you?" Fatou asked as sassy to David as he was to her.

"You think you're fucking funny, don't you?" he asked.

"You said it, not me," Fatou said. "But I don't wanna argue with you, David. I think we did enough of that yesterday."

"I'm not the one who's acting up," he said "You're the one who chose to ignore me, remember?"

"Like you couldn't call me, David," Fatou snapped. "My girl just got out of jail, and the nigga she's tryna get with got shot and is laid up in the hospital. At least I had a reason for being preoccupied. What's your damn excuse?"

"Don't try to turn the shit around on me," David replied, not knowing what else to say.

"Can we just talk about something else?" Fatou asked. "Yesterday's over, and we still love each other. We're still gonna be together, so why start off with bullshit first thing in the morning?"

"Cuz you're not supposed to just forget about a problem. You're supposed to fix it. Otherwise it'll just come back to haunt you."

"So, what's the problem, David? Tell me what you call a problem."

"You rubbing your ass all up on Ken for one. Must I continue?"

"I was wrong for that and I apologize," she said. "But you ain't have no business all up in my girl's grill either. Then you're gonna kiss her and shit."

"I kissed her fucking hand."

"It may as well have been her lips the way you were acting."

"Uh-Uh. You're exaggerating."

"I know what the fuck I saw. But the good news is that she'll be running the escort service for me. If you need to get some shit outta your system, you know where she'll be. Just make sure to leave a big tip. Business has been slow lately, and we can use the money."

"You're such a fucking smart ass," he said. "I'm not tryna fuck your girl. She's cute, but I already have the best."

"That don't mean shit, nigga. Men ain't never fucking satisfied."

"Anyway," he said. "What are you doing today?"

"I was gonna chill with Natali for a minute, help her get back on her feet."

"Then what are you doing?" he asked.

"I'm not sure. That depends on what she wants to do. A bunch of people are having cookouts, but I'm not sure I'm down for that after what happened in Brooklyn yesterday."

"I didn't hear you including me in any of your plans," he said.

"Natali doesn't have any other friends here, and I'm not feelin' you being around us right now."

"Stop it."

"No, seriously," she said. "I'm not saying that I'm mad or anything else. I'm just saying that maybe we should play it safe for a while. Besides, you need to check on Ken. You know how funny he is, thinking that nobody fucks with him and shit like that."

"Don't be tryna pull that business shit on me."

"But it was cool when you pulled the shit after I checked your ass in front of Joe-Joe for talking about my girl."

"That was different," he said.

"Different my ass," she snapped. "Hold on...what's up, Natali?"

"Someone's here for you," Natali said. "You'll never guess who it is. Just come out front."

"David, I have to call you back."

"See, your ass is acting up," he said.

"No, I'm not. Seriously, let me call you back."

Fatou hung up the phone and put her robe on. Then she walked up front to the check cashing business and was immediately stunned.

"Mati, what are you doing here?" she screamed excitedly. "How have you been?" The two women hugged tightly.

"I'm fine, child," Mati said. "The question is how have you been?"

"I'm doing OK. I can't believe you're here. Are you sure that everything is OK?"

"Well, Fifi lost a lot of business when you left and never got it back. So she's always pestering Lama about extra money. That's a hassle, but I can handle Fifi."

"And how is Lama?"

"Still driving himself crazy about you being gone. But you wouldn't know it. Patra just had twins. They have six kids now."

"I guess she got her man," Fatou said.

"You still love him. Everything he put you through and you still love him."

"I love him and I hate him. I hate him for what he did to me, but I love him for giving me the chance at a better life. I'm doing really good now."

"That's basically what I wanted to talk to you about. How good are you really doing, Fatou?"

"This business is wonderful. My apartment is in the back. And did you see my car out front? Things have been going great for me."

"You speak of money and material things. But how are you really doing? How do you feel about yourself when you're laying in bed at night?"

"Good, I guess—except for the fact that I can't go to sleep." Mati touched Fatou's five carat diamond bracelet and two carat diamond earrings.

"This was never you, Fatou," Mati said. "You were never worried about possessions like this. I've been hearing some very bad things. Now, seeing you with jewels that they've robbed from the motherland, I'm wondering if those things are true."

"I'm surviving, Mati. All I'm doing is getting my small piece of the American dream."

"Let me see your high school diploma. Let me see your class schedule for college. Tell me how your studies are going to receive your citizenship. That used to be your American dream."

"I was young and dumb, Mati. I was a victim in a society that victimizes people."

"And you were an angel, Fatou," Mati said. "You overcame some very rough odds and were still an example of how Allah wants us to be. It seems as if you have changed teams now. You are running a prostitution business like Fifi, you are selling drugs, and I even heard that you have murdered people. Tell me that my little angel hasn't transformed into this."

"This is the life I was given," Fatou said with teary eyes. "I don't have time to lay around and feel guilty. I'm too busy living. I'm too busy doing my best to survive."

"I spoke to an elder from the village," Mati said. "He tells me that you will never have peace until you have fellowship with peaceful people. You have to rid yourself of the demons you associate with. Allah has patience but only so much. Your dealings will be the death of you. One more thing…he told me to ask you if you feel like Allah has given you enough signs. Or do you need to have some more close calls?"

"I'm stuck," Fatou said, crying real tears. "The elder is an astonishing man, but it's gonna take some time for me. I have a lot of pain to overcome."

"You're traveling through dangerous territory, Fatou, and you don't have to. The lifestyle you're living is not in your nature. But you are almost a grown woman and have to find your own way, make your own mistakes. I'm not telling you to lose your independence. I am telling you that no one knows you better than you. If you can really sleep at night, then forget about everything that I've said. I don't think that you can, though. The special person that was inside of you the day that I met you is still inside of you. Come back into the light, Fatou. It gets hard for you to find your way in the darkness."

"Thanks for coming by," Fatou said tearfully. "I'll never forget what you've done for me."

Fatou walked to the door and let Mati out. She could no longer handle the conversation.

Across town in his hospital bed, Ken was also involved in a difficult conversation. He was talking to his friend, Jesse.

"That's fucked up! You ain't come through!" Ken yelled. "I'm in the hospital. It wouldn't a went down like that if ya black ass was there."

"Your peoples had your back man. What the fuck did you need me there for?"

"Cuz your ass said you was coming, nigga. And ain't shit wrong wit my peoples. I'm the one that's sittin' here fucked up."

David walked into the room as Ken was finishing up his sentence. "Let me go, nigga," Ken said. "My peoples is here. What's up, nigga?"

"You tell me, dog," David said. "You're the one sittin' here in the fucking hospital."

"Nah, I'm good," Ken said, bragging. "Them pussies can't take me out. I'm built for this shit."

"Them mothafuckas are gettin' on my nerves," David hissed. "I got sumthin' real sweet for them bastards."

"Wait until I get outta here," Ken said. "Them mothafuckas ain't gon' know what hit 'em when I step on their asses."

"I got your back, my nig," David said. "You just worry about getting yourself healthy."

"I'm good," Ken said. "Them mothafuckas that did this shit ain't gon' be good. But I'm good. Oh, where the fuck is Fatou?" David looked at Ken funny. "I ain't mean it like that, man," Ken said. "I'm saying, though. Wherever the fuck Fatou is, Natali can't be too far."

"Yeah, they're together," David said.

"Listen man," Ken said. "Fatou caught me off guard with that bull-shit yesterday."

"It's over," David said.

"For real, man, listen," Ken persisted. "We already discussed the shit, and you know I wouldn't disrespect you like that. She put me on the spot, and I ain't know what the fuck was going on."

"That's some personal shit, so don't you worry about it," David said. "But next time walk the fuck away from her dumb ass."

"True dat...You heard from the fellas?"

"Not everybody yet, but Donny and Joe-Joe are coming through," David said, smiling. "You know Joe-Joe's gonna let you have it."

"Yeah, that hatin' mothafucka," Ken said, laughing. "He's always giving me shit."

"I'm sure Fatou's gonna bring Natali here once she gets herself together. She might not come up though. She's probably embarrassed about the stupid shit she did yesterday."

"I won't be mad at her," Ken said, scheming. "Maybe I'll have some privacy for a while so I can bang Natali's back out."

"Fuck pussy," David snapped. "Get yourself together so you can get outta here and get back to that cheddar."

"True dat," Ken said as David got a chirp on his Nextel.

"I'll be right back, nigga," David said to Ken as he walked out of the room. "Yo, what's up, Underground?" he spoke into the phone.

"I'm checking on some funny shit for you," Underground replied. "But I'm not going say a word until I have more facts. I did put Nedley and Ramirez on that problem, though. L & I is checking into any infractions Motherland Taxi has, and Ramirez's people are rounding up as much of Salu's squad as they can. I told them I'm sure they're responsible for this gun shit on the street."

"That's what's up," David said.

"Just keep a low profile for a minute," Underground advised. "You can still make your money but try to hide out. Anybody who's tied to gunplay right about now is gonna be up shit's creek."

"I can lay low for a minute," David said, then he called Fatou.

"I'm at the hospital," he said. "Can you bring Natali up here to see Ken and let her drive your car back? We need to talk."

"OK, David, but I don't feel like arguing."

"It ain't like that," he said. "This is business. I'll chill up here until you get here."

David went to get a soda from the vending machine, then headed back to Ken's room. By the time he got there, Ken was asleep. He sat there thinking about business until Natali walked in.

"Let me holla at you," he whispered, walking out of the room. Natali followed him.

"I know about your business," he said. "And I also know that Fatou was involved in that business."

"What's your point?" she said.

"I fell for Fatou because I knew she wasn't a fucking trick," David snapped. "So if you're tryna make something happen with my man, you can't be sleeping with people for money."

"Why are you so interested in what I'm doing? How do you know how Ken feels about what I'm doing? How do you know that we haven't had conversations about what I've done? You're full of shit, David. I don't think what I do with other men has a damned thing to do with Ken. I think you're the one that has a problem with it."

"Bullshit," David said.

"Don't blame me for just being myself, David," Natali said. "You have a beautiful woman who holds you down all day, every day. That woman happens to be my best friend. Whether or not I decide to offer my services to other men is my business. If I start kicking it with Ken, then it will be his business. But it's definitely not your business. All you need to know is that as far as you're concerned, my services are not for sale. When you need some pussy, go get it from Fatou. I hope we understand each other. This conversation is over."

Natali stepped away from David and tiptoed into Ken's room, trying not to wake him up.

David stared at the door momentarily before walking outside to find Fatou. He flagged her down when he saw her, and they walked toward the car.

"What took you so long?" she asked.

"Nothin'. Just chilling wit Ken."

"How's he doing?"

"He'll live. His pride is hurt more than anything else."

"Who's gonna be holding him down while he's in the hospital?" Fatou asked.

"Nobody. He'll be out in no time, probably tomorrow. He can handle his business with his Nextel until then."

"And what do you need me to do?" she asked.

"Good question," he said. "You're gonna be running shit for a while. My connects told me to lay low for a minute. I'll be in the safe house. You're the only one who'll be able to find me."

"I don't know where that is."

"I'm about to take you there," he said. "But don't forget what I told you before. No one is to know about this place. Just tell mothafuckas that I had to go handle some business. If the lieutenants need me, they can just chirp my ass. Of course you can come through from time to time to take care of me."

"Take care of you?"

"I'm sorry, Fatou. Are you happy now? I was joking with you about Natali and let the shit go too far. I don't wanna sleep with her. I wanna be with you. Stop tryna put mothafuckas on punishment and shit."

"Sometimes mothafuckas deserve punishment," she said.

"And sometimes a woman should take care of her man, especially when she knows she's about to be stressed out and working her ass off for God knows how long. Running shit ain't gon' be as easy as you think it is."

"It won't be too bad," she said. "You already showed me everything, and I can always chirp you."

"That's true, but don't chirp me too fucking much. You have to trust your instincts when you're out there in the shit. Only call me if you have to. But I want you to holla at Underground and Eric as much as you need to. And Ricco's cool, too. When in doubt, you can go to him."

"So it's just gonna be me and your connects?"

"And you better do the damned thing, too. Show these mothafuckas what you're made of."

CHAPTER TWENTY-THREE

Massacre in Midtown

September didn't start out well for Fatou. Underground told her that his boss had given him strict instructions to get shit in order, since the country was placed on high alert because of threats from some extremists in the Middle East. That, coupled with his instincts, told him that her days of using the tunnels were numbered. He told her to do whatever she had to do, then lay low for a while.

Fatou was furious and called David with the details.

"What the fuck does he mean instincts?" she screamed into the phone. "Does he know how much money we could lose with this bullshit if I can't get away in a hurry? And what about the money that's already stashed?"

"I've known Underground for a while, and he is able to figure some shit out that has most mothafuckas baffled. But I think it's more than that. Underground has his hands on more classified information than those white boys in the FBI. When he says it's his instincts, I listen to his ass. That means he knows something he can't tell us."

"We're giving that mothafucka lots of cheddar to give us the scoop," Fatou said angrily.

"Look, the man is doing his job, but he still looked out. I think we better take advantage of that shit. I need you to come here and get my Hummer. It has bullet-proof everything."

"What the fuck do I need that for?"

"You have to move the money," David told her. "Every dime in the safe in the tunnel has to be moved. It's gonna take more than one trip."

"Shouldn't you be helping me do that? It sounds way too dangerous for just one person."

"You'll be all right. Just take the tunnel here so that no one sees you. When you get here, you can put on a disguise. You don't need to be looking like you're carrying millions of dollars with you."

"This is the fucking worst," Fatou said.

"It's only the third. Can anything else go wrong this month?"

Fatou spent the next several days transporting the money in the tunnels to the safe house. She also supervised the lieutenants, made pickups, and checked on Poncho to make sure he had the kitchen on lock. To say that she was beat was an understatement.

She also squeezed in an occasional client at her business. All the ladies knew that with Fatou's spare time was close to nonexistence, so having her braid their hair was a novelty.

Even her relationship with Natali was becoming somewhat strained. Natali always seemed to want to talk at night when Fatou came back from handling her business tired and cranky and just wanting to soak in the bath. She hoped her friend understood. Her mind was too clouded to speak about dumb shit.

It was four in the morning on September 10th when Fatou finally moved the last of David's money from the tunnels. She didn't feel like dealing with David, so she placed it in the safe in his house in Jamaica and headed back to Harlem. Since there was no traffic, it took her only a little over ten minutes to get there.

Fatou barely got in the house before she started pulling off her clothes. She headed straight for the bathroom and started running the bath. Once she got the temperature where she wanted it, she didn't even wait for the tub to fill up. She pulled off the last of her clothes and jumped in.

Ordinarily, Fatou could sit in the tub for an hour. But she started washing herself right away. She was dead tired and wanted to freshen up quickly before crashing into bed. Her plan was a success. She was sound asleep by 4:51 am.

Barely an hour later, at 5:50, Fatou seemed to be lost in a dream. Mati was standing over her talking about things an elder had told someone. The dream was weird.

After being shaken on her arm for a while, Fatou finally woke up to find that she wasn't dreaming. Mati was really standing over her.

"No...I just got to sleep," she said. "Let me go back to sleep."

"Nonsense, you have to wake up, child," Mati said. "You have to hear what the elder has professed in his dream."

"Come back later, Mati. Let me finish getting my rest. I'm too tired to listen to anything right now."

"Never say that you are too tired to hear the revelations of Allah. You must get up at once."

Fatou punched her pillow several times and finally forced herself to sit up.

Let me listen to what this bitch has to say before she becomes a pain in my ass, Fatou thought while staring blankly at nothing.

"The elder had a dream that two large metal birds would fly into the mountains, killing Lama for the way that he has treated you."

"Is this about Lama?" Fatou asked. "I don't give a damn about Lama."

"Hush, child," Mati said, frustrated. "I can look in your eyes and see that you still love him. And he loves you. That is why you must save him."

"Tell Patra to save him. He should want to live for her and that house full of kids."

"I know you're angry, Fatou, but you must hear me out. Lama says that the elder is an old-school fool. He won't listen to reason. But I checked in my dream book and know the elder speaks the truth. You must get Lama to stay away from tall buildings and mountains. And he cannot go near the airport for a month."

"And why should I do anything for Lama after the way he's treated me?

"Because you are an angel, and good always overcomes the lingering effects of evil. Speaking of which, the elder had a prophecy for you as well."

"Oh, really," Fatou said sarcastically.

"You must go back to making the world beautiful or else everyone you love will be taken from you."

"Haven't I suffered enough for one lifetime?" Fatou asked.

"It is Allah's will that you walk upright. If you lay in the pits with scoundrels, he cannot protect you from the harsh consequences."

"And what about when I did everything right and suffered? Who protected me then?" Fatou quipped.

"Close your eyes and you're guaranteed to see darkness. But if you open your eyes, you will see that Allah is everywhere. Open your arms so you can accept God's embrace. Do not close your mind to the goodness inside your soul."

"I'm doing my best, Mati. That's all anyone can do. I'm just making the best out of the life I've been given."

"I will pray for you, my child, so that you will see you've suffered enough. Only when you walk with Allah will your misery go away."

Mati walked out the room and Fatou sat up in the bed for a few minutes thinking about what she'd just heard. When she glanced at the clock, she saw it was only 6:35.

"Fuck. I've barely had an hour's worth of sleep."

She pulled the covers over her head to hide the sunlight, and drifted back to sleep.

About a half an hour later, Natali had finished her own bath and was about to go back to her room. Yet she paused when she heard some of Ken's conversation and decided against it. She headed straight to Fatou's room.

"Fatou, Fatou, get up," she said. "I need you to tell me what something Ken said means."

"No. No. No. No. No. No!," Fatou shouted. "I need some fucking sleep, Natali! Can't you tell me in a few hours? I'm tired, girl. I'm dead tired."

Frustrated, Natali stomped out of the room. When Fatou woke up, she was gone.

Fatou remembered that she had turned off her cell phone. When she turned it back on, she had many messages, several from David. She decided to call him right away.

"Where the fuck have you been?" David asked, without saying hello.

"Umm, I was dead tired. Can't I get a good night's sleep for once?"

"Fuck sleep. You never told me what's up with the tunnels."

"Oh, I get it," Fatou said sarcastically. "You're worried about me disappearing with your money. All of it's out of the tunnels, and only the last little bit is in the safe in the other house in Jamaica. Are you happy now?"

"Nobody said shit about you tryna play me out. Maybe I've been worried about your ass."

"If you say so."

"What's that about?" David asked. "I think you need to come over here so I can take care of you. It sounds like you're too stressed."

"Negative. I'm still tired as hell, plus I've been neglecting Natali and my clients. A lot of them are mad because their daughters didn't get their hair done for school. And poor Natali has been doing everything around here. Believe me, I could use a stress reliever. But if you want some pussy today, you're gonna have to come to me."

"I can't do that," he said. "And you're gonna have to chill with me pretty soon anyway. Underground told me about your conversation. You're supposed to be laying low too."

"How can I do that, David? Somebody has to deal with the lieutenants, be visible for the young boys and other soldiers, and I can't tell you how many times I've been back and forth to Poncho."

"That just means business is booming. But you don't have to do everything face-to-face. That's why we have Nextels to chirp each other. When you lay low, I'll just get Ricco to handle the face-to-face shit."

"Like the other mothafuckas ain't gon' be hatin' — especially Joe-Joe."

"Well, that's just Joe-Joe's fucking problem. Whatever I say, goes. I ain't tryna please his ass or nobody else's. Joe-Joe may have his shit tight in Brooklyn, but Ricco has connections in the whole city. Now when are we gonna stop goin' in circles so you can come over here and give me some of that thing?"

"Sorry, boo. I can't see it happening today. I'm gonna have to get with you tomorrow."

David and Fatou went back and forth about her coming to see him, but she didn't relent. Eventually they hung up, and she called a couple of her clients to let them know she was braiding hair for the next few hours.

When Fatou finished her last head, she tried to stay awake so she could talk to Natali when she came in. But she wasn't able to linger long. She decided to take a shower, hoping that Natali would come in by the time she was finished.

After rubbing herself down with body oil and getting dressed in her night clothes, Fatou walked downstairs to make sure Natali hadn't come in. Everything was as quiet.

I wonder where the hell Natali is, she thought as she walked up the stairs and crashed onto her bed, falling asleep almost instantly.

Like clockwork, Fatou woke up 6 am on the 11th ready to meet Poncho in Queens, then drop off her package to her connect in the mayor's office. Ordinarily, he got two bricks, but today he wanted three.

All went well with Poncho, and Fatou jumped on the E train to

Manhattan's financial district. Little did she know that she was on a collision course with Lama, who was just about to drop off a fare.

But as fate had it, the train stopped for a few minutes and all the passengers sat momentarily in the dark. When the lights came on and the train resumed moving, riders were told that they would have to exit the train on Canal Street, one stop before where Lama was standing in disbelief, looking up at the northern tower of the World Trade Center.

Moments earlier Lama had heard the deafening sound of a 747 flying too low before it crashed into the building, causing a massive fire. He was trying to explain what he saw to his dispatcher.

"No, really," he said. "Out of nowhere the plane slammed into the WTC One building. It is burning up, and everyone is screaming. This is very tragic. I am not pulling your leg."

As Lama described the north tower, he saw another plane heading toward the south tower.

"Oh, my God, the prophecy" he hollered, running back toward his car.

Lama remembered the revelation from his spiritual father that Mati had translated to mean he had to stay away from mountains, tall buildings, and the airport.

"Forgive me, Allah," Lama shouted as he continued to run back to his taxi.

By the time Lama got back in his taxi, the plane has crashed into the building. The tower collapsed on top of his taxi before he had a chance to drive off, killing him instantly.

Dust, fire, and terrified people ran everywhere. What had been called the most beautiful skyline in America had been replaced by a spreading dark cloud seen for miles.

As Fatou exited the train on Canal Street, she also saw the dark cloud.

Oh, my God, she thought. *What in the world has happened?* Knowing that she carried a backpack with three kilos of crack cocaine, she knew that she knew that she had to get away from the chaos. But she didn't want to blow her cover, so she didn't speak to the taxi driver who pulled over. She handed him a card for David's brother's alarm business in Brooklyn.

Fatou was on pins and needles during the ride to Brooklyn. She desperately needed to speak to David, but didn't want to call him until she left the cab.

When she finally reached her destination not far from the Brooklyn Bridge, she looked over at Manhattan and saw debris and flying paper drop from the burning twin towers of the World Trade Centers.

Smoke and flames were everywhere. She tried to imagine how many lives had been lost in the tragedy. After staring in amazement for a very long time, she picked up her Nextel and chirped David.

"Fatou, you're all right," he said, answering her chirp.

"So you already know. This is a disaster."

"Where are you?" he asked.

"I'm in Brooklyn, near your brother's store. Since they stopped running the trains, I had to catch a cab from Manhattan. You have to come here, David. I'm scared. And I'm still dirty."

"I'm on my way right now. Don't go into my brother's store. Just try to blend into the crowd outside. I wanna talk to Underground on the way there to see what he thinks."

"OK, baby," she said. "Just hurry up—please!"

David chirped Underground, who answered right away.

"What's up, David?" he said. "I can't talk long."

"I'm on my way to pick up Fatou in Brooklyn. What's the best way to get out of this madness?"

"David, I told you to lay low," he said worriedly. "With this craziness going on, you can't depend on the police. I'm sure they haven't finished picking up all the Motherland Taxi people. It's dangerous out there."

"I'll be careful. But you have to help me out. I hear on the radio that bridges are closing and there are detours everywhere. I need a fucking escape route."

"I'll chirp you. I gotta go," Underground said hurriedly before turning his attention to the business at hand.

David wanted to be careful, so he called in some insurance. "Joe-Joe," he said. "Fatou is stuck in Brooklyn and it's a madhouse. I'm on my way to pick her up in your squatter. She's on Fulton Street not far from the Metro. Tell your peoples to look out for both of us. I have a funny feeling, man."

"No doubt," Joe-Joe yelled. "I'll get everybody on the same page. Be careful out there, nigga."

"True dat."

As David headed toward Fatou, she remained gripped by the flames, the smoke and the occasional groups of white people walking through downtown Brooklyn. Undeniably, they were all walking from Manhattan, since they couldn't catch a train or bus.

The blare of the sirens from fire trucks, ambulances, and police cars didn't do anything to calm her nerves. To the contrary, they made her feel more uneasy than she already did. *Gypsy Cab and*

Motherland Taxi would make a killing today, she thought. But in reality, both companies were busy worrying about other things.

Gypsy Cab had been on a frantic search for Lama. They hadn't heard a thing from him since his last transmission, moments before the second plane crashed into the south tower. They were unwilling to accept the obvious. Lama had perished in the catastrophe.

Motherland Taxi was on another mission. They were desperately seeking David and Fatou. They were focused only on cutting off the heads of their number one rivals in the drug game and not on making a killing driving hysterical Brooklynites back to their homes.

As Fatou paced nervously, David finally chirped her, speaking without waiting for a response.

"Start walking toward my brother's store. I'm coming around the corner right now."

Fatou breathed a sigh of relief as she hurried the rest of the block to the alarm shop.

As David slowed to open the door for her, a gunshot rang out. Fatou dove into the car, quickly closing the door.

"We're in the shit right now, baby, so straighten that shit the fuck up!" David screamed.

"But so many innocent people are dying right now. This is a tragedy for everyone."

"Fuck 'em," David shouted. "Do you see Salu's crew behind us, chasing us? Don't you know they're shooting at us? Pull yourself together and get your heat out. Chirp Joe-Joe too and let him know what's up."

Fatou pulled out the Desert Eagle 44 Magnum that Ken had given her and checked to make sure the clip was loaded.

"That's some power but use that shit1" David yelled, pointing toward the back seat.

Fatou looked behind her and saw an AK-47 with a ribbon of ammo hanging down from underneath it and a handheld rocket launcher. As she was looking, a bullet broke the back window. She screamed.

"Mothafuckas!" she shouted. "Y'all wanna play wit me, let's fucking play!"

She grabbed the rocket launcher and like a pro directed a shot at the first of the three taxis chasing them. Her first shot hit the cab head-on, causing it to flip into one of the other taxis. The third was able to swerve away from danger, but had to brake and back up before it could resume chasing David and Fatou. It lost vital time and distance.

Wanting to take advantage of the extra seconds, David told Fatou to put the weapons in her backpack. While she was doing so, he turned left off of Atlantic onto Bedford, and parked right before Fulton.

"Come on," he shouted. "Give me the bag and call Joe-Joe. Let him know to meet us in three minutes on DeKalb and Bedford."

"You're taking the tunnels?" Fatou asked. "You know there's gonna be people down there in all this shit."

"We can't worry about that," he said. "We're tryna save our asses."

David unlocked the manhole cover and they escaped from visibility as the third Motherland taxi driver pulled up behind Joe-Joe's squatter.

"Fuck!" he shouted, wondering where they could have disappeared.

After running two blocks in the tunnel, a group of emergency workers appeared about a block and a half behind David and Fatou.

"What the fuck are you doing down here?" they yelled in the distance.

"Don't look back," David shouted to Fatou. "And don't slow down. Fuck them niggas. We only got about a block left."

The emergency workers started chasing behind David and Fatou, but they weren't really running fast. They didn't have any weapons and were fearful of what might happen if they actually caught the trespassers.

As David and Fatou left the tunnels, one of the workers called in the breach of security to Underground and explained the situation.

"No, boss," he said "I don't know how they got in and I don't know how they got out. But they didn't bother anything as far as I can tell."

"Well, don't worry about it then," Underground said, sensing it was David and Fatou in the tunnels. "Go ahead and finish up what I asked you to do. I'll get another team to double check that area."

When Underground chirped David, he responded quickly.

"My bad, Underground," he said. "We're running for our fucking lives out here."

"Just be careful," he hollered. "And don't get caught in my tunnels. If you do, I don't know you."

David didn't respond, and Underground didn't anticipate that he would. David knew that Underground couldn't risk his career by vouching for him, and Underground knew that David couldn't risk his life by respecting his wishes and staying out of the tunnels.

David and Fatou didn't even get a half a block on DeKalb before they saw Joe-Joe and his posse driving toward them in a group of cars. One of Joe-Joe's soldiers opened the door for them, but David didn't get in.

"Nah, I need to holla at Joe-Joe," David said

When they jumped in Joe-Joe's car, he looked at them funny.

"That's what the fuck I'm talking about," David said "How the fuck could they recognize Fatou with this disguise on? Sumthin' ain't making fucking sense to me."

"I don't know, man," Joe-Joe replied. "Do you think you were followed?"

"If they woulda seen me by myself, they could'a been at me. Why the fuck would they wanna wait until both of us were together?"

No one answered the question because no one knew the answer. The four cars continued to drive slowly down the streets of Brooklyn.

Joe-Joe pointed out to his captain and general the snipers he had stationed on rooftops throughout the borough.

"With all the chaos," he said, "I wanted to make sure that we're ready for anything and everything."

"I see your work, nigga," David said, sounding impressed.

"This shit has to stop," Fatou said.

"What the fuck are you talking about?" David and Joe-Joe asked her simultaneously.

"Since you're ready for their asses, David and I can act like bait to draw those bastards out. Let's get rid of these mothafuckas once and for all."

"I'm wit that," Joe-Joe said.

"It sounds dangerous, but it can work," David added, co-signing Joe-Joe's endorsement of the plan. "But your snipers have to be on point to pick those mothafuckas off if they get too close."

"You ain't said nothing but a word," Joe- Joe said before pulling out his two-way radio. "Y'all niggas stand by," he shouted into the radio. "We're about to put some mothafuckas outta their misery. Be on y'all p's and q's, and I'll let y'all know what's up in a minute."

"So we're really gonna do this?" Fatou asked.

"It sounds like a plan to me, baby," David said. "Don't be scared now. It was your idea, remember?"

"I ain't scared," Fatou said matter-of-factly. "I've always been built for this shit. Salu and his squad are about to find that out the hard way."

"You don't even know the half of it," David said, taking out his Nextel to chirp Sarge and Rottweiler.

"Yo," Rottweiler answered.

"Are y'all niggas still in Manhattan?" David asked.

"Yeah, man," Rottweiler said. "That little shindig that Ricco had last night was off the hook."

"Where's that nigga at now?" David asked.

"He's probably sleeping in a pile of throw up with all that shit he drank last night," Rottweiler said, laughing.

"What about Sarge?" David asked.

"That nigga's out of it, too."

"Well, wake their asses up," David said. "Tell one of Ricco's bitches to make some fucking coffee. I'll hit you back in exactly five minutes. And y'all need to be totally alert to hear what the fuck's going down."

"No doubt, nigga," Rottweiler said. "I'm on it."

"What's that about?" Fatou asked.

"You know me, I like insurance," David replied evasively.

Five minutes later David chirped Ricco.

"Yo," Ricco answered, sounding sluggish.

"Mothafucka, have you had your coffee?" David snapped angrily.

"I'm good," Ricco said.

"Man, we ain't got time to be bullshittin'," David said. "Wake that ass up...Is Sarge there?"

"Yo," Sarge responded in the distance while Ricco held in the button on his Nextel.

"Y'all mothafuckas better get y'all shit together," David said. "Drink some coffee, and I'll call y'all niggas back in three minutes. And y'all better be bright eyed and fucking bushy tailed."

David shut the phone down and looked at Joe-Joe.

"Take us back to DeKalb and Bedford so we can pick up your squatter. We have to split up and lure these mothafuckas outta hiding."

"I want a scooter," Fatou said emphatically.

"We gotta stick together, boo," David said.

"I'll ride alongside you, but I'll be on the sidewalk," she said. "I feel more at home on a scooter."

David gave Joe-Joe a look, signifying he agreed with Fatou, so Joe-Joe chirped his cousin that everyone called Pretty Tony.

"Yo," Pretty Tony answered.

"I need to get a scooter right away. But it's gonna have some battle scars when it's over with," Joe-Joe said.

"True dat," Tony responded. "Just come through."

Joe-Joe drove by Tony's to get the scooter. When he saw Tony, he wanted him to follow him.

"Yo, dog," Joe-Joe said. "Follow me to DeKalb and Bedford. I want you to ride with me when they get out."

"Word, son," Tony shouted eagerly. "We about to get it the fuck in. That's what the fuck I'm talking about."

When Joe-Joe pulled up beside his squatter, David jumped out and immediately chirped Ricco.

"Yo," Ricco answered, more lively.

"You got your game face on, nigga?" David asked.

"True," Ricco answered.

"What about Sarge? Is his thumb still up his ass?" David asked.

"Nah, I'm good," Sarge answered.

"Well, listen up. I want y'all to lock Manhattan the fuck down. Rottweiler, you take all of Central Park. Sarge, you take the Lower East Side, near the United Nations to the bottom of the park near Grand Army Plaza. Ricco, you basically have Midtown, the Garment District, and the Theater District. Y'all got survival packs on you, right?"

"Yeah," the three lieutenants answered in unison.

"Then Ricco, you need to get the connect at my2way.com to call all your soldiers with the code. Let them know that Rottweiler is in command in Central Park and Sarge has the Lower East Side. Then make sure they put their two-way radios on the right channels. Rott, you got the park on channel two; Sarge, the Lower East Side will be on channel three; and Ricco, your area will be on channel four. I'll be on channel one so I can hear y'all. Get as many of your soldiers up on roofs as you can without being caught by hotta. You know it's a fucking madhouse out there. One last thing…Rott and Sarge, y'all are in Ricco's back yard, so show him respect. He's in charge of the operation in Manhattan."

"True," the two brothers both answered.

"Alright, I'm out," David said. "I'll hit you back in fifteen, Ricco. Everything should be set up by then."

"Wait...what are we doing after that?" Sarge asked.

"Just get set the hell up and wait for Ricco to tell you," David snapped. "Ricco, like I said, I'll hit you in fifteen."

Thirteen minutes later, David was standing in the shadows near Joe-Joe's squatter. Fatou was beside him sitting on a scooter.

"Give me a kiss, baby," David said, walking up to Fatou.

He grabbed her tightly like he didn't want to let her go, then planted the most passionate kiss Fatou had ever had on her lips.

"Look at me," David whispered, exploring Fatou's eyes with his.

Fatou lifted her head to meet David's eyes. She saw a seriousness that's she'd never seen.

David reached into his back pocket and pulled out a ring.

He placed it on Fatou's finger.

"It's not worth much cheddar, but it was my grandmother's," he said. "I want you to have it."

"This is the most precious gift you've ever given me, David," Fatou said, tearing up.

"Well, no matter what happens here today," David said, "I want you to know that I love you. I really, really love you. Never forget that."

"Do you know that you've never said that to me without joking around before?" Fatou asked. "You're making me cry."

"You can cry later when we have sex on the beach after all this shit is over," David said. "Now we gotta go handle this business."

David sighed, then picked up his Nextel to chirp Ricco.

"Yo," Ricco responded.

"Are the snipers on the roofs?" David asked.

"All throughout Manhattan."

"Do y'all have wheels?"

"We got hella niggas wit SUV's, squatters, scooters and bikes. And they all have their two-ways on 'em."

"That's what's up," David said. "All right, here's the plan. Any and every fucking Motherland taxi you see in Manhattan gets bum-rushed. Don't take no fucking prisoners or ask any questions. Oh, and one more thing."

"What's that?" Ricco asked.

"Be careful out there."

David put his Nextel up, then gave Joe-Joe the signal on his two-way radio.

"You and me have the only radios that can hear everything that's going on in Manhattan and Brooklyn," David told Fatou. "Be safe, baby."

David got in the squatter, and Fatou put her helmet on. They drove off in search of their enemies.

CHAPTER TWENTY-FOUR

The Aftermath

For many hours, Salu watched the television reports about the destruction of the twin towers. And for the same number of hours, he hadn't heard from his soldiers in the field.

One by one, his drivers were being picked off, and it seemed that there was nothing he could do about it. His enemy was too organized and his plan appeared unbeatable.

"We have to do something quick," Salu yelled at his cousin, Jesse. "We're moving to plan B."

"What's plan B?" Jesse asked.

"Retreat," Salu yelled. "Tell everyone to retreat. I need time to think. We can't lose our whole squad."

Jesse radioed the remaining drivers and told them to get out of their cabs and take refuge in the nearest restaurants and coffee shops.

"Don't worry about your cabs," Jesse said. "They will be safe. Our enemies don't want your cabs, they want your asses."

"I think I may have something," Salu said after Jesse finished dispatching the information. "Let's grab their loved ones. Kidnap them. That'll throw them off track for at least a while until we can regroup and get organized?"

"That's risky," Jesse said. "David and Fatou don't have any family here. And Fatou would probably pay us to kill her husband, Lama. So he's not valuable to us. The two of them aren't close to anyone else—just each other."

"That can't be right," Salu said. "There has to be somebody! Where's your Benedict Arnold? Maybe he can help us."

"I don't know," Jesse said. "Let me chirp him."

Jesse chirped his connection but got no acknowledgement. He tried him again four more times. Finally, he answered.

"What?" he asked, breathing hard. "Can't a nigga bust a fucking nut in peace, damn?"

"Nigga, all hell is breaking loose, so you gotta get your ass outta that pussy," Jesse hollered. "We need some information about who David and Fatou are close to. They're on a rampage and we've gotta slow them down. We're losing too many soldiers. If we kidnap a mothafucka, maybe that will slow their asses down."

"Neither one has family here," his connect answered. "and I can't think of anyone that they're close enough to to give a shit about."

"Think, motherfucker, think!" Jesse yelled. "What about that other bitch? You think she knows anything?"

"Other than how to suck a mean dick, I don't think she knows shit. She's been locked up, remember?"

His woman got mad at the statement and pushed him away before she hopped out of the bed. She lingered by the doorway before going downstairs and heard enough to get her moving.

"I have to warn my girl," she said to herself as she quickly put on her clothes, grabbed her purse, and tiptoed out the door.

She walked away quickly, taking out her cell phone and chirping her girlfriend repeatedly.

"I'm kind of busy right now," her girlfriend finally answered.

"I'm riding on a scooter."

"Well, pull over, bitch," she said. "This is too fucking important."

"Wait a sec...OK, what the fuck is it?" her girlfriend asked.

"It's Ken," she said. "He's fucking two-faced. He's on the phone right now talking to Salu's people. I think he's tryna set y'all up. They're gonna try to kidnap somebody you care about."

"Do you hear this?" Fatou asked David.

"Loud and fucking clear," he said.

"Natali, are you still with him?" Fatou asked.

"Hell, no!" she yelled. "For all I know, he could'a tried to kidnap my ass!"

"Well, go somewhere safe so we can send somebody to pick you up," Fatou said.

"No," Natali snapped. "I don't know who I can trust. I'm not going nowhere with anyone but you."

"But I can't get you. I'm on a scooter."

"I'll get her," David said. "I'll follow you, and she can ride with me."

While David and Fatou were racing to meet Natali, Ken was creeping around his lay-low spot in Brooklyn looking for her.

"I'm sorry, girl. Stop acting so fucking sensitive," he said as he looked in closets and anywhere else she could hide.

"Oh shit!" he exclaimed. Her clothes and purse were gone. "The bitch left!"

He quickly chirped Jesse.

"Yo, you think of sumthin', mothafucka?" Jesse asked.

"Nah, man," Ken said. "Natali left while we were fucking talking."

"Do you think she heard anything?" Jesse asked.

"She had to."

"How could you let her leave, man? You gotta go find that bitch."

"It don't matter now," Ken said. "I'm sure she's already run her fucking mouth to Fatou. I gotta get the fuck outta here. If Fatou knows, David knows. If David knows, the whole crew knows."

"Calm down, mothafucka, and think," Jesse said.

"Fuck you, nigga!" Ken snapped and put his Nextel away. He ran to the window and peeked out the curtains. He didn't know what had happened to the twin towers, and the extra activity on the streets made him even more frazzled.

"What the fuck is going on? Let me get the fuck outta here!" he said out loud.

Ken quickly stuffed a duffle bag with his heat and all the money he had stashed in the house. He dashed down the steps two at a time and opened the door, ready to disappear into the crowds when he heard a familiar voice.

"Going somewhere?" David asked.

"Yo, what up, nigga?" Ken said, trying to play it cool. "I need to take care of sumthin' real fast. What's poppin'?"

"Don't play with me, mothafucka," David snapped as Fatou emerged from her hiding place and hit Ken on the head with the butt of her gun, knocking him out cold.

"Let's put him in the trunk," Fatou said, grabbing his arms from behind.

"What?" she asked when David didn't move.

"I'm sorry," David said, snapping out of it. "I just can't believe that my nigga would turn against me like this. I never would'a thought some shit like this would happen with him. This is fucked up."

"I agree, David, but we gotta get the fuck outta here and stop drawing attention to ourselves. Let's get this nigga in the car."

They put Ken in the trunk and tied his hands and feet before closing it. David drove off in the squatter with Natali riding shotgun, and Fatou drove off next to him on the scooter.

"So what did you hear?" he asked Natali.

"I'm not sure," she said. "I think they're tryna figure out who's important to you and Fatou. My guess is they wanna kidnap somebody. Whatever it is that y'all are doing, they think if they kidnap somebody, they can make you stop."

"Those fucking pussies," David hissed. "They can't just man the fuck up and fight like troopers? They wanna put civilians in the shit."

"Can I ask you something, David?"

"What? You know Fatou is riding right alongside us."

"It's nothing like that," she said "And you already know I wouldn't play my girl out."

"Uhm hmm."

"Anyway," she snapped. "Why the fuck are all these white mothafuckas in Brooklyn?"

"You don't know?"

"Know what?"

"Some terrorist mothafuckas hijacked some planes and flew them into the World Trade Center. Both of the twin towers got fucked up. Manhattan is locked the fuck down right now. Where the fuck have you been? It's been on the news all fucking day."

"I was busy," she said.

"I bet you fucking was."

Natali rolled her eyes at David and didn't say anything else to him the rest of the trip.

When they arrived at David's, Redd was waiting for him in his ride. Redd got out of the car immediately when David pulled up.

"What the fuck were you saying, nigga?" he asked David soon as he got out of the squatter.

"I'm saying that your boy, Ken, is a bitch," David hissed. "Help me get his ass out the trunk."

They dragged him into the house and threw him on the carpet.

"Shit!" Ken barked as the pain woke him up.

"What the fuck's up, nigga?" Redd asked. "I've been hearing some shit that don't sound too good."

"I don't know what you're talking about," Ken lied. "What kinda game are y'all niggas playing? What the fuck am I tied up for?"

"You're tied up cuz you're a bitch," Redd yelled. "How can you sell out the squad?"

"Fuck you. I ain't sell shit out. That mothafucka right there is the only nigga that sold out the fucking squad," Ken hissed, looking at David.

David got close Ken and kicked him in the side.

"Mothafucka, all I did is put paper in your broke ass pockets," David shouted. "You're the one here without no fucking loyalty."

"Yeah, blame me," Ken said sarcastically. "I been wit ya ass since day one. But what do you do? Your ass gets pussy whipped and you smack me in the face over some bitch! Me and all your fucking lieutenants."

"You turned on me over a piece of ass? Ken? A piece of fucking ass?"

"This ain't about pussy, nigga," Ken said. "This is about you giving away our organization over a piece of pussy. We were a group of tight mothafuckas that never let a bitch come between us. You threw salt in the mothafuckin' game."

Fatou screamed and headed toward Ken.

David grabbed her before she could reach him. "Let me handle this," he said. "Can you and Natali leave us alone?"

Fatou looked at David sideways.

"This is fucking business," he snapped.

Fatou started walking up the stairs and Natali followed her.

When they were out of earshot, David whispered to Redd. "Is Joe-Joe almost here?"

"He should be."

"Well, let's finish dealing with this shit when he gets here."

They waited for a half an hour, and Joe-Joe still hadn't shown up. David decided to chirp him.

"Yo, nigga," Joe-Joe answered.

"Where the fuck are you? We're waiting for your ass."

"I'm in the heat of battle, man. We're storming Motherland's fucking dispatch. We're taking all those mothafuckas out!"

"Man, later for them pussies," David hissed. "We told you we had some serious business to discuss over here."

"I'm in the shit right now, man," Joe-Joe said. "What the fuck do you want me to do?"

"That depends. What's the situation over there?"

"Give us about five minutes, and these mothafuckas will be history," Joe-Joe replied.

"Well, snatch that fucking pussy ass Salu up and bring his ass here. I need his ass here like yesterday."

"Understood," Joe-Joe said before putting his Nextel away.

"I guess we're gonna make this mothafucka sweat," David said as he turned to Redd.

"Nigga, fuck you," Ken shouted.

"Cover his fucking mouth up," David ordered. "I don't wanna hear shit right now from this bitch ass nigga."

David walked up the stairs and left Redd to handle Ken.

"Don't take none of that shit to heart," David told Fatou after he walked in the bedroom.

"I told you them niggas would feel like that," she said.

"It don't have shit to do with that," he said. "Yeah, the mothafucka's jealous. But he ain't jealous of your position. He's jealous cuz I'm fucking you and he's not. Now that's a bitch ass reason to turn on your crew."

"David!" It was Underground on the Nextel.

"Yo, what's up, man?" he asked Underground. "Excuse me a sec, Fatou."

"Hey, I'm not gonna be running all around this fucking house," she snapped.

"Nah, I don't mean you have to leave," he said. "A nigga can't have good manners and shit? I said that cuz I stopped talking to you and started another con…"

"I know what's going on," Underground interrupted David.

"What do you mean?"

"The media is focused on the towers, but I know about your fucking war with Salu!" he shouted "His dispatch is just a couple blocks away from the mayor's office, for Christ's sake!"

"That little situation is almost over with," David said.

"Well, I hope you don't think that's the end of it," Underground said. "There's gonna be a big investigation. You think you had to lay low before? You ain't seen shit yet!"

"You think mothafuckas know who I am?" David asked.

"You're killing mothafuckas left and right. There're taxis all over the city with their windows shot out. The city's being hijacked in the middle of the afternoon! Do you think it fucking matters if they know who the fuck you are? Heads are gonna roll until somebody figures out who the fuck you are."

"I feel you," David said. "Well, let me try to put an end to this shit. Can I chirp you later?"

"Yeah, you can chirp me," Underground said, frustrated. "But make sure you end your fucking war before you do."

David didn't answer. He turned to Fatou sadly.

"This is a sad fucking day," he said. "You know what I have to do, right?"

"What?"

"Don't act dumb, baby...you know."

"You have to take Underground out so he won't identify us?" she said. "And Eric and Poncho?"

"Nah," David answered. "He doesn't know Poncho. But Eric and Underground do know each another. We can't take one of them out without taking out the other."

"It is sad. You're right," Fatou said, tearing up.

"Yeah. This day's gonna end with me having three less friends than

I started with. I guess I just have to chalk it up to the game."

Natali walked to the room and stood in the door.

"Joe-Joe's here," she said.

"Thanks," both David and Fatou replied to her glumly.

"Well there's no sense in putting it off," David said. "We gotta do what we gotta do."

CHAPTER TWENTY-FIVE

Cleanup Time

After nightfall, everyone left David's house in two cars and drove to to the Verrazano Bridge. Joe-Joe and Redd held Ken over the side by his legs.

"It didn't have to be like this, man," Joe-Joe said tauntingly. "Why'd you have to turn your back on your homies?"

"Fuck y'all," Ken yelled. "Just get this fucking shit over with." Ken spit toward Fatou.

"Are you happy, you little bitch?" he hissed. "This is all your fucking fault."

"Let his ass go," David snapped. "I'm tired of hearing his turncoat-ass mouth."

"No," Fatou yelled, walking over to where Ken was hanging.

Before anyone knew what had happened, she pulled a straight razor out of her purse and sliced his throat.

"I said to call me Miss Bitch," she hissed sinisterly. "Now y'all can drop that motherfucker."

She pulled out a handkerchief and wiped her hands. Then she threw the knife and handkerchief over the side of the bridge.

Lastly, she squirted some sanitizer on her hands and rubbed them together until they were dry.

David, Redd and Joe-Joe looked at Fatou in astonishment. Once again, her uncompromising wrath took them all by surprise.

"Let's go," she said.

Natali greeted her with a nervous stare.

"You killed Chyna, didn't you?" she asked.

"I can't remember," she answered. "It was either me or David. But she was a snake in the grass. She robbed me and you of a lot of money. She had you thinking that I turned my back on you. The bitch got what she fucking deserved."

"Well, I don't know if this means anything to you," Natali said, "but I never flirted or anything with David."

"What are you telling me that for?" Fatou asked.

"You have a very bad temper," Natali said. "I don't want to have you thinking anything that's gonna make me end up in a river."

"I love you, Natali," Fatou said. "You don't have to worry about that."

The two of them hugged while David looked at them in the rearview mirror.

David and Fatou went into the bedroom while Natali, Redd and Joe-Joe remained downstairs.

"It's time for part two of the plan," David said.

"I guess it is," Fatou agreed.

David chirped Underground and got him to meet him Brooklyn.

"That's real suspicious," Underground said. "They're only letting emergency vehicles cross any of the bridges into Manhattan."

"Man, you have the biggest fucking juice card around," David said, gassing him up. "But if you feel like that, why don't you get Eric to take you across Wallabout Bay in his boat? I know he has clearance too."

"Yeah, that'll work," Underground said "Now what is this you asked me to do?"

"Pick up a package for me," David said, smiling, believing his plan would work.

"I ain't fucking with no drugs," Underground objected.

"It's not drugs," David said. "It's Salu and his punk ass cousin, Jesse. I hid them in that warehouse we used to meet at in Manhattan."

"And what am I supposed to do with them in Brooklyn?" Underground asked.

"Nothing, we'll handle all that shit ourselves," David said, ending the phone call.

About an hour later David, Redd and Joe-Joe stood staring over the side of the Brooklyn-Queens Expressway not far from the Brooklyn Bridge. Redd was holding the handheld rocket launcher, waiting for the signal.

In the distance, they could see lights approaching in the water. David pulled out his binoculars to get a closer look. It was definitely Underground and Eric riding in the boat with a tied up Salu and Jesse.

David's two enemies were wearing Islamic garb and made to look questionable. David heard on the news how law enforcement had started profiling anyone who appeared to be of Middle Eastern descent.

"That's them," David said. "Are you ready?"

"Like a mothafucka," Redd said.

He steadied himself and fired a shot at the boat. The rocket hit the boat head-on, causing it to blow up. A red fireball lit up the sky.

"That's the end of that," David said, trying to disguise his sorrow for having to kill Underground and Eric. "Y'all can take me back to Fatou's wheels. I'll holla at y'all later. It's been a long day."

When they got back to David's house, Natali excused herself. "I know y'all have to talk," Natali said. "Do you mind if I lay down for a while?"

"Go ahead," David answered. "But don't get too comfortable. We ain't gonna be here too long."

Natali walked away, leaving David and Fatou alone. They sat on the couch and cuddled.

"This feels good," Fatou said.

"But you know we can't be here too long."

"Don't remind me."

"So now you see how fucked up the game can be," David said, pausing to give Fatou a peck on the lips. "I've been dealing with this shit for years. It's a wonder I can even function normally anymore."

"Let me ask you a question," Fatou said. "And don't lie."

"What?" David asked suspiciously.

"Do you wanna fuck Natali," she asks. "I mean, I see the way you look at her."

"I'll answer your question if you answer mine," David said.

"I gotta hear this," Fatou said, laughing. "What?"

"Did you wanna fuck Ken?"

"I just bodied fucking Ken," she hissed. "What the fuck are you talking about?"

"You bodied him because he turned on us," David said. "But

before he turned, did you wanna fuck him?"

"I'm not that kinda girl," she said.

"What the fuck does that mean?"

"I'm old school. I would never sleep with one of your friends."

"But did you want to?"

"How could I want to if he was your friend?"

"We're not getting anywhere with this shit," David said "Let's start packing. You know we have to leave."

"And where are we going?"

"Any suggestions?" he asked.

"I don't care," she said. "As long as we're together, I don't care where we are."

"How are we gonna get Natali back to Harlem?" David asked.

"You're still worried about her," Fatou said sarcastically. "But I ain't mad at you. She is very pretty. Just do me one favor."

"And what's that?" David asked, laughing.

"Just don't lie to me about it and try to be discreet. I don't wanna hear anything about it."

"You're funny," he said.

"I'm not finished," Fatou said, interrupting. "And a fuck is a fuck. Don't ever take her out or anything like that. Pay your money at the escort service like anybody else."

"You're funny as shit," he said.

"Are we clear, nigga?"

"Whatever."

"Deny the shit as much as you want as long as we're fucking clear."

Fatou kissed David on the mouth, then got up. "I'm going to pack.

I'll come down with Natali when I'm done so you can get your shit together and we can get the fuck outta here."

Fatou walked away leaving David sitting on the couch thinking about everything his squad had survived over the last few months, knowing they wouldn't have made it if it wasn't for Fatou.

My baby came here from West Africa and took New York City by storm, David thought to himself, smiling before he nodded off to sleep, safe, sound, and poised for his next battle.

EPILOGUE

Fatou and David took a romantic vacation in Kingston, Jamaica, David's hometown, so that they could clear their heads and spend some quality time together.

Before leaving, David ensured that their remaining lieutenants — Ricco, Joe-Joe, Redd, Donny, Sarge and Rottweiler — would be holding down the fort until they returned. Fatou had Natali run the escort service and check cashing business while she was away.

Fatou enjoyed snuggling with David on the flight but hated the extra precautions that were being taken after the terrorists' attacks. They waited in line for hours as airport personnel inspected luggage, shoes, passports, everything.

As David slept, Fatou thought about the conversation she'd had with Mati regarding how Allah had said that everything would be taken away from her if she kept up her unfavorable lifestyle. She also wondered how David would react to her leaving the game now that he had chosen her as his successor in the event that anything happened to him.

I just want to be happy, Lord, she prayed. *I just want someone to love me.*

She snuggled tightly with David and tried to put everything out of her mind. Slowly, thoughts of drugs and money and death were replaced with thoughts of water skiing and sunbathing naked on the beach.

She thought about Lama and his death at the scene of the World Trade Center attacks. She thought of Patra raising Lama's children. She thought of having David's children.

They were about to be a world away from the rough streets of New York. So she put her mind on hold and didn't think about all the battles she knew she would face when she returned.

Will I be ready when I come back to New York? she thought to herself.

The better question was, would New York be ready for her?

FATOU

Returns to Harlem

Part II of the saga of a West African girl in Harlem

A new novel by

Sidi

PROLOGUE

December 13, 2001

New York City

Fatou La Princesse was sitting inside her boyfriend David's plush Jamaica,Queens brownstone, crying uncontrollably while trying to hold a conversation with two of New York City's finest.

To the detectives, the house was a mansion. Dt. Sergeant Peterson glared at the huge fish tank built into the living room wall, thinking it probably cost more to build than the row home he grew up in.

"There's no sign of forced entry, ma'am," Peterson said, "so your boyfriend must have known the perpetrators."

So your boyfriend must have known the perpetrators...so your boyfriend must have known the perpetrators.

Dt. Peterson's words lingered in Fatou's mind hours after he had left the scene. David was completely paranoid, and he certainly would not have let someone into his home that he was beefing with. Besides, with all the warnings and close calls they had had before visiting David's hometown of Kingston, Fatou was sure her man would've had his heat ready if anything looked suspicious.

"This means that one of my lieutenants must have done this shit," Fatou said to herself.

"Did you say something?" Fatou's best friend, Natali, yelled from the kitchen.

"No. I was talking to myself."

Natali sighed before placing her cup of coffee on the table and walking into the living room to join Fatou.

"You know it's been a couple weeks," Natali said. "You're barely eating. Your drop-dead figure has done just that—dropped dead. Pretty soon people will be wondering if you're using that shit you're selling."

"Is this your way of making me feel better?"

"It's called tough love, Fatou. How many motherfuckers do you think David killed in his life? I'm sure you know what karma means."

"Fuck karma, and fuck you!"

"Fuck me, Fatou?" Natali asked. "Fuck me? Since when did you start saying fuck you to me? I've been in your corner since day one, remember?"

"Well, be in my corner and stop badgering me."

"I'm not badgering you, girlfriend. I'm just telling you that some risks come with the territory. When you live a cutthroat life, you can expect to have a cutthroat death. I don't know why hustlers get so bent out of shape when one of their homies die. It's the t-shirts, the soap on cars, the retaliations on everything moving. Rest in peace! Give me a fucking break. Somebody needed to tell the mothers of all the people your man killed that their kids should rest in peace."

"Leave me the fuck alone, Natali!" Fatou shouted.

"I'm not bothering you, girl. I'm just giving you my opinion."

"Well, when I want your opinion, I'll give it to you. Matter of fact, take my keys and get the fuck out. I won't have your ass in my man's house another second talking shit!"

"Look, girl…" Natali started.

"Not another fucking second! Get the fuck out, bitch! Get the fuck out!"

Natali walked out the door and Fatou slammed it behind her before she broke down in tears and crumbled to the floor.

"Why? Why? Why? Why? Why?!" she screamed.

Two hours later Fatou woke up. She had fallen asleep while still lying on the carpet just in front of the door.

"Forget about everything I said I was going to do," she said. "Forget about leaving the game. I'm gonna find out which one of our lieutenants killed David if it's the last thing I do.

"If motherfuckers don't know what no justice, no peace means, they're about to find out. David was the only thing that kept me from losing it half the time. But he's gone now, so what does that mean? Whatever the fuck I wanna do, I'm gonna do. And God help the motherfucker who's behind this shit. Ain't a corner on this earth they can run to. Miss Bitch is back, and she's on a fucking rampage. Let me get up and get my shit together. My fucking vacation is over. It's time to send other motherfuckers on vacations—permanent ones."

Mandingo
The Golden Boy

A new novel by

Sidi

PROLOGUE

Denise Jackson

January 2003

Although I'd been with boys before in high school, that's just what they were—boys. And none of them had the length and girth of the grown-ass man standing in front of me. I swear to God, he has to be longer than a ruler and wide enough to fuck up some of my internal shit. Still, I have to go through with this. That's the only way I'm gonna know if he'll be to women what I am to men—the best damned sex money can buy.

I'm scared to ask him to continue taking his clothes off. The bulge in his boxers is very impressive, and I'm afraid his dick is gonna spring out and knock me into the wall or something. To allay my fears, I try to concentrate on a different part by turning my attention to the rest of his body.

The muscles ripping out of his chest and arms make him look like a Mr. Universe contestant. Yet he's not so diesel that it's a turn-off. His six-pack stomach and his thighs are so lean and developed he could race against a horse. He's a strong stallion, alright. The stud-muffin every woman dreams about but never has the chance to experience. I'm about to audition him to make sure he's capable of making their wildest dreams come true. Well, at least those women who can afford him.

"Do you want me to take these off?" he asks in a heavily accented voice.

I feel the lump in my throat grow larger.

"Sure, sweetie," I answer as calmly as I can. "Where'd you say you were from? Africa?" I ask him even though I already know the answer.

"I am from the Mandingo tribe," he replies proudly.

"Nigga, you ain't never lied!"

As he pulls his boxers down, I see it's going to be worse than I thought. He's got a good twelve inches and he's only half hard.

Goddamn! I say to myself. *Some serious fucking is about to go down.*

CHAPTER ONE

Mandingo

As Denise steps out of her dress revealing a silky Victoria's Secret chemise, all of my problems become irrelevant. All that matters to me are the ample breasts straining to stay inside her negligee. Her thighs are thicker than those of any of the pale faces that walk the halls of Columbia University and her butt is a sight for sore eyes. I look up into the air and thank Allah for also giving Denise the brains to make it into one of the toughest schools in America.

I've been lusting after Denise since she befriended me a year ago when I first arrived here. I guess the connection that blacks in America have with each other kicked in when she saw me. Back then, she didn't know I was African. I guess all she cared about was that I was one of the few dark faces in the lily-white crowd. I didn't care what the reason was, though. All that mattered to me was that she was the prettiest woman I'd ever seen in my life and she was talking to me. Just a few words and I was making plans for our wedding and honeymoon, especially our honeymoon.

Regrettably for me, I learned that there were a few problems with the plans I was making for Denise . First and foremost, she is what Americans call a carpet-muncher, meaning that she is attracted to other women. That difficulty alone loomed largely enough but, additionally, her occupation was another disqualifying factor. To put it bluntly, she was a high priced call girl, and I was a broke college student. We were definitely not a match made in heaven.

Even though Denise and I became close, I always beat her upside her head with questions about why with all that she had going for herself would she still decide to degrade herself by selling her body. She'd always say, "You're my boy but your broke-ass is just like all those other niggas trying to get some pussy for free." She had a point, but I still wasn't wrong. There are a million things a woman can do besides prostituting herself. All it takes is a little hard work.

Damn. Now I feel like a hypocrite. I'm talking all of that trash about Denise but the only reason she's about to give me some is because she wants to make sure I'll please the rich clients she has lined up for me. But hell, any excuse to be with this bombshell is good enough for me. She has a body like Vivica Fox and a face like Stacey Dash. Allah forgive me for the illicit acts

I'm about to commit but I don't know a man who's strong enough to withstand her charms. I'm so glad Karen Steinberg told her about our little run-in.

Karen was a country girl from Kentucky who put the C, O, U, N, T, R, and Y in the word. I swear if you look in Webster's you'll see a picture of her smiling face right next to country. But I ain't mad at her though.

For one, she's one of the smartest people to ever graduate from high school in her state. How else do you think she got here? Poor white trash can't afford this place just like we can't.

The other reason I ain't mad at her is she looks like a blond-haired, blue-eyed Daisy Duke. Keep it real, your eyes are glued to the TV, too, whenever you can catch the Dukes of Hazard reruns on Spike TV. What man wouldn't be lusting after Daisy Duke? Not to say that I was lusting after Karen Steinberg, but I noticed her.

Karen Steinberg has breasts similar to Denise 's and long, flowing legs. She's pretty much the classic white bombshell. Kinda tall and slim with big titties. She does have a little phatty for a white girl. Yet, still, like I said, I wasn't all big on her. She stepped to me.

I was in the cafeteria one day when she came in. A couple of the resident loudmouths started talking trash to her after she grabbed her food so I motioned for her to sit with me. I guess I just felt bad for her. And I knew that the only reason they were clowning with her in the first place was because she wouldn't sleep with any of them. Nevertheless, I was certain that they would calm that shit down once she sat with me and I wasn't wrong. Soon as Karen Steinberg's ass hit the chair all of her hecklers became mute church mice. The resulting silence gave us the perfect opportunity to hold our own little private conversation.

Karen wanted to know what it was like in Africa. She asked if we still ran around hunting bears with spears. Although I thought that was an ignorant, racist question, I also found it amusing that those myths still exist.

I didn't answer her, Instead, I asked her if she still wrestled the pigs in the slop pen. She started laughing. I guess she got my point because she changed the subject.

She asked me why blacks got mad about some myths and were quick to cling to others. Of course I didn't know what she meant so I asked her to be more specific. Her response made me fall out.

She said, "You got mad about me asking you if you were a hunter but if I asked you if you had a big, African dick you would have been quick to agree with me."

After I finished laughing, I said, "That's because your first assumption was ridiculous but your second is true."

"Yeah, right," she said. "Everyone knows that the myth about black guys being bigger than white guys. It's legend."

"Nah, baby girl, it's an actual fact," I said proudly.

"Well, show me," she replied.

"What? You can't be serious."

"I'm dead serious," she said, unaware that that was the beginning of the end for her.

We went back to my dorm room and I put on some reggae. I thought Shabba Ranks was appropriate for the moment.

I started gyrating my body to the rhythms of Shabba as I undressed. I could tell that she was more than impressed with my body. After watching her stare at my chest and arms, I decided to rub some baby oil on them to make them glisten. I planned to intensify whatever pleasure this naive white girl was feeling as she lusted over my African features. And, truth be told, she had know idea what the fact of my being of the Mandingo tribe meant. She was definitely about to find out.

When I finally got down to taking off my boxers she gasped. "Is that thing real?" she asked.

I grabbed her arm and led her to me.

"Come on over here, girl, and find out."

She started stroking my dick while she kissed my neck. I could feel myself starting to elongate. Soon I would be at my full fifteen inches.

I smiled when her kisses went from my chest to my stomach. She looked in amazement at my python and muttered repeatedly, "Oh my God."

"Don't pray to Jah now, baby girl," I said. "Your mouth got you into all of this trouble you're in."

I got tired of playing with Karen Steinberg so I finally grabbed the top of her shoulders and guided her down to her knees.

"So, what are you going to do with this big African dick?" I asked her. Without responding, she showed me.

Believe me when I tell you, the myth about white girls knowing how to suck a golf ball through a straw is not a lie. Come to think of it, a redneck, country-ass white girl has even more skills than a regular one. I didn't know that then, but I do now. But I'll tell you about that later. Let me get back to Karen Steinberg and her talented mouth.

At first, she kissed the tip. It was like a series of quick pecks on the lips. But instead of it being my lips, it was the round, sensitive head of my dick.

Out of nowhere, she glanced up at me with the most devilish grin I've ever seen then she took the plunge. She skillfully took me inside her mouth and wrapped her lips around my dick as if she was giving it a bear hug. All the while, she stared deeply into my eyes.

There's something about a woman looking in your eyes while

she's pleasuring you orally. It's a reassurance that lets you know that she knows exactly what she's doing and who she's doing it to. And she was doing it to death.

She bobbed her head up and down as her mouth made slurping sounds each time she swished her tongue.

"Suck that big, African dick!" I demanded, encouraging her.

I doubt that she needed my encouragement, though. She was already going to town.

When her oral prowess started to feel too good, I wanted her to stop. I wasn't going to let her get away with just a Lewinsky. I wanted to pound her white pussy for all it was worth, especially because of the dumb shit she said to me earlier.

"Are you ready for me to ruin that white hole?" I asked.

She started shaking her head and mumbling through slurps on my dick. Yet, that wasn't enough for me. I wanted to hear her speak in plain English.

I pulled my dick out of her mouth roughly and started smacking her in the face with it.

"Beat me with that black dick, Mandingo," she said while catching her breath. "Beat me with it."

I had never understood why my uncle Moriba cheated on his wives even though he had three of them and therefore shouldn't have been bored with any of them. But as I was severely degrading and disrespecting Karen Steinberg, the reasons started to become clear to me.

I would never be seriously involved with Karen Steinberg. But she's a master at sucking dick so I wouldn't mind letting her do it to me again. I just didn't want her to feel like I thought she was special.

She had given me some oral sex that made me go berserk. And I was about to get some white pussy for the first time. I didn't care about Karen Steinberg so told myself I could do whatever I wanted with her wothout explaining myself. She really didn't fucking matter to me then. So I fucked the shit out of her that day.

Karen Steinberg was every man's fantasy—a piece of ass you could do whatever the hell you wanted with none of the bitching and moaning you usually had to deal with. She was the perfect "other woman" to me. She could have been any of the women my uncle Moriba cheated on his wife with. But that day, she was my first victim at Columbia.

After smacking her repeatedly in the face with my dick, I was finally ready to fuck her.

"Turn around," I yelled at her.

"You're too big for that way," she said with pleading eyes.

"I'm just a man about to prove that certain myths are not myths. Just turn the fuck around and take what I'm about to give to you."

Karen Steinberg remained on her knees while she turned

around slowly...cautiously...deliberately.

I paused to stare briefly, somewhat in awe at how nice her ass was for a white girl, round and plump. It definitely wasn't a wide, board butt like other white chicks. It poked out just the way I like it.

After putting on my Magnum condom, I nudged forward to tease her with the tip for a moment. She rocked back eagerly. I knew that wouldn't last for long though. Her ass was about to run for the hills when I really started giving her the dick.

For fifteen minutes, I gave it to her an inch at a time. As every minute passed, I gave her another inch. By the time it reached ten minutes, she was ready to pass out. I was having none of that, though. I smacked her ass really hard until it turned red. I giggled to myself, pleased at how it wiggled like jelly. She looked back at me speechless. I could tell that she wanted to holler or scream or moan or at least tell me to stop smacking her ass so hard. My dick must have been killing her. Her breaths were caught somewhere in her throat. She wasn't able to make the minutest of sounds.

After I had made her take all of me, I started growing bored with the silence. I decided it was time to make Karen Steinberg get a sore throat.

I braced myself carefully behind her and grabbed her small waist tightly with both hands. I rammed myself into her as hard as I could. With each thrust I got more turned on by the way her ass was jiggling. Not to mention her whimpering had me really feeling myself. But it was still not enough.

I rocked back enough to totally remove myself from her then thrust myself back in. She let out a loud shriek.

At that point, I knew I had her where I wanted her so I started repeating the process of taking my dick out and thrusting it back in.

"Oh shit, Mandingo! Goddamn. Oh my damn. Fuck!"

Karen Steinberg was shouting out combinations of curse words I'd never heard before.

Yeah I thought. I was wearing her ass out.

I had no idea about Karen Steinberg's previous sex partners. But I will say that she had one of the tightest pussies I ever had. At the time, I thought that she was so tight because white men have little dicks. My experiences with other white girls after Karen Steinberg clued me in that it wasn't true. It was just her. With that little-ass pussy, I must have been killing her.

I rammed my dick in and out of Karen Steinberg for about ten minutes until her shit started to get to me. Then I put the whole thing inside of her and started grinding it as deep as I could. If I remember correctly, I think I felt my dick hit her kneecap. I don't fucking know how and I know I didn't care. All that mattered to me at the time was that she had some good-ass pussy.

I can't even say that her shit was good for a white girl. She could have been red, black, green or orange, it didn't matter. Her shit was popping. It may have been the best shot in my life. That's why I kept fucking her even after that night. And I'm glad she wanted more. I thought it would just be one and done after I degraded her the way I did.

When I felt myself getting ready to come, I pulled out of Karen Steinberg and pulled the rubber off. She sighed as if she felt instant relief then I started smacking her in the face with my dick again. Eventually, I shoved it in her mouth and started barking out commands.

"Suck this big, black dick you white whore," I yelled at her. "Suck it," I repeated over and over as she obliged me.

After a couple of slurps from her talented mouth, I think I shot a gallon of come into her mouth while holding the back of her head to ensure that she didn't move. Once the last drop came out, I relaxed and slumped backwards.

She started gagging like a five hundred pound man was choking her with both hands. Then she ran to the sink and continued to gag while simultaneously spitting into the sink. Finally, she stomped over to me and preceded to tear me a new asshole.

"You have some fucking big-ass balls, you freakin' African," she screamed. "Some big-ass balls."

"What the fuck is wrong with you?" I asked, pretending to be totally oblivious to her issue.

"You fucking come in my mouth? That's what you do? You fucking come in my mouth?"

"What do you mean?" I said. "If you weren't cool with it, why the hell did you let me finish? You should have pulled away."

"No. You should have pulled away like any other man who had some fucking respect for me would have done."

"But you liked it..."

"I liked it?" she said interrupting me. "You think I fucking liked it?"

"Yeah. That's what white girls do. Black girls front like they don't like it, but white girls will gladly swallow your cum."

"Well, this one won't," she yelled, scurrying around looking for her clothes.

Once I realized she was serious, I apologized over and over. But she wasn't beat.

"No, you meant to disrespect me, Mandingo, so why should I accept your apology?"

"Because I really am sorry."

"You're not sorry. If you were sorry, why did you laugh at me then?"

I'd almost forgotten that I had laughed. The whole situation was so fucking unexpected it caught me off guard. I didn't think she heard me. Still, I wasn't laughing at her. I was laughing at the situation. And she had to admit it, it was a funny-ass situation.

Who starts gagging like that after you take your dick out of their mouth?

At any rate, I didn't tell her what I was thinking. She probably wouldn't have looked at things the same way as I did.

Surprisingly, we were able to peace everything up that night. Or so I thought. To this day, Karen Steinberg stills mentions the time she says I disrespected her.

That night, though, after sulking for what seemed an eternity, she started complaining about not having an orgasm.

"How could you say that?" I asked. "You were screaming your fucking lungs out."

"I was screaming because I was in pain, you asshole, not because it felt good."

Karen Steinberg's words hit me like an unexpected sucker punch. But it wasn't because I was so big on her. I thought hard about what she said. Other women in my life had screamed like hell, too. I always thought that my dick was the bomb to them. But apparently I had the game totally fucked up.

"If I was hurting you, Karen, why didn't you say so?" I finally asked.

"Why should I?" she replied. "Your intention was to show me that black men have bigger dicks than white men and that you did. What reason did I have to just give up the fight before it even started?"

"All I know is that if someone is hurting you then you let them know. Hell, if it was a sister she would have said something," I said, trying more to convince myself than her.

"That's what you think, Mandingo, but you're wrong," she said sweetly. "Trust me, you're not just big because you're black. You're big for any man. And any woman who's had some of that big-ass dick was in pain. They were probably just too proud to tell you."

Out of nowhere Karen Steinberg started smiling.

"Correction. They probably didn't want to further inflate your already humongous ego."

"I'm not conceited."

"No one is saying you're conceited, but you do have a big-ass ego. Let a woman compliment you sometimes. You don't always have to give yourself props."

Clearly, my dick had Karen Steinberg talking crazy that night but her words did put a heart into what had previously just been some nice titties and a plump ass. Plus, I was still kinda upset about her not having an orgasm.

"Did I ever tell you that you're smart, Karen Steinberg?" I asked her.

"I guess I should be worried," she said. "You're compliment-ing me. What the hell do you want?"

"Why do I have to want something?" I asked.

"Because men always do," she said. "They treat you like shit on a regular basis because they want something. Then they act like you're the fucking queen of England."

"Well, regardless if I want something or not, I've honestly always thought you were smart. Why else would you be here?"

Karen Steinberg never answered me. She just rested her head on my shoulders.

"I'm still turned on," she had said. "My pussy is sore as all hell, but I'm still turned on. Do you think you can finish the job without trying to kill me?"

Without answering, I pulled her over to me and started kissing her neck. Before long, I started hungrily sucking on her titties.

It's baffling to me why I hadn't touched her titties before despite being so big on them. I guess she was right about me not caring about her. I'm not sure I ever started caring. But I was sure that I didn't like the fact that she didn't come. I remember thinking that the only way I was leaving that night without her having an orgasm was in a body bag.

After sucking on her titties long enough to get hard again, I laid on top of her and eased myself into her. She wrapped her legs around my back and we started grinding together in rhythm.

"Yes, Mandingo," she moaned. "This is how you're supposed to give a girl some of this big-ass dick."

I have to admit, it felt a lot better doing it slowly and carefully than it did acting like I was running a hundred yard dash.

She let me lead for a while then she asked me to let her get on top. I didn't care. As long as she didn't ask me to stop. I was possessed by the thought of making her come wildly and crazily.

Wildly and crazily, it's funny I use those words. That's exactly how Karen Steinberg started acting when she got on top.

When she got on top, she started grinding on me like she was riding a horse. It was kind of exotic. But it wasn't anything to write home bragging about. Then something changed. She started moaning really loud and hopping up and down harder and harder on my dick.

"Yes, Mandingo," she shouted. "Fuck me with this big black dick! Fuck the shit out of me you motherfucker!"

Karen Steinberg really started wilding out. She was bouncing on me like she was crazy. She had a hand full of my chest with her nails and was pounding me into the bed. It's a good thing I didn't have a girlfriend at the time or I would have been in trouble. I didn't care, though. The shit was starting to feel real good. And the way Karen Steinberg was acting was turning me the fuck on.

Before I had a chance to come the second time, Karen Steinberg let out a really loud shriek then slammed her pussy down hard on every inch of my dick. I could feel her pussy pulsating around my dick and before long she started to shake. Her eyes got really big and she became extremely quiet with the exception of her heart beating like an African drum roll.

She stayed that way for about three minutes then she lifted her head off of me and started kissing me on my neck and chest.

"Damn, this dick is good, Mandingo," she stammered. "Goddamn this dick is good."

Before I knew what was happening, her mouth had found its way back down to my dick. She was sucked it like I was about to give her a million dollars or something. Of course, it didn't take long for me to get ready to bust.

Since I felt it coming, this time I started pulling away. But she wouldn't let me pull away.

"No!" she yelled. "I want to taste you this time. I don't want to waste a single drop."

I never told Karen Steinberg what I'm about to say. In fact, I've never told any woman what I learned that night. I found out that if you don't just try to go for yourself and actually keep the woman's enjoyment in mind then you will enjoy the sex just as much as she does, if not more. And she may let you get away with a few things she would have ordinarily freaked out about.

I can't believe that she let me fuck her again after I came in her mouth. Then she let me come in her mouth again and swallowed it.

I have never been mad at Karen Steinberg since that day. Now, today, not only am I not mad at her but I love her. That's right—I love her. If you saw what I am seeing right now while Denise is undressing you would understand. I'm the luckiest man in the world right now because of a country-ass white girl named Karen Steinberg.

Like Don King says, "Only in America." Only in fucking America.

ABOUT THE AUTHOR

Sidibe Ibrahima, affectionately called "Sidi", was born and raised in Africa's Ivory Coast. In 1982 he moved to Germany and attended university. There, he developed his entrepreneurial spirit. In 1995, he returned to the Ivory Coast and opened Sidibe & Freres Distribution, an import/export company.

In 2000, able to speak seven different languages and write four, Sidi came to America. He got a job working at a jewelry store for $3.50 an hour and driving a taxicab. As soon as he managed to save $600, he opened his first bookstand in Harlem.

In addition to selling books, Sidi began reading them, many from new publishing companies, and sharing them with other book vendors. With his business savvy and his networking skills, Sidi expanded his business to five bookstands—one in every borough of New York City.

Over the years, Sidi has helped promote many authors—Teri Woods of Teri Woods Publishing, Shannon Holmes of Triple Crown, Danielle Santiago, author of A Little Ghetto Girl in Harlem, and Treasure Blue, author of Harlem Girl Lost to name but a few. On the distribution side, Sidi has assisted Culture Plus and A & B distributors and Say U Promise publication.

Recently, he's worked with Ashante Kahare, author of Homo Thug and has helped his novel to become a bestseller.

Sidi's "start small but think big" attitude has helped him become the most well-known seller of African American books in New York City. He is constantly sent books to review and blueline proofs to approve prior to going to press. Sidi has his finger on the pulse of the African American book patron and a natural instinct for and knowledge of the ever-increasing market for urban literature.

In response to market demand, Sidi has created Harlem Book Center (HBC), a publishing and distribution company based in Harlem. Its first release was *Fatou: An African Girl in Harlem*, a novel Sidi penned himself. Both HBC and "Fatou" are doing extremely well and Sidi expectations have already been surpassed. His hope is to grow HBC into a huge publishing and distribution conglomerate operating both nationally and internationally.

With his natural talents and instincts, Sidi has already accomplished many things in his young life. And his future promises to be exciting and successful. Be sure to visit Harlem Book Center at (www.harlembookcenter.com) or visit him online to keep abreast of current and ongoing projects.

Harlem Book Center
106West 137th Street Ste 5D
New York, NY 10030
Tel: +1 646/739-6429